TREMORS

AND

TRANSFORMATIONS

A Collection of Short Stories

MICHAEL RANIS

Publishing Coordinator – Sharon Kizziah-Holmes
Cover Design – Jaycee DeLorenzo

Paperback-Press
an imprint of A & S Publishing
A & S Holmes, Inc.

ISBN -13: 978-1-951772-67-3

DEDICATION

To all those who put decency ahead of money

"Decency is indecency's conspiracy of silence."
George Bernard Shaw

"Don't Overestimate the decency of the human race."
H.L. Mencken

CONTENTS

PREFACE

As I was walking out of the bridge club in South Miami, a gentleman that I am, I held the door open for Beverly D. She thanked me and quickly turned to ask, "Whatever happened with the Swiss drunk? You know, what was his name?" I told her I would eventually write a second book, and Andreas would reappear. I was not sure what that second story would tell, except that it would be in Brazil. Beverly was happy to hear that. She eventually also published a positive review of Opaque Blue. She joined a few others who praised the book; luckily, there were no pans. But then, whoever writes a negative review unless they want to protect their status as critics or get paid to do so?

When I finished writing Tremors and Transformations, the second tome of short stories to follow Opaque Blue published a bit over a year earlier, I felt a measure of elation. I did not contemplate writing another book when Opaque Blue was launched, but here it was. It happened much faster than expected, in part because, like most my age, I was self-quarantined—with a lot of time at my hands and little else to do but write. I can only watch that much Netflix, and my head turns to mush if I read for four uninterrupted hours—is that a sign of old age? Since my newly arrived loving dog sleeps endless hours, I might as well become creative.

I struggled with the choice of a title for this compilation. I ditched one because it focused on one story at the expense of others; I chose a second, but it also got tossed when I judged it overly dramatic or pretentious. I settled on "Tremors and Transformations." It is not perfect, but at least it reflects themes touched one way or another in this tome.

This title certainly reflects my state of mind these days. These months have been quite hard on my soul; a measure of sadness has often crowded it. My mental processing struggled to understand what was happening. The disenchantment with American politics has been haunting me and producing sleepless nights. Many current politicians-- a bunch of second-hand car salesmen would do no worse than them—have willingly turned their backs on a

1

myriad of democratic principles. Like many others worldwide, I had long ago become convinced that this country was the beacon of democracy. And yet, recently, I feel I am living in a country that resembles Bolivia, where I was born, or any number of authoritarian regimes I had studied as part of my earlier profession as a political scientist.

And in the middle of all this, I watched in disbelief countless cases where intelligence, science, knowledge, and truthfulness are rejected and substituted with outright lies, conspiracy theories, and violence. I am dismayed by the gutless performance of a significant subset of the media. They seem afraid to confront political leaders and opinion makers and demand better; instead, they talk to like-minded individuals, create an echo chamber, chiming in and repeating the desired and expected cacophony.

Above all, I abhor the inhumanity so often displayed as of late. We all watched the killing of a man, as a policeman presses his neck with a knee while the poor man begs to breathe. We heard about the unwillingness to allow sick passengers to get off a cruise ship that has turned into a virus hive. And lately, we heard of the wanton eviction of renters locked out of a measly income because of the pandemic.

In a way, it feels good to realize that there is a message embedded in most, if not all, the stories. I sought to look for "decency" when I was saddened by so much indecency around me. Let's be clear, by "indecent," I do not mean "vulgar," but, using the definition in Merriam Webster: "not conforming to standards of taste, propriety, or quality." For me, at this time of so much anger and nastiness, I would narrow it down to propriety. But that is just me. I also hope to make a statement in opposition to ignorance and blind frivolity, both irritate and frustrate me.

How pretentious of me to come out with a new book? After all, I got no training to be an author, and I would not describe myself that way when asked for my profession. I had never taken a course in literature or writing. Nonetheless, I plunged. A few factors made me do it. A story did not make it to the first book because the editors believed that a roughly two-hundred-page book was optimal; furthermore, it also needed rethinking and rewriting, but I had reached writers-exhaustion by then. Above all, though, there were all the positive comments from those who read the first book.

I will be eternally thankful for their uplifting, warm words. There was the commentary of my good friend Ian who thought I would write a novel next, and Allison, who said she would be happy to read more. Whether the readers chose to write me a note or published a review, I got lots of encouragement from what they said about Opaque Blue.

Is there an evolution in my writing? Maybe at the margins. As I read more short stories by well-known authors, I noticed that they often were notoriously shorter than what I had written in 'Opaque Blue.' Here, I was at least successful in keeping a story truly short in a couple of cases. In another story, I also used a technique that I saw in another book—a compilation of much shorter stories linked by a common theme and under one title. Two other stories also depart from the old as they are somewhere between a tragic parody and a fable. Notwithstanding, for good or bad, I have to admit that I have not radically "changed my spots."

In Opaque Blue, I paid homage to my Mother using tidbits of information she shared with me over the years; I wrote a story which, to a great extent, was an accurate biographical account. Now I give my dear father his due. I had a different set of data from which to glean and build a remarkable story of change.

As in Opaque Blue, my previous experiences as a student and teacher of political science found a way into this book. Several stories reflect my feelings regarding the pandemic and unhappiness about what the United States is going through. Libertarianism and poor public policy are pushing the country to records no one should want: most deaths on an absolute and per-capita basis— what a terrible statistic that is!

Several books have influenced my thinking and writing, and I found it appropriate to acknowledge them, primarily since I refer to them. In proper sequencing: In the story about the professor, I mention Marx's "The 18th Brumaire of Louis Bonaparte". I also quote from Aristide Zolberg's "Moments of Madness." And Viet Thanh Nguyen's "The Sympathizer." My views on the current political debacle have been shaped by E. Posner's "The Demagogue's Playbook." The Kryptonia fable was written as I was reading J. Maarten Troost's "The Sex Lives of Cannibals"; I refer to it because his depiction influenced my imagery of the fictional country in my story. Woody Allen's "The Insanity Defense"

3

became part of my research for "Being Like Woody." Saul Below is mentioned twice in this book. "Henderson, the Rain King" is mentioned in "The Professor," and "More Die of Heartbreak" is alluded to in "Weenie Salchicha."

A short time ago, I got a present; it was a mug that said: "I am a writer; Anything you say or do may be used in a story." "The Urn" is based on a story told by Nancy S., and Lily R. provided useful information for "Vilde Chaye;" Tatiana was based on a story told by a friend with a similar sounding name (she knows and approved the story). I thank all those who have impacted this book in one way or the other. Obviously, hold only myself responsible for what appears here.

Good friends always lend a helping hand. And that was the case here too. I am thankful for Claire Alpert, Frida Baranek, David Rosenblatt, my daughter in law, Francesca, and my son Ethan's careful reading and comments. "Sounding boards" are critical to any writer, and David was particularly valuable; he read most stories with a warm heart and a lucid mind.

When I was in dire need of fixing typos and other errors in an imperfect edition of Opaque Blue, Sharon Kizzia-Holmes of Paperback-Press lent me a helping hand. They published the second, clean edition of that book. I was delighted that she agreed to publish this book. Her assistance in all regards was invaluable.

I benefitted from the editing help of Holly Atkinson of Evil Eye Editing and Timothy Kowarsky. who also made several constructive literary suggestions. Jaycee DeLorenzo helped with the design of the book covers.

THE TRANSFORMATION OF PAPI

Some writing is confessional; others are apologetic. It is not particularly pleasing to admit that only recently, many years after his death, I understood my father's dedication to community work, his continuous effort to instill specific values, his passion for history. It is not that I did not love him, for I did; I just did not fully "get" him. This realization came through full force while composing this piece.

I had landed a couple of days earlier and was eager to see Vera. I wanted "us" to work out. She had sent me multiple "selfies" while I was away. It seemed she was trying to remind me of her existence; perhaps it was her way to assure I stayed on the straight and narrow. After all, she was a relatively new divorcee and remained suspicious about men our age looking for young cuties replacing the old and trite at home.

I had told her that before meeting her, I had planned to go wild in Russia. I had heard that nightlife was total debauchery; photos and videos proved this. I would enjoy that turpitude while also attending the soccer world cup. Now that I had fallen in love with her, I would be an angel: go to museums and the theatre instead. Nonetheless, she seemed wary and vigilant, as anyone who had recently been hurt would be, I thought to myself. I may have sowed the seeds of suspicion with my honesty. Still, I was annoyed with her frequent phone calls and texts during the trip. It was not that she called but that she was more intent on asking where I was and where I was going, rather than how I felt. I got the sense I was spied upon like she did not trust me.

We agreed to meet two days after my return—on Saturday; she reserved Fridays to see her mother. She would come over to my place, I would cook some fish, and we would enjoy a bottle of Sancerre I had reserved for a special occasion. I was looking forward to seeing her. I remained committed to making this relationship work.

As soon as she came in, I sprung on her: "Look, you thought I was making up a story. My feet were bleeding all over. Those awful blisters everywhere—my heels, my soles, my toes. How stupid I was not to take the right shoes to the trip!" She sneered at my display, giving a strong indication that she was not particularly interested. "Tell me everything about the trip" was her way to change the topic.

"The last game I saw was England against Colombia. A great game. My father would have loved to be there. He was such a soccer fan! I kept thinking about my father as I struggled with pain and the long walk to reach the subway—the stupid organizers had sent me the wrong way. I had to climb up and down staircases and walk-through dim tunnels to arrive at the subway station. It was the sort of tenacity my father had, I thought. I still loved him, even though he had been dead for decades. Why is it, Vera, that we suddenly get so emotional about certain people, even if they had passed many years earlier?"

I took out a bunch of photo albums—they were a treasure I'd carried with me from house to house, city to city, continent to continent, throughout my many job-related moves. The photos went as far back as the 1920s when my father had been a very young German soldier in WWI. "Look, he was a good-looking man." I turned to a picture taken when he was in his early twenties. "Too bad I didn't inherit his looks."

As I headed to the subway station on that hot Moscow night, bleeding and in pain, I kept thinking about my father. It was not just the soccer that he'd loved so much. I appreciated his interest in history and his perspective—how he was able to interpret significant events that had disrupted his life; how he revered the actions of some courageous men and women that changed what seemed like the inexorable trend of global domination by Nazi Germany. Once, while discussing the collapse of Hitler's forces in Russia, he said, "Like most young men in their twenties, I once favored socialism—I would have had no heart otherwise, but wisdom turned me into a man with a strong distaste for the 'Dictatorship of the Proletariat.' Still, what the men and women of Stalingrad and the Russian army did to Hitler's armies and the Fuehrer's grandiose plans to spread malice, racism, and antisemitic vitriol was so dramatically important. We owe them a huge debt of gratitude." Remembering these words, I decided to visit Volgograd—the renamed city that had once been Stalingrad—and pay my respects.

Vera did not seem interested in what I was telling her, but I was determined to go on. It was as if the trip to Russia had unleashed a torrent of memories about my father, remembrances I needed to share with someone. The one, I thought, that would be close enough to show interest and listen.

"But what about the nightclubs you wanted to visit. Did you go to any of them? Were the women half-naked as you hoped, expected?"

I ignored the nasty innuendo and replied: "I had dinner at *Propaganda* twice. The managers regularly turn the restaurant into a sort of nightclub. On both occasions, the live band played jazzy style tunes, and the audience was thrilled. One time, the bold guy on stage appeared to be a star with some reputation—people were pushing their way forward to get a closer look and take a picture. I got seated in a corner by that stage. The band leader noticed our similar 'hair-styles' and smiled. There were no half-naked women. But being there reminded me of the period when my father lived in Berlin. I am sure you saw *Cabaret*, the movie with Liza Minnelli. It portrayed the late 20s early 30s Berlin when Nazism started rearing its ugly head. Berlin had become one of the three largest cities in the world. All that construction was good for my father financially because his business sold construction steel wholesale."

I frantically searched the photo albums to find the right pictures and got excited when I finally did. "Look at these people, ready for a masquerade ball, their funny hats, looking like Turkish businessmen at the bazaar. Looking at the women reminds me of the Great Gatsby—F. Scott Fitzgerald's nearly autobiographical work.

I know these were very commonplace in that period of hedonistic indulgence. My father had no qualms about being part of it. At the time, he enjoyed Karl Valentin, the cabaret comedian, like everyone his age. Look, there he is in front of a nice car—I have no idea what model it is, but it does not look shabby. Here he is walking with his first wife and their dog. He lived it up in those days of the early and mid-30s."

Vera interrupted me; she declared she was famished and wanted to eat. I put the albums to the side and turned toward the stovetop.

But my mind was still on my father's life-history. I thought to myself, isn't it odd that decades after a loved one died, our memories resurface when we look at old pictures. I suppose that's the way you pay homage.

I almost burned the salmon rummaging in my cerebral depot while Vera changed into 'something more comfortable,' which essentially meant her underwear and a tunic. It was late summer, and she was always sexually ravenous.

She wanted to know what I had done in Russia other than visiting stadiums or watching soccer matches at some restaurant or bar. She still seemed to probe for indiscretions. I told her about the Hermitage, the art museums, and Bulgakov's house because I loved *The Master and Margarita*. I'd also gone to the Kremlin. And because my father still occupied my thoughts, I mentioned that he'd passed on to me the appreciation for politics and history. Going to see the Kremlin did not suggest that I appreciated Putin's Russia, just like touring Tiananmen Square did not honor Mao, or visiting Peterhof Palace would not be bowing to the Russian Czars. I told her about the beautiful subway stations, probably the most elaborate on the planet. How amazed I was at Moscow's grand broad avenues and how striking the difference was with Volgograd's impoverished and dilapidated look. My little tour was interrupted by her sitting on my lap and kissing me. We headed to

the bedroom, and carnal desires took over.

Whether it was jetlag, her body heat, or the upheaval caused by reflections about my father, I woke up around 2:30 in the morning. I slithered out of bed and sat next to the photo albums still lying on the dining room table.

I searched and quickly found a picture with my father and many other newly immigrated Jews looking out a window with Israel's flag gently blowing in the wind. I checked the photo's back, and it confirmed my hunch—the date, written in pencil in my father's handwriting, had been the 30th of November 1947. The day after the United Nations had affirmed the establishment of a Jewish State. It had not been a unanimous vote, rather a nail-biter. The US brought along a good number of countries; the Arab States, alongside many "non-aligned countries," had voted in the negative. Looking out that window, these men and women were celebrating a vote that reflected redemption. They understood that the vote embodied efforts to make up for the Holocaust and the guilt associated with many shameful decisions blocking desperate Jews from entering the United States and other countries. Supposedly, it also was the, only partial for sure, redress for the murder of millions of men, women, and children, whose sole fault was being Jewish.

Vera was Jewish too, a "Jewban"—a Jewess of Cuban descent; I am convinced that she never had the same intensity of feelings toward the Holocaust. My parents were lucky. They had not gone to concentration camps or suffered any bodily injury. Yet, growing up in Bolivia, my generation was raised on the knees of remembrance, of "never forget" —the Shoah was a constant presence in our education. When I was a child, many teachers and community leaders said that Israel would ensure no such Holocaust ever recurred. It was an exaggeration, but I now understood why they said it. It established why we should cherish an independent Israel regardless of where we chose to live.

Looking again at the picture, I saw men wearing suits that looked secondhand. It caused me to reflect on my father's enormous economic difficulties as he tried to build a new life in Bolivia. Suddenly, I was too tired to continue this voyage into the past and went back to bed.

After breakfast, Vera told me she needed to run some errands and would return later in the afternoon. I was happy to be left alone with my memories and my sudden need to pay homage to my papa. Vera's disinterest was only an obstacle in my pursuit. Having been blessed with an acute sociological perspective, I soon realized that my father had gone through a tremendous personal transformation between the early years of Nazi Germany until he'd left in 1939 and what became of him in La Paz.

Years back, I had uncovered a document left untouched and

unexamined in a box of old papers. It was a two-sided, print shop-prepared announcement of the departure of the MS Hermonthis from Hamburg; it would traverse the Panama Canal and stop at various ports, including Arica, Chile. Among the twenty-four passengers were my father and his wife at that time. The date of departure was the 29th of June 1939, a bit over a month before WWII erupted. I got goosebumps thinking, what if it would have been later? Would he have been allowed to leave? Would the boat have made it? How terrifying close it all was.

The decision to flee Germany was not an easy one for many like my father. *Kristallnacht* (The Night of Broken Glass) was the event that spurred his thinking. Living in Berlin, he witnessed the burning synagogues and smashing of store vitrines firsthand. If before he had been hopeful that Nazi Germany would be a fleeting episode of a turbulent Weimar Republic, that illusion vanished overnight. Here is what he told me when I was mature enough to ask and listen:

"I decided that they were going to apprehend us all. There were rumors of incarcerated Jews; people getting picked up on the streets here and there. I concluded this would become much more general, much more pervasive. And then, they would kill us all." He got animated as he said, "No, this is not a, by hindsight exaggerated, version of what transpired. I have the best proof. That night I told my wife that we were moving out of our apartment, and we would be living in hiding until we found a way out."

They never returned to the apartment and sent non-Jewish friends—they had several—to gradually fetch their belongings and bring them to the place of hiding.

When Vera returned from her chores, I told her what I have been doing. She pretended to be interested. Pretended? I was unsure whether she cared or not, but usually, I knew when she was fully there, listening, attentive. Now she was playing with her fingers, arranging her clothes, looking bored and impatient.

"Can you imagine?" I asked. "Here is a man who did not even finish high school because his parents wanted him out of the house where too many had to share limited meals and off to learn a trade and support himself—a widespread thing in those days. He had the wisdom to foresee what would indeed befall German and, eventually, European Jewry. Many German Jews relied on their military service, on whatever medals of valor decorated their chests, and trusted that this would protect them. My grandpa on my mother's side was one of them. My father did serve, even enlisted before he was eighteen, and served as an artilleryman. Only a few months, mind you, because Germany surrendered, but he probably saw the horrors of that war up close. He did not get hurt, though. Anyway, he chose not to have such pipedreams and engage in comfort-providing self-deceptions. I am so proud of him!

"He would not have had the opportunity to tell his tale if Bolivia had not issued the visas. It matters little that some politicians stuffed their pockets with bribe money sent by American Jews. That a package deal largely organized by Eleanor Roosevelt was behind this. Yes, that same woman who allegedly spoke derisively about Jews as a young woman developed a soft heart for suffering Jews. Seeing the obstacles that prevented Jews from migrating to many countries, including the US, Mrs. Roosevelt was committed to helping. The bottom line is he made it there. He knew little about Bolivia, like most arriving there. He knew about La Paz being very high-up—fifteen thousand feet up! He knew there was a beautiful mountain overlooking the city. Still, the name Illimani was challenging to pronounce by a person speaking only German. It is gorgeous, come." I took her by the hand and showed a watercolor painting I'd made of the majestic, snow-covered mountain peaks.

"It was not easy for these, virtually penniless, Jews arriving in La Paz—the immigration of Jews bulged from about twenty families before the 30s to over seven thousand.

I once remarked that maybe he should replace the old, terribly scuffed, brown bag he carried to work. He sat me down next to him and told me the story of that bag. "I carried it up and down sometimes very steep, cobbled streets of La Paz, carrying goods bought from one immigrant family and trying to sell them to another. How hard those years had been! How different from a life of comfort in Berlin. The bag reminded me of old times; it made sure I remembered and appreciated the better times that eventually would come to be."

Vera felt the need to react. "Seemingly, the good old times we saw in the pictures we saw yesterday were gone forever. Or did he turn into a fun-loving person when economic conditions improved?"

I loved the opportunity to haul out the albums one more time.

"I cannot tell you if Kristallnacht did it. But clearly, the hedonist turned into a different human being. I can guess that when in Berlin, he concentrated on two issues: how to manage his construction steel wholesaling business best and how to have as much fun as possible on any given evening. To be sure, it was not just parties. He went to operas and concerts. He told me he loved operettas—but I could not understand how they were different from operas for a long time. Did it have anything to do with slimmer ladies singing at the end? He told me about the *Three Penny Opera*, Brecht, and Weil, as if I would automatically recognize the names. He somehow got to own a bunch of 78 rpm records from which I had my first exposure to Beethoven and Schubert. You, Vera, can blame him when I drag you to concerts at Arsht." I said this with a smile, trying to be humorous and make the conversation less somber. "These pictures tell me that the energy he had spent hedonistically was now being funneled to doing good things for the community of immigrants."

Suddenly I was filled with nostalgia and sadness. I had lost my father too early—I had only been twenty-one—and it left a hole in my heart. I closed the albums and said to Vera, "Let's go and buy a terrific snack—I am hungry. You have not eaten anything this good in your life."

She gave me a nervous smile; she was conservative by nature—not in terms of her approach to politics, which was a mixed bag but daring to do new things, such as trying exotic foods.

We headed to Calle Ocho and walked into a somewhat austere restaurant where I ordered two *salteñas*, one with a meat filling and the other with chicken. As we waited, I explained to her that the name linked these fantastic empanadas to the province of Salta in northern Argentina, yet many considered it a Bolivian dish.

We each had half of the two *salteñas*. The juice was overflowing, dripping on our hands, and threatening to spill over to our clothes. We laughed about our struggles. Vera surprised me with her positive reaction. She liked the chicken version better but agreed both were "delightful"—how careful she was with her words!

"When I was in my early teens, I would head to the store my

parents owned to help with whatever my father was willing to let me do. Around lunchtime, I would head to a store that only produced *salteñas,* these ever so tasty snacks, by the hundreds. I would bring back two for everyone working at the store, including my parents, the sales personnel, and Eduardo, the older man who carried heavier merchandise packages. It was always a half-hour feast. I have had versions of these in several cities, in Zurich, London, New York, and Miami. Everywhere, even in upstate New York, I searched for a place that would sell them. They were always good, but none compared to the originals from the Calle Loayza."

It suddenly dawned on me that I better stop this voyage into history or lose the shaky relationship with Vera for good. Her dour demeanor, the reluctance to smile at comic situations, told me about a particular personality, ingrained as mother's milk. Right now, I looked at her and saw a Modigliani female portrait, except for their excessive neck length, which Vera lacked. In his paintings, women also showed little propensity to laugh, their lips tightly collapsing into each other, as if they were preventing humor from piercing through them and cracking the sourness. I wondered if she had tolerated my nostalgic trip but was at the brink of screaming, "Enough!"

We went back to her apartment. She had to work the next day, and it was more convenient if I stayed over at her place, allowing her time to prepare her workday, clothes, and ready her mindset. It would also prevent delving into more albums. She often exhibited a degree of insecurity about her performance at work, a direct consequence, I thought, of her obtaining her doctorate at a relatively late stage. I guessed she was doing fine, at least in terms of her superiors' evaluation. I was much more concerned about her students and underlings. I heard stories that appalled me. Occasionally she was outright nasty—as if that power trip gave her more satisfaction than producing good work.

The next morning, back at my apartment, and now alone, I took another look at the photo collection. I enjoyed this moment of quiet intimacy with my somewhat-dimmed-by-time remembrances. I paused in front of a picture of my father and me marching in a parade. It spoke volumes. I recalled people telling me that the crowds watching the Independence Day parade from the sidewalk oohed and awed about this little boy—I was probably seven years old—marching with

his father. Years later, Mom told me she'd made my pants using the cloth of an old skirt. Only then I could not realize how poor my parents had been. One can also see how proud my father was. He had his son alongside him. He was also leading a group of Jewish athletes, all Maccabee members because he was that organization's president. On that day, schools, foreign organizations, and trade unions marched through La Paz's streets and up to the central plaza where the presidential palace is. They were paying respects to the president and the country. My father was always grateful for the opportunities given to him and other jews by Bolivia.

My recollections and other pictures provided additional material to hint at the main issue: a man, my father, who underwent a massive conversion from the days of pleasure-seeking predisposition, ethnic and religious agnosticism, proud Berliner, to becoming this community member bent on doing everything possible to strengthen, better, and contribute to the congregation of fellow immigrants who had made it out.

It was not the only organization he'd dedicated time to, but *Macabi* was, in a way, his baby. He'd presided over this entity for many years.

There were dozens of pictures in these albums showing him surrounded by young immigrants in athletic events, all women and men in their shorts and running attire.

They really must have felt cold, considering La Paz's temperatures rarely rose above fifteen degrees Fahrenheit. He was much older than these athletes. He was not even a great athlete as a young man. Maybe just a decent bowler in Berlin or an above-average ping pong player later. But he was incredibly dedicated to making the organization a vibrant, lively entity. People saw that and kept reelecting him to be its president or a member of its board.

He loved sports and sports events. He went with his soccer fan friends to Chile for the 1962 World Cup (I was upset I could not join them!) and Munich with my mom for the tragically interrupted Olympics. He took me to soccer matches played at the local stadium. Rarely was this high-quality soccer—a conclusion I reached later in life when I saw better playing elsewhere. But clearly he thought that inculcating in me a love for soccer and other sports was an excellent idea. He succeeded.

I could not conclude that he had gone through a radical alteration had he just devoted time and energy to his beloved Maccabee. But, as my mother sometimes bemoaned, he spent three, four weeknights attending meetings of the oversight council of all the Jewish organizations, the school board, and the "*Gemeinde*" that concerned itself with German immigrants and had its synagogue.

And he did all of that in the face of significant headwinds. When my mom deplored his time commitment to meetings, she might have thought, "We have a small child, and we are not well off; maybe it would be good to give more time to both." She consented, nonetheless.

My mother was very influential, and a reason my father's business flourished. The primary input was to import quality household goods from Europe. Casa Ranis, over time, became a well-recognized name.

Until I was about nine, we lived in tight quarters. The apartment's central location was convenient; it was also near the store. But the three-story building was above a movie theater, strangers frequented its hallways, and the staircase routinely smelled of urine. When they finally were financially stronger, my parents bought a house; it was farther away from the city center but more peaceful. It was a significant improvement in our quality of life.

Vera called that afternoon to tell me that she was coming over at around 7 p.m. She wanted to talk about something important. I had my premonitions but decided not to waste time guessing. I told her that I'd had no time to shop for food, and it would be best to head out to one of our favorite restaurants. She came a bit later than expected, and we headed out. There was no indication of what she wanted to talk about, as she acted normal.

At one of the Wynwood restaurants specializing in small tapas dishes, she told me that she had been thinking about our relationship and wanted out. She declared she did not love me any longer. I produced a sour smirk. There was no use in telling a friend, sexual partner, housemate to reconsider when they say they want to be gone. I asked her to pack whatever belongings she had in my apartment and return the keys to me. I detached her key from my chain. I asked the waitress to prepare two leftover bags with the food we'd ordered but had not tasted. I certainly had lost my appetite.

There was no use in even trying to fall asleep. I had encountered breakups before. Too many, to be honest. It never becomes old hat or less painful. I was miserable that I had been trying to convince myself this would work, even though she had been selfish, too frequently heartless. I do not deal well with that type.

A couple of days later, the albums I had been looking through before the breakup were still on the dining room table. I decided to look through them one more time. I saw pictures of my parents and me from when I was in my late teens and early twenties. The photographs had been taken in Israel and brought to life other memories.

I remembered my father's Yishuv activities as sources of pride and joy, but also moments of painful conflict. He did not do it for money; on the contrary, my parents were donors. He did not do it for power; he was a consensus seeker rather than a power grabber. And he did not do it for applause. While he was recognized for his work during events like the community gathering for Israel's independence day, he also had to tolerate innuendo and malice related to the fact that he was a Yekke (a German Jew) in a predominantly Eastern European community. But he did plow ahead anyway because he had to, because of what was happening inside his soul.

Postscript

All that dedication to the Yishuv, all that excitement about Israel, had produced its effect and an unintended consequence. When I was barely fourteen, I announced to my parents that I wanted to move to Israel. I often equated my parents' reactions to this request to WWIII. My parents were facing in-house turmoil, an insurrection. I argued that it would be suitable for my education. It fit the Zionist ideas preached at home, by teachers at school, and by leaders at community events—it was making all those big statements and pronouncements into reality. A Zionist should move to Israel. And it would be good for them, too. They complained that I was forcing them to sell the store. I retorted that their quality of life would be better. They wondered if I had thought about where and when, and I said that I knew of boarding schools where I could stay until they, hopefully, joined me. They were unhappy about having to change their lifestyle, abandon their circle of friends. I told them I felt abused by mine. They eventually surrendered.

The album dedicated to my bar-mitzvah had a picture with my father. Our faces close, radiantly smiling. The photographer had thought it was such a good photo it needed to be on the front page. He'd polished it to take away any distracting items and highlight our happy faces. Whenever I think of my father, this picture springs to mind.

After his untimely death, my mom gave me a letter my father had left for me. The issues addressed there seemed unsurprising and appropriate. He asked me to be kind to Mom—after all, only a few years earlier, I had been a rabble-rouser, inflicting pain on both parents. He also wanted to remind me one last time of often repeated phrases. Sayings like "Speaking is Silver and Silence is Gold," which he uttered on a daily basis as I exited the black DeSoto to enter the school building.

I now regret not to have followed that directive enough. I did better with the other two—he frequently implored me to stay on the golden, narrow path and repeated it in writing here. And he also repeated what he told me often: to work hard to merit whatever I would inherit from my parents.

Those were not the words of a Valentin but a transformed Maccabean.

THE GRANDCHILD, THE PROFESSOR AND JOE SIX-PACK

By way of a Prologue

Paraphrasing the twisting of a Hegelian thought, another philosopher with incisive views argued that great history repeats itself, except the second time it is a laughable farce. Why was I reminded of the opening paragraph in the "Eighteenth Brumaire"? Because during a speech that followed the Capitol's seditious storming, one Congressman compared what had transpired with the collapse of the Roman Republic more than two millennia back. At best, I reflected, this was a bit of hyperbole.

Not that we should lament this, but the replica of the collapse of the Roman Res-publica got its farcical, atonal, ugly, hypocritical version on 1-6-2021 when the American Capitol got stormed. And here we thought that the new year would be better! Despite it being highly unnerving and deplorable, the clownish version of 2021 was nowhere near a threat to this Republic's collapse. And in that lies part of the satire.

I know; many were horrified by the events. They were shook-up and forced to lift their ostrich heads from the sand and remove the

Disneyland mouse ears. After all, there were many antecedents: the plot to kidnap and kill the governor of Michigan, the armed clashes in Oregon, the militia support for the baby-faced murderer in Kenosha, and so forth. And in all these instances, you could hear a crowd of politicians, headed by the President, who either applauded outright or shamelessly excused, justified, half-heartedly denounced. "Good people on both sides" kept on ringing in my ears.

Why was it farcical? Because despite the bloodshed, five individuals did die, and despite the rattled nerves of good people who could never have imagined what they were seeing, the clash seemed more like an excursion than a battle. Indeed, a lot less belligerent than the police and national guard soldiers' expulsion of Black Lives Matter demonstrators the previous summer. Observers appropriately drew critical comparisons.

It was clownish because many participants were more interested in selfies than in pursuing their loudly clamored changes. They so enjoyed their poses: feet up on the desk of the number one Democrat in the House or stealing/carrying her lectern into the Rotunda and posing for yet another photo-op, or showing off a trim, half-naked body, while appearing shirtless but with lots of paint and Viking-like horns as if ready to get on some theatre stage rather than stage an insurrection. It seems that there were leaders who planned, some inside cooperation and intelligence, all indicative of sedition's pervasiveness amidst us.

There also was property destruction and other disgusting acts, but not the burning down of the building as it may have been in ancient Rome. All that was followed by a nearly voluntary retreat that seemed as theatrical as a scene in a bad Hollywood movie. Certainly, there were some terrible characters there, men and women intending to kill and maim, but, in a way, the mob spectacle drowned the visuals, voices, and actions of the most sinister.

It also was an event full of hypocrisy because of the fake-filled reversals produced by covert promoters and facilitators, politicians who dashed to the senate floor to rebuke and denounce what they had been smiling at and instigating over the last months.

And yet, the dispersing crowd of nincompoops, the Joe-Six-Packs in this story's title, could not point to any achievements.

Yes, they caused tremors and fright. But the American Republic had survived the assault intact. Not because of its defenders' heroics, not because a leader, least of all the President, redirected the hordes, but because the stupid crowds had no clue what to do once they were able to march into the building, almost unimpeded (a tragicomedy, per se).

Other than several arrests and whatever legal consequences they may face, the most prominent effect was the fissures and splintering inside the Republican party. Something that the crowd and the insurrectionists probably did not fathom.

I observed with a measure of sad puzzlement that the critics were much more concerned with "how the World viewed this all" (for sure an abhorrent shocker, but not one with immediate consequences), rather than what to do about these people to prevent a recurrence in the future? How do we educate them? Change their hostile hearts and delusional minds?

This prologue is written to provide a bookend of sorts to the story to follow.

The story

Gene often expressed how impressed he was with Ron, his grandchild, the first of three. He wished he had been as precocious, curious, and inquisitive at the age of seventeen. Ron wanted to learn, was eager to read, and sought guidance from those with knowledge. As Gene told his daughter, Ron's mother, "If only I could have been less "full of myself" at that age! I was too arrogant to open my eyes wide enough to see, too self-absorbed to fully lend my ears and hear all that was said, too confident of being on the right path to seek advice actively. Ron is just so much better."

It was the summer of 2019 when he approached his grandson with a proposal. "How about you and I take a weeklong trip to Chicago? I want to show you the university campus, hang out at some remarkable places I used to visit while a student there, and walk around the near-Northside of Chicago with its impressive architecture. Maybe years from now, you will remember the trip with a smile."

Gene felt he was getting old. His health was fading. He wanted

Ron, and others, to remember him positively, yet he was aware that his life achievements lacked the kind of notoriety that would stand on its own.

Ron was not prone to overreactions—his serene nature permeated every aspect of his being. He smiled at his grandpa and suggested a three or four-day trip. After all, he did have a summer job at the library and did not want to miss too many days. If those days included a weekend, the damage would be negligible. Elated to have found a compromise, they jointly looked at the calendar and chose a three-day weekend with suitable late-August dates.

"How come you went to Chicago, Grandpa? You never told me that story. You have so many wonderful tales. But about this, I only know that you got your Ph.D. from the University of Chicago in the early '80s."

Gene figured the three-hour flight would be shorter if he gave a more detailed response. "While an undergrad at *La Universidad Catolica* in Santiago, I hoped to join the Chilean diplomatic corps. I was majoring in Poli.Sci with a minor in philosophy. But I also was interested in history and the economics of developing countries. In other words, I was a rather confused kid. My cousin, a famous economist at Columbia University, came to speak at a conference, and I seized on the opportunity to ask him what he thought I should do. His answer was unequivocal: 'A B.A. is nothing these days; you must get at least a master's degree.' I asked the professors at the university whether I should pursue a degree in Santiago, and their answer was also direct: 'You are already teaching us here; we cannot add much to your education.'

Gene smiled at Ron's reaction to that last statement. "Wow, *Abuelo,* that is some compliment!"

"I began the process of searching for a university. Should I go to the USA? England? The Sorbonne? When I got accepted to Oxford, Columbia, and Chicago, I asked Trevor Jones, a visiting scholar, where I should go. His response also was unqualified: Chicago was the mecca of the social sciences. Quite honestly, I would have preferred one of the other options. England would have been nice; I always had a soft spot for its culture and quaintness. New York, so lively, would have been exciting, and I could be near my cousin. On the other hand, Chicago was a bit of an enigma—I knew so little about it, but it seemed so pedestrian—

an industrial hub filled with glamourless smokestacks. I knew no one there. I remember my first thought was, 'Didn't Al Capone cause all that mayhem in Chicago?'

Nonetheless, I was going to study, not for a holiday. I heeded the advice I got, and I am glad I did. That is why we are on this plane, heading to Chicago.

Ron turned toward Gene and probed, "Were you surprised by what you found in Chicago? In America, in general?"

"My impressions of the US were a concoction of images provided by books, movies, and the negatively infused perspective of my professors in Chile—most of whom had leftist inclinations. Yes, I was surprised. Soon, I realized that the America I was getting to know was more neurotic, more alike the characters in *American Beauty,* than the innocence portrayed in *The Graduate.* I am not sure you saw either movie; maybe you should look them up.

"When it comes to American politics, I also found out that the picture I had formed in my mind was a lot more complicated than the Chilean academics would have it. They were correct in pointing out the strong individualistic strand in the American political creed. But even in that regard, there are shades.

"One of the Chile professors was big on a relatively new paradigm in the political science of the day—it was called 'political culture.' It suggested itself as a revolution in how politics is viewed and examined, and in a way, it was. Until then, all the work concentrated on leaders, rulers, kings, presidents—what they did or did not do. Political culture wanted to study the population and its beliefs about the regime, elections, and public policy issues.

"I had real problems with the assumptions underlying the methodology. Can one rely on the veracity and honesty of the pollees? Were the survey responses an output heavily influenced by opinion-makers? If there were doubts about these matters, what worth were the conclusions reached when running statistics and formulating hypotheses?

"Yet, there was one useful feature of this approach. It wanted to inquire into other actors rather than the elites, political leaders, kings, presidents, and prime ministers.

"In Chile, I had this professor, Hurtado, who claimed that a country's political culture is a great determinant of how its politics function—who will get elected, what choices they will make, even whether it will be a parliamentary or presidential system. He described the American political culture as extremely individualistic, as opposed to community-oriented. He linked it to the protestant religion preferred by many Americans. And he completed his portrayal by heavily leaning on Max Weber's 'The Protestant Ethic and the Spirit of Capitalism.'

"I see you're frowning, Ron, and I understand. I, too, was very skeptical of the direct linkage, the exaggerated assertions, the simplicity of the argument. In Chile, I voiced my disagreements and had heated debates with Hurtado. Strangely, my dear *nieto*, Hurtado's bombastic statements, as crude as they sounded, stuck in my head and popped up from time to time. They still do these days.

"I don't get it! What has that Protestant Ethic to do with how one votes?" Ron's voice was a bit strident—more than Gene ever heard before. In a way, it was nice to see him this animated. "We are not religious at home, so I am not sure I follow the argument, and it may well be my lack of education."

"I am going to try to keep it short, Ron. That Ethic says that if you fulfill your purpose on Earth—meaning work hard, be thrifty, achieve what you can, seek success, all of which per your self-interest, you will be well rewarded in the afterlife. So, the explicit emphasis is on you as an individual, and the antithesis would be doing things for the communal good or with the larger society in mind.

They say that in the USA, many vote with their pocketbook. Many claimed after the last election that people voted without regard to the impact a Trump presidency may have on society. They just wanted to pursue wealth. Does this help you, Ron?"

Ron was silent, but his face showed that he was mulling things over. Gene understood that it might have been a bit too much information for a youngster.

"I know you are not a Trump supporter," Ron suddenly said. "But I want to understand better why."

Gene did not respond but made himself a mental note to tackle the matter dispassionately, logically, and objectively during this trip. He hoped that in time, Ron would understand his distaste for the current president.

"I think it is essential to approach the study of politics from a second angle: the role played by elites. In the founding fathers' view, the elites' role was critical for a Democracy to function properly. Even in those days they were well aware of multiple elites and the possible clashes between them. On the one hand, there was the landed aristocracy; on the other hand, the lawyers, the merchants, and financiers, all better-educated city dwellers. Furthermore, one could differentiate elites on a geographical basis. That is true today as well.

"Elites play a vital role in the political analysis of any country. When it comes to the US, I think many on the East and West coasts have myopia. They believe that they have a monopoly on opinions, especially when it comes to politics. They may be extremely influential when it comes to fashion, taste, and the arts. But when it comes to politics, you better pay a lot of attention to the middle of the country—the Midwest, the South--any place in the Central and Mountain time zones. These folks may even disdain the New York and Los Angeles elites. Does that matter? Because of the country's political system and factors like gerrymandering and the Electoral College, it matters a lot!

Objecting again in an unusually high-pitched voice, Ron said, "Wait a minute! Many may not have liked the outcome, but I thought The Donald won the elections fair and square. It was legit."

Gene saw he needed to expand a bit more. "Of course, it was. But let's analyze it a bit further. The American system is unique. In most presidential systems, a president is elected based on a straight formula—you get the most votes, you are the president. The concept of a simple majority is clear and self-evident—a robust but straightforward construct.

As you know, in America, the Electoral College (an elitists design of the Founders) is the final step in determining who wins the presidential elections. That institution reflects a weighted system in which some states count more than others. We know the founding fathers wanted to decentralize power and allow the states (and principally their elites, I should note) to impact the nation's politics. But as is the case with most systems and political structures, the gains on one side of the ledger may well be offset by losses on the other. Disadvantages may counter the benefits.

"As you know, Ron, Clinton won the popular vote, but Trump won the presidency. Swing states and their relative importance in the Electoral College determined the outcome—it was all legitimate, as you say. But it left a bad taste for many on the losing side.

"To reiterate, you need to understand the politics and the voters in the middle of the country. Those states that voted Trump into power. You can't just read *The New York Times* and *The Washington Post*—you must read the *Chicago Tribune* and the *Dallas News*. You can't just go by what New Yorkers and Angelinos feel—you have to understand what is said in Pittsburgh, Dayton, and Kalamazoo."

As the plane approached O'Hare, Gene asked Ron to look out the window. "Look at that vast land underneath you. No surprise that Carl Sandburg described Chicago as the city of broad shoulders. He told of a city struggling to develop its own identity while shouldering the American economy in meaningful ways. His poem 'Chicago' is very telling of the city at the time of WWI when it was barely seventy years old."

They had landed, rushed to the rental car agency to sign papers, hopped in the car, and headed south. It had been a long time since Gene had been on these roads, but the signage was clear, and his GPS guided them smoothly to the hotel on 53rd street. He intended to pass on his experiences as a graduate student—staying in Hyde Park would provide a suitable background.

The drive along Lake Shore Drive passed a large swath of land known as the ghetto of South Chicago. Gang wars and violence dominated the scene these days. From the highway, one sees burned down buildings and windows with no curtains or covers. Ron asked whether it was as dangerous in the old days.

"One of my favorite memories from those days are the multiple visits to 'Theresa's,' smack in the middle of the ghetto. It is now closed but used to be a renowned small bar providing a stage for some of the country's best musicians. In that basement, they played mostly blues and some jazz; musicians like Junio Wells and Buddy Guy. The performances I saw were beautiful, and I fell in love with that music. They used to say that anyone who became great passed through Theresa's at some point. It may be an exaggeration, but there is a book of photographs about Theresa's.

At that time, it opened me to music I had paid little attention to beforehand. Was I scared to go there? I would be the one driving since I could pack five to six passengers in my second-hand Plymouth. Yes, I was concerned about theft or vandalism, but nothing ever happened. One night I saw a couple of unaccompanied white women listening to a blues band. They did not appear worried, even though many feared entering the ghetto! It was an eye-opener. Taking the risk was worth it. Summing it up, the situation is worse today than then, but there were incidents even at that time.

"Let me be totally clear, Ron, no murder, and no crime can be excused. We often glide into forgiving transgressions by explaining the causes. Poverty is horrendous, overbearing in its impact, all-encompassing in its effects, relentless in its persistence, and oh so brutal to climb out from. All those half-burned buildings, torn rags covering the windows to provide some privacy, testify to the desolation of poor black America—not just here but all over the country. Again, it is not a justification for gang-warfare, but the two are intertwined.

"There was little interaction between the students and the community of mostly Blacks surrounding the campus. Nonetheless, one of my earliest friends was a black man who taught at the neighborhood school. He lived with his mother, perhaps because he never could amass enough money to move out of her house. Maybe all of that combined to cause him to stay single. I could not pierce the layers of privacy he covered himself with—he changed subjects when conversations became a bit more personal. All I know is that he was a sweet, gentle person with sad eyes. Over the years, I remember him fondly when I recite his favorite phrase: 'Don't look at me with that tone of voice.' I think it is a beautiful phrase."

"For dinner, I am very tempted to go to the Medici," Gene said to his *nieto*. "It is just a normal burger and such joint, but it would bring back fun memories. The Medici reminds me of get-togethers with friends, lively discussions, laughter. The restaurant and its famous gargoyles have been around for decades. I would say it is a landmark in the community. It is one of several restaurants I would like to revisit."

Soon after registering and dropping off their suitcases, they headed to that restaurant a few blocks from the hotel. The evening was a bit muggy, as summers in Chicago can be. When Ron asked about the friendships of those days, Gene's eyes got moist.

"These were special people—I had a group of friends that were a bit rowdy, adventurous, and fun. They smoked cigarettes and drank—mostly beers. We went kayaking down the Fox River in Wisconsin. With the adage of 'the more, the merrier,' we loved to gather around the largest table in a Chinatown restaurant or, maybe, nearby Greektown. At least once or twice a week, we would get together at a seedy bar 'Jimmy's,' loudly discuss bridge hands we just had played at the club or something else.

"The other group was well-behaved in comparison. They did not smoke or even drink that much. They impressed anyone as the more studious type. I nicknamed them the 'ice-cream-party friends;' I thought that was appropriate since they often had afternoon gatherings; around a table were several ice-cream buckets. It also reflected their innocent sweetness. They were all very bright, and a few came across as the most exceptional people I would ever encounter."

As the salad arrived, Ron turned severe. "I have been thinking about what you said about political culture and elites, Grandpa. Can you tell me more about it?"

Gene looked pensive before he responded. "Let's start with a basic premise: who cares what the populace thinks if the ruler is a king? Or, more clearly, political culture is only of relevance in the context of a democracy. Okay?"

Ron nodded.

"We know that elites exert an influence on voters. Who are these elites? What are they after?

"You doubtless have heard of Plato. One of his treatises was about the ideal form of government; it examined Athens's experiences as a polity. He thought that a democratic government was far from perfect. He feared that an uneducated mob making decisions about peace and war and other important matters would be disastrous. He much preferred some wise men ruling a polity. As a utopia and in abstract, the concept may have its appeal, but not so much in reality. Who would pick these wise men? How do you ensure they do not turn tyrannical? Despite the obvious objections, the notion that we might be better off if a few wise men have the reins of power has lingered forever—well beyond Athens and Plato. Subliminally, the debate between those favoring some form of benign elitism and the majority rule is still hovering around today.

"To elucidate further, let's look at two massive events in the history of democracies. The French and American Revolutions were the most important assault on monarchic rule and launched the spread of democracy across many parts of the world. Who were the leaders (the elites) of those revolutions? Many early French revolution leaders were philosophers and, well respected through the ages, political thinkers. But they quickly lost control. The country's politics turned into a chaotic and bloody mess. Many early leaders were guillotined or murdered; extremists demanded more aggressive corrective measures and would stop at nothing. We know the eventual outcome: a thirst for order established Napoleon as the eventual emperor—a new king! It was not all in vain, but surely many would end up disappointed by the turn of events.

"The American version also centered around a cadre of wise men. To this day, the Founding Fathers are revered as near demigods in our political discourse. Even if they were intelligent and farsighted, their outlook was shaped by the conditions of their time. Their tolerance of, and lip-service to slavery, running in direct contradiction to the tenet that all men are created equal, is one example. Their fear of a despot ruling from Washington was also sensible, given what they'd fought against. Still, the decentralized system created was messy and partially responsible for the Civil War. It also provided the foundation for the love affair with guns—such a curse on the country today. Bottom line: wise men are not infallible. On the other hand, no one would argue against the notion that democratic rule was an improvement relative to royals' despotism.

"I get what you said, Grandpa, but what has that all to do with political culture and with the election of Trump?"

"Again, the change in how we study politics that came in the second half of the twentieth century was focused on understanding what the population at large thinks. These men and women were, after all, the voters who would elect not only leaders but also shape public policy, the direction laws would take, and the character of the regime at large. Once more, we have the schism—politicians, political thinkers, political philosophers, and opinion shapers—journalists and media pundits, influencing the masses' thinking. They were quite conscious that they would affect popular thinking; this was the case in the '50s as much as it is true today. Many of these opinion shapers were well educated, from wealthy families, and if not already part of the elite, leaned towards elitist notions themselves. See if you can find a tape of William F. Buckley's TV show—he was a conservative thinker, he also was smart, pompous, and very sure of his elite status and the value of every word he spoke. It will clarify what I am saying. These elites felt entitled and obligated to guide the nation.

"Of course, politicians contending for the presidency are always vying to shape the political culture. One poignant example we saw was when Hillary Clinton described some of Trump's supporters as a 'basket of deplorables.' In effect, she said that these people were too stupid to understand what is right for America. The unfortunate comment, one of many foolish and insensitive remarks that came out of her mouth, exuded elitism. They also hurt her badly in November 2016.

"Underlying all that I just described to you is one central argument: elites influence what regular folks think. That fact is running parallel to the nearly universal transformation from monarchies to democracies. Conceptually, democracies and elites have an uneasy coexistence at best—at worst, they downright clash. But it is impossible to deny that we find both in just about every country, even in the most democratic countries. Some say that Jefferson exhibited the clash better than anyone else. He wanted to appeal to the masses but, at the same time, preserve all critical decisions to a small elite of educated men.

"Enough, for now, dear Ron. You must be bored to tears. Let us enjoy our Medici Burger and take a stroll down this street once we're done."

They walked down to Powell's, the used bookstore where Gene had bought his first Saul Bellow book. "A few days after I found out that the author and U of C faculty was chosen as the recipient of the Nobel prize in literature, and so proud to be here, I made it a point to come here and get a Bellow book. The first of many. 1976 was an exceptional Nobel season since Milton Friedman of the

Economics Department also was selected. The book I bought, *Henderson the Rain King*, had a tremendous impact on me. How he made me sense and smell the setting that Henderson encountered in Africa!"

They headed toward the hotel by walking down Harper. Gene remembered that some forty years back, he had been on this street looking for the house of a remarkable professor whose specialty was the Middle East, an area utterly distinct from philosophy and epistemology. Gene had been part of a small group hosted by the professor—no credits or exams were involved. They would sit on couches, chairs, or the floor to discuss philosophy books. He seemed to remember that they convened once every two weeks. The material was difficult and reviewing it when the stars were out, after a long day of classes and library work, was even more difficult. He admitted to Ron that he'd fallen asleep a couple of times as they talked about Wittgenstein or Husserl and how embarrassed he was! He was sure others had noticed him dozing off. Grandpa and grandson had a hearty laugh.

The next morning, they looked for Gene's favorite diner for breakfast. As they walked to the place, Gene reminisced: "We, that is the 'rowdy group,' would gather at the Agora on weekend mornings and chat about bridge and professors before we embarked on schoolwork at the library, a bridge game at International House or anything else. Sometimes our table would have up to eight or nine people sitting almost on top of each other as we laughed about a story told by Ned, two David, or Tom." But there was no more Agora; instead, there was a restaurant serving Asian food. Gene was visibly disappointed. They asked around and discovered that nearby was another diner with a Greek name called Salonica. Gene was sure the food would be fine, but the memories slate would be left wanting.

From there, they went to the center of the university—the Quadrangle. Gene turned quiet. It was like he had embarked in a time machine, and all sorts of memories crowded his mind. He apologized for having engaged in nostalgia.

"One day, I was walking over to my office using this exact path. I was carrying two bulky boxes. I tripped over something; I do not know what. The boxes opened as they crashed to the floor, the contents dispersed all over—these were the infamous IBM cards. I am sure you have no idea what I am talking about. In those days, we entered data into a computer, and large mainframes spat out a multitude of these cards. Sometime later, anyone could take these cards and reproduce the data collected. As long as the cards were in the correct order, that is. The scene was a mess, and I am sure I was as red as a tomato. I also was furious because I would have to go back to the lab and create these cards all over again—what a nuisance!"

Ron cackled but chose to focus on a positive piece of information. "You had your own office here?"

"Yes, I was the assistant to two professors and occupied an office in that building over there." He pointed to a more modern structure, very different from the older buildings surrounding the Quadrangle. "I would help students with whatever questions they had and conduct research for the two professors—both remarkable individuals, I should quickly add. They both were so smart, so well-read. They were different personalities, and their methods of doing political science were dissimilar too. One was much more a data-driven person; the other was almost an artist. I respected the former but was much more empathetic to the Renaissance man that was Ari. One of his seminal articles is relevant to the conversation we were having. In that wonderful piece, he compared periods of rebellion and discontent in Western Europe, mainly France. He looked at the student rebellions of 1968, the much broader turmoil of 1848, 1871, and some other important dates. This 'Moments of Madness' article draws primarily on literature and looks at other societal manifestations to describe how pervasive these tumultuous times were. 'Politics bursts its bounds to invade all of life,' he wrote. Critical to him was to point out that at such crucial moments, the elites would sense the masses' disenchantments and even join in, despite some awareness that this may cause their downfall. It is a fascinating article, and I hope you can read it when we are back in New York."

They entered the magnificent library at one side of the Quadrangle and walked around the premises quietly. Even in summer, there were many people (mostly graduate students working on their dissertations).

When they left those premises, Gene remembered an awful incident he'd witnessed while in the library. "Forty-odd years back, I was sitting at one of those big desks working away when a younger student, probably an undergraduate, sat diagonally across from me. He eventually put his feet on the table. It bothered me as I thought it was bad manners, but I said nothing. About ten minutes later, the young man chose to take off his shoes and socks. At that point, I turned to him and said, 'Really?' The young man immediately took his sharp pencil and stabbed his hand while asking if I was happy now. I was horrified, took my belongings, and moved away."

Ron was incredulous, and Gene felt the need to explain.

"I think undergraduate students often felt stressed by the fact that this university was primarily attended by, and catered to, students seeking higher degrees. Undergraduates would often register for courses also offered to the graduates. They automatically felt like second-class citizens—they knew less, were often struggling to understand the discussions, were less eloquent in their oral answers and written essays. It was an unfair situation for them."

Gene regretted telling him about the episode—he feared he had darkened the visit with it. They needed change. "Enough roaming around here. Why don't we head to the city and see what we can discover?"

They took the Metra train that dropped them off smack in the middle of the Loop. They saw the giant red Calder that has become an iconic symbol of the city, then headed to the Magnificent Mile with its very fancy shops.

Gene wanted to make sure his grandchild had a historical understanding of Chicago. "Somehow, this relatively new city attracted and created wealth and the need to satisfy the tastes of the wealthy. So, even though the uninformed impression is that this was a city of hard-working hicks with unsophisticated tastes, you walk around the wealthy areas of near uptown, and you realize that there is great variety in this city."

They joined a tourists' filled boat that traversed the Chicago River and afforded a good look at the architecture in that area—the Wrigley and Chicago Tribune buildings, among others. To see some of the architecture close up, they walked through the area's quaint streets immediately north of the Magnificent Mile. Some of these unique streets, Gene noted, could just as well be in Europe.

"One could ponder," said Gene, "what went through the minds of the mayor and aldermen of that time when they chose to name one street Goethe, another Shubert, and another Schiller. Conscious of Chicago's image, the politicians wanted to make the city look universal and cultured. The effort did not fully succeed—you may even say it backfired. Many locals chose to pronounce these streets names as *Go-etie* and *Skyler*—a factoid my very amused Evanston relatives told me several times.

"I do not know, Ron, if you are aware that Chicago was nicknamed 'Second City' for the longest time. Second, of course, to New York. In fact, that is the origin of the famous comedy group. They included top names like Bill Murray, Tina Fey, Stephen Colbert, the Belushi brothers, and Alan Arkin. The notion that Chicago was not New York, second in class, was pervasive with heavy baggage hovering over the city in the '70s. I heard references to it when discussing the arts, quality of life, sports, anything. The official nickname, Windy City, almost got replaced by this more derogatory term. Wind blowing across Lake Michigan and producing frigid winters was a force of nature—but being second to some other first was something that could be, needed to be, turned-around; but what would be the secret sauce that would cause it to happen?"

Gene had secretly planned that he would pretend to be much younger on that Friday night and lead his grandson to a fun evening full of music. He wanted to visit the place that had once been The Earl of Old Town. Here he had been exposed to American folk music—a genre he knew nothing about—and, to his surprise, he'd taken a liking to it. He'd particularly enjoyed a young woman who had sung Joni Mitchell and Judy Collins songs; he often hummed "Both Sides Now."

He checked out the internet, and found a nearby Vietnamese restaurant, Pasteur, that they might enjoy—it had good ratings. Also nearby were a few exciting places worth exploring, absorbing the vibes, having a beer, and moving on. Just like in the old days...

The Earl of Old Town had become the Corcoran Pub and Grill, and they no longer played folk and country in the premises; still, Gene was surprised how little the furniture and interior had changed.

Gene noted to Ron, "I was walking this street, saw a sign' Live music here' and walked in. I had no idea I had entered an institution with a remarkable history. When I later asked local friends, I learned a lot more about the place I had visited. I returned to it a few times."

After they finished their beers at the pub, they moved on. They went to a jazz venue called the Green Mill Tavern. It had a lot of history. Sinatra had sung there, Greta Garbo had frequented the place, and, most strikingly, it had been a favorite of Al Capone; not surprisingly, it had become a must for tourists and locals.

Preparing for the outing, Gene found that the area was sprinkled with other popular music venues. He did not want to engage solely in nostalgic excursions. After the Green Mill, they went to the Hideout. The place was hopping—a large crowd, mostly young, multiracial, gay, and straight—danced to the light rock tunes played on stage. They finished their musical tour at the Empty Bottle, which Gene picked because it had been described as an Indie Rock club. It was possible that both Gene and Ron were already too tired or overly exposed to different musical venues, but their stay there was short. They hailed a taxi back to the hotel.

As they entered the hotel lobby, Ron stated, "This was a great outing, Grandpa! A lot of fun. Thank you! You were not just a student in Chicago, and I am secretly curious about your romantic life during those days."

Gene produced a wry smile and shook his head. "No, Ron, we will not talk about that. At least not on this trip, or at this time."

They woke up rather hungry. Gene thought that going to the Mellow Yellow for breakfast would be an excellent way to satiate their appetite. Amazingly enough, this was another place that had withstood time—their specialty pancakes, crepes, and waffles continued to delight forty years later.

For the last day of their visit, Gene chose the Art Institute, a museum well-liked by art lovers. Seeing American Gothic and The Old Guitarist would be enough to make an art connoisseur's day. Still, there was so much more: Miro, Monet (thirty paintings!), and Toulouse Lautrec, alongside Van Gogh, Renoir, and Cezanne. For those looking for modern art, there was Jackson Pollock, Jasper, and Warhol. Gene insisted that because architecture was an essential component of what Chicago meant to many, they should see the drawings and models made by Frank Lloyd Wright—Gene mentioned that Hyde Park had some buildings designed by him, but they ran out of time to see them.

They spent over four hours there and felt exhausted by the end. Gene noted that when he'd taken Ron's mother and uncle to the Pompidou in Paris as teenagers, they'd had a lot less stamina and patience. He and Ron smiled about that.

They headed back to Hyde Park, and when they settled in Gene's room to put up their tired feet, Gene wondered aloud if Ron was up for a somewhat offbeat last evening. "I used to live in an apartment that was part of university housing. You could rent it at a subsidized price, and it was furnished. It was better than the tiny bedrooms of the International House. At the corner of that block on South Dorchester was this place called Ribs and Bibs. I checked last night if it still exists, and it does! We could order the food for pickup or delivery if they have that, stay in the room, and watch the US Open—I know you are a tennis fan."

Ron was happy. He said that he appreciated what his grandpa had organized, but he had reached his limit—his sensory system was satiated. He would rather have something more mundane. He was very amenable to Gene's idea. It also made sense since they were flying back to New York early the next morning.

They reconvened around 7 p.m. and ordered two racks of lamb and some corn-on-the-cob. "Just like in the old days!" Gene exclaimed.

"Delicious!" Ron managed to say as he was licking his index and middle fingers.

Ron suddenly lowered the TV volume and said, "There was something you said early during this trip that bothered me, and I wanted to discuss it with you a bit more. You seemed to distinguish between elites and masses, but that seems like such a foreign concept to an American—it seems more European."

Gene nodded that he was happy to engage, but he thought for a while before responding. How could he stay succinct and not give a dissertation that could take hours?

"Every society, no matter how egalitarian its predisposition, has leaders, has elites, has people who, because of their knowledge, wealth, military service and rank, or the ability to bring food to the tribe, are anointed implicitly or explicitly as leaders. We can talk about Amazons in the jungle, chieftains among the Sioux, or the secretary in an even smaller society like an Israeli kibbutz.

"We should acknowledge that most elites try to secure their privilege. They want to extend the presumed expiration date or pass it on to their next of kin. It, of course, was anti-democratic. People are uneasy about such efforts. It produces a clash. If you take a closer look at American history, you will find the Roosevelts, the Vanderbilts, the Kennedys, the Bush family, and many others toiling hard to produce dynasties. So, even though there are constitutional limits on an American president, there are no significant obstacles to ensure that elites do not try to protect their advantages forever. The notion of elites in America is not as foreign as you may think.

"What about the notion of 'masses'? Here, too, there is plenty to talk about. Your hunch is right that it smacks like a European phenomenon rather than fitting the USA. The notion often gets associated with the working poor, the proletariat, in the Marx-Engels discourse. But that is a narrow interpretation. How about the underprivileged, the disenfranchised, the people that feel powerless? In the Marxian perspective, they were bound to rebel against power. It was the expected outcome of a historical dynamic, part of the dialectic process.

"When we use a wider lens, other concepts enter the fray. When I was here, a professor with a robust mathematical bent pointed out an axiom we can call 'the numbers game.' The 'masses' are, by definition, more numerous, and in a democracy that favors the plurality of votes, the masses should win. And the easy assumption is that those masses would vote for candidates that help their economic and social condition.

"Makes perfect sense, except it is not so! Forty years later comes a guy who publicly declares that the masses can be duped. Yes, I see your lips moving, and I am confirming that I am referring to Donald Trump. He made several such statements, and they are public knowledge. What does that say? It says that he was confident he could manipulate the masses—or at least some of them. It also says that he looked derisively at those he was counting on! But, unfortunately, it also says something about the masses. Was he the first to discover this? No way! He just used his oratory style to exploit it better than other politicians of both parties. That's why many critics called him a dangerous demagogue.

"Enter Joe Six-Pack! Have you ever heard of him? I cannot tell you when precisely this imaginary folk-non-hero entered my consciousness. But we have seen TV characters like Archie Bunker exemplifying this Joe. The hallmarks of the personality? A certain boorishness and a matching unwillingness to become better informed. The reliance on the tube as the sole source of information—instead of, let's say, newspapers with their more critical look or, heaven forbid, books.

"The Archie character has racist inclinations, which sometimes get a cute portrayal as if being a racist could ever be cute. Unsurprisingly, there is a related intolerance of other religions, to sexual preferences considered outside the norm—primarily gay men and women."

Ron suddenly interjected with a voice denoting clarity. "And nothing is easier to accept than the need to reject the stranger, the outsider."

"Sitting in front of the TV, drinking a six-pack, and getting satisfaction from that is part of the portrait. It is derogatory. It may even be a bit exaggerated—like any caricature or cartoon is. But there is something real and meaningful in this fictional character.

"What leaves me unhappy—what I see as disconcerting and alarming is that it has dramatic consequences for how our democracy functions. Take these statistical data to elucidate you: white men without a college degree are about forty-plus percent of the total population. In Michigan, one of the states that swung in Trump's direction, only about twenty-five percent of all white folks twenty-five and older have a college degree. This segment is large and only shrinking gradually. They are a crowd that feels humiliated and diminished by the educated elites. They want revenge and redemption.

"The manipulation of the masses is as old as... At least, as old as Shakespeare, who portrayed it beautifully in the masses' response to the two competing orators after Julius Caesar's murder. Brutus speaks first, and the crowd cheers. After that, Marc Anthony delivers the famous 'Friends, Romans, Countrymen,' and the same crowd goes wild supporting him.

"In what could be considered a modern version, Trump has been accused of playing cultural wars to win the election."

"He is appealing to a crowd of Joe Six-Packs," Ron interjected.

"Yes. He rallies the masses against Mexicans, other foreigners, Muslims. If you are an 'anti-authoritarian'"—and here again, Gene used two fingers in each hand to pass on the idea that he just coined the label—"what do you do about this? How do you fight it? You know the answer is educating those masses to be more discerning, less gullible, less willing to be duped, but that is an uphill battle you may well lose. Calling some people deplorable certainly was not the way to counter it. It just played into his hands. But it was the best indication that the Clinton camp realized what was going on, was exasperated by it, and incapable of countering it.

"Now, three years into his presidency, we are witnessing how he is trampling over cornerstones of our democracy. He is using the Justice Department as a weapon to pursue self-interest. He continually abuses the 'Separation of Powers' concepts as he refuses to comply with Congress's demands, and so much more.

"Unfortunately, the Joe-Six-Pack syndrome is facilitated by an affluent society that likes an uncomplicated, easy life: go consume, go shopping at Walmart, don't bother reading a book. It also likes easy answers rather than complex ones. It prefers slogans to science and guns over conflict resolution. As Viet Thanh Nguyen so aptly notes, our notion of being super. We are a country so smothered by a sense of greatness that there is no need to read, work, improve—we are simply great! The nation is so complacent that leaders feel the need to wake it up. Time and again, we hear them use the old Kennedy exhortation: 'Ask not what this country can do for you...' The unwillingness to take the more challenging road of being better educated, more informed, listening to science rather than schemers, connivers, and charlatans is strident.

"When I moved from Chicago to New York, it seemed like I entered a somewhat different world. Many seemed to be proud to read *The New York Times*, be more knowledgeable, better informed. I eventually recognized that, in their folly, they thought the rest of America was like them. When Trump got elected, many voiced frustration and dismay, how could they vote for him? This self-deception, this belief that people in Arkansas, Tennessee, and Nebraska are of the same mindset, created an analytical gap preventing the understanding of the Trump surprise.

"So, dear grandson, you now know that this country's political culture is highly bifurcated and likely to stay like that for a long time. You ask the elites, and you get one answer, and you ask Joe-Six-Pack, his answer will be different. We may get lucky and have people in power who are benign in their elitism. Or we may get unlucky and have a president who exploits this fragile regime to his benefit. To those who would tell you that the US is a strong democracy that will not allow such abuse, we now have evidence that urges us to say "hogwash." Our Founding Fathers were wise men, but the polity they created is a fragile structure indeed. Philip Roth wrote his 'Plot Against America' to warn us. We are now witnessing a somewhat different kind of attack on our democracy. Sometimes I feel like I am back in Latin America with their typical disregard for law and the Constitution.

"There was one instance in our recent history when the population was ready to shake up the system—America's own Moment of Madness. It was when they clamored for Nixon to go home. That is as close as we got to a European style rebellion. I don't think we may see another such moment anytime soon, but who knows?"

Ron looked at Gene with appreciation. "You have clarified things to me, and more than that, Grandpa, you have taught me how to think about political issues. Maybe I will become a political scientist someday."

Gene smiled and suggested he should follow his heart in choosing a career.

Nearly a year passed after that trip to Chicago. One evening in late June, Gene's phone rang. It was Ron. He had not seen children or grandchildren in weeks. The self-imposed quarantine induced by the pandemic had finally made him a homebody. After the usual, "How are you doing with all this shit?" back and forth, Ron's voice got more excited, and words were jumping out of his mouth.

"Reflecting on what is going on, I remembered your mention of 'Moments of Madness.' I finally read the article today. Do you think we are going through our own 'Moments' right now?"

It was clear he was alluding to the explosive demonstrations decrying the murder of George Floyd and clamoring that "Black Lives Matter."

"I am so pleased you read that article and linked it to what we are going through, Ron! And yet, one more thing: I came to this country because Chicago was the best Poli.Sci department in the world. Education, knowledge, and excellence in all science matters were what the USA meant for me and many others looking up to this country. It is incredible to me that these days we are turning our backs on science and scientists. That, riding the Joe Six-Packs of this country, the president has turned to an anti-science leader, just because what the scientists were saying did not fit his reelection plans.

"And, by the way, Professor Hurtado visits my busy mind once again as he points out: 'See, there they go again. Those hyper-individualistic characters claiming that wearing a mask is a right rather than a societal obligation to prevent the spread of the plague.'"

Ron's response was young but genuine. "Wow! I did not think about those two points, Grandpa. Nice! I, of course, agree with everything else you said."

"One more thing, Ron, I just have finished an outstanding book. It is by Eric Posner. It is called "The Demagogues Playbook." It touches on all the subjects we discussed during our trip: "Elites," the "Mob" (which I preferred to call "Masses"), the undemocratic character of the current inhabitant of the White House. He even refers to Plato, Shakespeare's "Julius Cesar," and, of course, the Founders. I think I am going to send you a copy of the book.

He thanked Gene one more time for the trip to Chicago and their lengthy political conversations.

Gene still felt upset after hanging up. The terrible numbers of dead and sick, and the inability to have a well-defined, organized federal response, angered him. Then he calmed down. A light smile came to his lips as he thought that the trip to Chicago had been a good idea.

DANIEL Z"L

The terrible news hit me hard. Daniel's girlfriend called to tell me the story. She had gotten my number from his mother, who was too decimated to contact me. He had been standing at a designated plaza for hitchhikers—a place where civilians pick up soldiers to offer a ride, and then he got shot.

I turned on the radio, just to make sure—as if such terrible news could ever be said in jest. The army station's newsflash was terse. It announced that Sergeant Daniel P. Z"L had been one of several soldiers shot. Two men on a motorcycle had opened fire on the soldiers standing there, killing Daniel and injuring three others. The announcement concluded by saying that the assailants, members of the PLA, had been caught and were awaiting trial.

After the shock, I became upset: why did he have to expose himself like that? Daniel was not inclined to stupidity or carelessness. I knew him well enough to make this statement with certainty. He knew the risks—surely, he'd read about similar situations ending poorly; he read about assaults identical to the one that cost him his life. Maybe the poor man thought it would never happen to him; perhaps he thought it was a low-risk undertaking. Even in a country with a high dose of terrorism, most soldiers hitchhike often. Maybe he just was exhausted and wanted to make it home as fast as possible.

He was planning on joining Tel Aviv University to pursue a degree in Economics. He was looking forward to the end of this dour chapter of his life. He'd gone into the military service full of hope, patriotic fervor, and conviction, and by the time he'd finished his first six months, he could not wait for the long, three-year service to be over. Some evoke religion or philosophy when reflecting on events such as this. They say, "One proposes, but God disposes." Others, the more agnostic, conclude that "You can plan from here until eternity, but something will always knock you out of your imagined trajectory, your planned path."

I guess he was waiting for a ride to take him home for the long week preceding his release from the long military service. It made his death even more painful. His life was cut short about two weeks before his army release. Mentally preparing for the burial that afternoon, between bouts of tears and a few smiles, I recalled the history of our friendship.

The first time I met Daniel, we were about sixteen years old. He struck me like an utter abnormality. He was so blond! That he was an American by birth could hardly be surprising; still, his features and his hair color did not match what I had seen or expected Jewish youngsters to look like—he was an even blonder Robert Redford. He did not have the physique or the height to be a movie star but otherwise had a perfectly shaped face, blue eyes, and intensely straw-colored hair. I wondered if this boy could be anything but superficial and dull. I was hesitant to form a closer friendship with him. In Mexico City, where I was born, I had two friends. We called ourselves "Los Tres Bandidos." We were similar in upbringing, education, and the Zionist fervor inculcated by the teachers. It was only a slight exaggeration to say we would die or kill for each other. I could not imagine Daniel being one of us.

We met at the boarding school called *Alonei Yitzhak* (Isaac's Oaks), which hosted many foreign-born boys and girls whose parents, like ours, did not live in Israel. Placed in the middle of the country, near impoverished *Binyamina*, and next to an even smaller village with, I guess, as few as eight streets, named *Givat Ada* (Ada's Hill). The area was primarily agricultural, with its primordial coloring the pleasant green of orange trees and vineyards.

I learned that the adjacent village's only coffee-shop could provide a slight variation from the mediocre food at the boarding school. I walked over there for a somewhat stale pastry and a soda. Apparently, Daniel got enticed by the same opportunity. So our first meeting took place there. The conversation was in English because our Hebrew was still rudimentary. He told me he was from a location near New York City—"Englewood, on the New Jersey side." And I said to him that I'd gotten lost in Macy's when my parents had taken me to the Big Apple and Miami to celebrate my thirteenth birthday—it was my Bar-Mitzvah trip. I told him how frantic my mother had become at my disappearance, and we had a good laugh.

"Maybe we can dare travel to Tel Aviv to watch a football match some Saturday," I suggested. He looked at me apprehensively; the only football he knew was American Football (a Jets fan, he stressed), and he was a bit leery about going to Tel Aviv. How would we get there? How would we find the stadium? I told him, "I will find out more, and we can see if it makes sense."

I bumped into Daniel (he hated being called Danny) in the eating hall two days later. "I have good news. We can take a bus from *Givat Ada* to *Binyamina*'s train station. Once in Tel Aviv, we would take a bus to Bloomfield Stadium in *Yaffo (*Jaffa in English). Presumably, the game next Saturday is a dandy—*Hapoel* Tel Aviv is playing *Hapoel Haifa.* They are among the top five right now. I am planning on going. Hopefully, you can come as well."

Daniel agreed. Bright and early that Saturday, the only day we had no classes and didn't have to do the everyday upkeep work, we started our journey. We waited for a good while until the train came. Daniel was thoughtful when he suggested we find a printed schedule to better plan our trip back. "I came from a country where no one took the train," I said, to excuse my poor preparation.

Once we arrived in Tel Aviv—a place full of people, cars, and general commotion—we looked at each other as if to say, "Now what?" We saw an information desk and asked how to get to the stadium. Once again, this was more complicated than initially thought. We had to take two buses and walk a bit to make the forty-minute journey, but, the nice elderly lady added, we should arrive with plenty of time to buy tickets and see the 1 p.m. game.

My first impression of *Yaffo,* with its older buildings and mix of

Arabs and Jews milling around, was somewhat disconcerting. We were just two boys born in foreign lands, with limited knowledge of one language and zero of the other, and we were still trying to find our way to the stadium, for which we did not know the Hebrew word. There was also the issue of being hungry. We were famished and had no clue where to go. From the corner of my eye, I saw a line of mostly men waiting to buy what, considering the hour, was probably lunch. I grabbed Daniel, and soon enough, we had a pita bread stuffed with some greens, spicy sauce, hummus, and what I later discovered was considered the best Falafel in the whole country. All that for approximately USD 1.50. I loved it, Daniel less so. It was the first of several incidents that led me to conclude that this American boy—one would assume worldly in all respects—was, in many ways, provincial or insular. His taste buds, just like his concepts about ethnicities or music, showed limited worldliness. Furthermore, he showed little curiosity or fascination with discovery.

Once done with lunch, it occurred to me that I could ask for directions to the game in a different way. I grabbed a youngster and asked, "Where?" in Hebrew. Then I made a gesture to indicate doubt, followed it with a kicking motion, and *"Hapoel Tel Aviv."* The response was immediate and in quick Hebrew phrases. I had no clue what he said. He noticed his silliness —talking in a language we did not understand—and motioned to follow him. Three blocks down this boulevard, one left turn, and we could see the stadium that would stage the game.

It was not easy to explain the rules of the game as it was going on, and distractions abounded, but I tried my best, and whether he was just pretending or genuinely interested, Daniel seemed to enjoy the match. Maybe it was the fact that we witnessed a rarity: the two teams managed to score many goals (the Tel Aviv club won 5-3).

The thought that the return trip would be relatively easy was dispelled by reality. But we learned, and laughed, about the new country's idiosyncrasies. We found out that navigating back was complicated. We boarded a bus, and I asked if we were headed toward the train station; I'd memorized the appropriate phrase on the way in. Suddenly, from all corners, men and women of all ages talked to us, argued with each other, and pointing in all directions.

Daniel and I looked at each other, utterly confused. We barely understood some words and were still unsure if we were heading in the right direction.

Suddenly, a large man with a big baritone voice and a huge mustache screamed, "Silence!" Everyone quieted down. He was not wearing military fatigues or anything that suggested authority, but he had a remarkable presence and stopped the mayhem. He spoke clearly in good English and explained we needed to go across the street, hail the same line bus going in the other direction, and after—he halted to count—eight stops get off. I admired his clarity—I would vote for him to be president in my native Mexico! We had a big laugh about the whole episode.

Daniel and I lived in different quarters with different roommates; I was in group *Alef* ("A"), he was in *Gimmel* ("C"), so we did not share the same classes. Thus, we did not run into each other often.

I was disgusted by the kitchen area's sights and odors, where the school's students took turns washing dishes and cleaning the mess in the shared dining room. Just picture emptying the big plastic bowls at the center of the tables containing all the leftovers offloaded to expedite the subsequent cleaning. Yuck! I had found an excuse to skip that chore, something about the humidity affecting my knees (I did have a cartilage problem common to growing kids). I got to work outdoors, excavating the ground for the installation of sewage tubes. It allowed me to develop some muscle strength and breathe fresh air. I also loved David, my direct supervisor, the one in charge of three handymen who took care of all the school's physical installations. I was happy to work with him; he was a Holocaust survivor, had a kind smile, and was patient with me—a boy that had never worked in construction before, lacked in strength, and made mistakes. The solitude of this work allowed reflection but also reduced my interaction with other children, including Daniel.

Just before the summer break, we bumped into each other, walking through one of the many garden-surrounded paths that, in hindsight, were so enchanting. He asked me what my plans were for vacation, and the conversation revealed that we both were headed west to visit our parents in Mexico and the US. I said something along these lines: "I am certain that my flight will stop in New York. My father plans to meet me there and accompany me on the last leg to "DF" (short for Mexico City). Maybe I can convince him to spend a couple of days in New York on the way in or out and find a way for us to get together. It would be so awesome to meet you there!"

Daniel's response was typical. "Hmmm. Maybe we can make it work. I will give you my phone number in Englewood."

If I had suggested something like this to one of my Mexican *compadres,* I am sure the response would have been more effusive. But this was Daniel.

I found his number in my wallet and rang him. My father was so wonderful; when I proposed stopping in NY, he said that this would only be possible on the way back.

"Your mother can't wait to see you, and she would kill me if I delayed your arrival so you can have fun in the Big Apple."

I got lucky that it was Daniel who answered the phone. I did not want to explain to anyone who I was and why I was calling. "Hey Daniel, how about you come into Manhattan, and we go to Radio City Hall for their afternoon show? My dad thinks he can get tickets."

Daniel's response was the typical "euphoric" same. "Hmmm. I have never been to Manhattan. Let me talk to my mom. Call me back in thirty minutes?"

I was so amazed. How was it possible that this boy, this family of his, never had made it across the GW Bridge and into Manhattan? People in Bangladesh and Korea would die to spend a few hours in that city. That was so weird to me.

His mother agreed that he could come in, and we would meet him at Penn Station, where the bus would have its last stop.

We saw the show; it was so different from anything we had seen before. Daniel was happy he'd come, and I was glad to bond a bit closer with this buddy.

We were back in *Alonei Yitzhak* in late August. Daniel was elated to give me his good news. "My family is moving to Israel; they bought an apartment in Tel Aviv. I probably will join them sometime later this school year. Let us stay in touch, Yossi."

It took a while for all this to materialize, but by February, Daniel was packing.

Two weeks later, I got a letter from him; he described the new environment, new school and included his new address and phone number. There were no cellular phone numbers in the 1970s, and so our contact was primarily by letter. He asked if I wanted to stay at his parents' apartment for the Passover break. I was thankful for that invitation since I had nowhere else to go. Being one of those remaining at the boarding school while others went to family or friends left you very aware of how alone you were.

His parents were older than I expected. We were sixteen at the time, and his father was over sixty-five and his mother three years younger. I found out that Daniel had a half-brother and half-sister who shared the same mother. They stayed in the United States in Dallas, Texas. They were not interested in living in Israel and, according to Daniel, were not particularly interested in anything that was related to the country or their Judaism.

Daniel's father, Theodore, had been born in what the Brits had officially called Palestine. His parents, Russian Jews, had emigrated in the early 30s. They decided to join a cousin that lived in Brooklyn before WWII started. I told Daniel that I envied him for seeing and talking to his parents any time he wanted to. I did not think my parents would immigrate anytime soon. I had siblings younger than me; they were in Mexico and needed their parents.

The four days I passed at their house were pleasurable and cemented a friendship born out of thin air.

Daniel entered his eleventh year at the local municipal high school while I continued at the boarding school. We met during holidays and summer vacations. Usually, we spent time in Tel Aviv. But we also took trips: down to Eilat and up to a kibbutz near Tiberias. We chatted about what we were planning on doing after high school. I told him that my parents were adamant that I come back to Mexico; they missed me. I convinced them that I needed a college degree and would pursue a business/economics degree from Tel Aviv University. My status in Israel was not as a citizen but as a temporary resident. It allowed me to bypass the compulsory military service. Daniel told me that he'd obtained his Israeli citizenship a couple of months after his parents had arrived and would enter the army once out of high school. I sensed our paths would deviate at that point and wondered what that would do to our friendship.

We graduated high school roughly at the same time. I went

home for a couple of months and left my belongings in Daniel's room until my return. I thought I was lucky to have a good friend whom I could approach with such matters. Upon my return, I picked up my stuff and moved to the dorms adjacent to Tel Aviv University. I would start classes in early September.

Meanwhile, Daniel would enlist in October. We got to see each other a couple of times before then. He told me that he was looking forward to serving.

"It is what you do when you love your country. I know it sounds corny, but that is how I feel. There are a couple of things that worry me, though. One is my father. Back in the US, he had a light heart attack, and the doctors say he has heart disease. I hope that he will not stress out about me. The other concern is over the type of service it will be. I do not want to be one of those despised armchair soldiers sitting in the *Kriya* (the complex of buildings housing all sorts of Ministry of Defense office-personnel) and pushing papers from one stack to another. I have no way to solve the first issue. Concerning the other, they have asked me to take a bunch of psychometric tests—five rounds! They called me first, and I did it. They said nothing. Two weeks later, they asked me to come in again. I called to tell them this could be a mistake; I had already done it. But they told me there was no mistake, and they expected me on the date and time in the letter. I did not call them when they sent another letter, and then a fourth and a fifth. Yes, the tests were getting a bit more complicated and intricate every time."

I smiled and cracked a joke. "Maybe they are looking into you being the head of the army."

He promised to keep me informed.

A week later, the phone in the dorm rang, and Daniel sounded excited. "I have this friend, Meir, whose father knows about the operations of those in charge of the enlisting process. Through them, I found out that I am enlisting together with a group selected to be air force pilots!"

"That is tremendous, Daniel." I was impressed.

"It is ridiculous! You know I wear contact lenses because I do not have perfect eyesight! They will remove me from the group in no time. I suppose you know that they do not have pilots with imperfect eyesight."

"No, I did not know that. I am so sorry, Daniel. Hopefully, all these tests will allow you to service the country in a fulfilling way!"

"I hope so. But this mess is not encouraging."

I must admit that the story had two effects on me. I was almost on the edge of my seat, waiting to see where Daniel would end up. The other was that I became doubtful that any large organization could manage its affairs in a rational, best methods, optimal results way. Even the so-highly lauded Israeli army could mess up.

The saga that ended so tragically had just begun, and, for the most part, it would not be a good story at all.

I have read accounts about basic training in the American military; it was body-punishing and ego-degrading. Daniel told me that he experienced the same, was prepared for that and had no complaints. The travesty was that his path for the next three years was as disappointing as it was contrasting all those psychometric tests. For the first three months of his service, we expected not to have the opportunity to meet or talk. He did call the first free weekend he had; he was very eager to speak to me. He could not tell his parents how unhappy he was. After all, he was the reason they'd migrated from Englewood. He could not talk to Varda, a girlfriend he met at the local high school—she would not understand.

I drove over to his parents' house, and from there, we went to a local coffee shop. Daniel was very agitated as he told me the story:

"You will not believe what transpired! You are in the area where everyone convenes, and your deployment for the next three years, maybe for your whole life, is determined. You are called into one of the wooden bungalows, and in front of you are two lower-ranking officers. They looked bored with their work. It is all routine. You are just one more cog in the machine."

"You have been recruited to be a pilot," one of those paper-pushers told me. I am sure you are aware because your group probably chatted about it."

"Yes. I know. That is an amazing collection of smart individuals. The problem is, I do not have perfect eyesight. I wear contact lenses. No one asked…"

"Oh! Officer One exclaims and asks me to go back to the tent. You will be told where to move next. No one says sorry we were so stupid; no one bothers to lift my spirits after the abrupt dismissal. You are just a screw that did not fit the hole."

"Two hours later, I was asked to go to a different bungalow. I met a soldier, I think a sergeant, who told me I had several options for my three-year service. 'Options' sounded like an excellent way to appease me. You can become a nurse, a member of the military police, or a truck driver. I was flabbergasted. 'What about using my skills, my English? What about all those psychometric tests? I guess being a nurse will allow me to learn something, so that's my pick. But wouldn't an intelligence unit or the military spokesperson-office be more suitable?"

"We will get back to you tomorrow once we make our decision."

Daniel told me he had a sleepless night. The military police are looked down upon in the country—they hate it. Truck drivers, he guessed, were probably among the less educated servicemen. Why on earth were they giving him such poor choices?

The following morning, he found out the decision—he would spend three years behind the wheel, usually in a truck. He could not believe it. He was so shocked, so saddened by what they had decided.

I never heard him this sarcastic: "I am going to learn how to drive a truck! Yippee! Three years of this, Yossi. Three years!"

All I could muster at that moment was, "Sorry, Daniel. I understand how you feel. Maybe you can find a way to serve near Tel Aviv and start attending university during your off times. I have no idea if you will have a way to get this done. Regardless, please remember I am your friend. I am there for you at all times."

I had not heard from Daniel for two months when suddenly I got a call. He was coming home for a two-day visit with his parents. He was planning to see his girlfriend, but maybe we could all go out together on Friday night—a Yaffo nightclub would be fun. I called Lea, a classmate at the university. She was excited about finally meeting Daniel and his girlfriend, Varda.

Lea and I had met on campus. Mexican origins were a significant factor in our comfort being together. When you are a member of a smaller community in a large city like Mexico City, everyone sort of knows each other—we all had common friends, attended each other's family events, gossiped about the same people. But beyond that, Lea was smart, pleasant, and attractive.

I did not know Varda well; we only met briefly once before. My first reaction was that while Daniel kept his Hollywood looks, Varda was as plain as possible. Her shoulder-length black hair, inexpressive face, freckles—the whole package was uninteresting to me, but she was Daniel's girlfriend, and he clearly liked her and, judging from that Friday, the way she was all over him, she wanted him too.

The Yaffo place was one of three big venues that provided the same entertainment program and identical food menus. It was amazing that these establishments seemed content to match each other's offerings rather than outbid each other to win a broader clientele. Usually, all three were packed—enjoying the heyday of this sort of nightlife. The offerings included a well-known singer or group, a comedian, a magician, and some acrobats. The food was also limited, and the most common drink those days was beer—the better-off clientele drinking an imported brand.

I do not know if it was Varda or any beers he might have had before, but Daniel did not seem as sad and frustrated as he had the last time. I was happy about that. He did not say too much, but he was never too talkative. He did not project the same moroseness of last time, and it proved to me that we humans accept almost anything.

I called him the following day just to get the chance to have a one-on-one chat. "Are you okay?" I inquired.

He told me he had concluded that he had no choice but to accept his fate. He was counting the days to his release, and he still had well over two-and-a-half years to go. But there was nothing he could do about his situation. He'd asked if he could join a more interesting group in the army—even the group in charge of criminal investigations inside the hated military police, or the liaisons to the foreign press (because of his English), or an "intelligence" unit. They told him that unless he knew someone or knew someone who knew someone, i.e., if he did not have "Protekzia" (the sort of corruption and bribery that greases much of what happens in the country), he had zero chance for a reassignment. After a few months, he was redeployed to the South. His base was in the middle of the Sinai desert.

As one can imagine, we saw each other much less frequently. Daniel came home every two weeks for short weekends, and when he did, there were parents, the girlfriend, and sporadically some other friends or visitors from abroad.

In February of 1973, when his service was more than half over, I got a call in the middle of the week. The words were almost unintelligible, but I understood that his father had died from a massive heart attack early that morning. They allowed him to fly back home, and I was one of his first phone calls. Of course, I would attend the funeral.

I went to his house the following two evenings for Shiva prayers. Neither of us was religious, but traditions help in times of sorrow. He told me that a corporal had woken him up sometime after 4 a.m., and he'd immediately guessed that it was about his father. All he managed to say to the corporal was, "Is he dead?"

He was concerned about his mother and how she would handle becoming a widow. She had few friends in the country, and he was not nearby either.

"Maybe you can ask them to redeploy you?" I suggested. "In any case, if she needs anything, I will be happy to help. Anything."

Daniel went back to the Sinai but asked to be relocated closer to home to be near his mother. His request was denied. It provided another nail in the coffin of how he felt about the army and his service.

Weeks passed, and as always is the case, with time came a measure of healing. At least Daniel was comforted by Varda's presence and dedication. His mother, on the other hand, was not doing well. Daniel told me, "She is so lonely! She sits on the balcony, staring out, presumably to see the goings-on in the street, but probably just contemplating the empty space left in her heart."

1973 rolled on, the hot summer led to the Jewish High Holidays, and Daniel was still in the Sinai. So, I called his mother and offered to go with her to the local synagogue. Though I was not religious, I figured she wanted to pray in memory of her husband.

On that day, she said, "Yossi, please stop calling me Mrs. Norman. My name is Nora."

Daniel called me after that and expressed his deep appreciation.

The Yom Kippur War started, and because we were all in shock, and the country seemed to fall apart at the seams, there was no ability to call Daniel and make sure he was well—the automated announcement repeatedly stated that all lines were busy. However, I was able to reach Nora, his mom, after several days of trying:

"Can you imagine, Yossi, suddenly at 8:30 last night, Daniel showed up at my front door. He wanted to make some quick steak sandwiches while we talked. He needed them for his colleagues, waiting a few blocks away. I was so perplexed by the request but so happy to see him. He says he is okay, just exhausted from the endless driving and nervous about what the country went through the first few days. But he also told me he was more confident and relaxed about the war by now."

I told her I was thrilled to hear that he was all right and even more that he could see her.

After the announcement of the ceasefire, Daniel was able to come home for a couple of days. I met him at that time. Obviously, I was very keen to hear how he'd managed to see his mom in the middle of the war. He pulled me to the side and asked me to swear that I would never say anything to anyone.

"I could spend years in jail if this reached the wrong ears. You will not believe this. I am at the base, and suddenly my boss calls me and says that I am about to have a special mission. Two dozen Egyptian commandos were caught and imprisoned. They had to be transported in two buses to the jail near Haifa, where all military prisoners are normally held. I would be in charge of their transport. Of course, there would be military police on the buses as well. I convinced the other driver and the four military policemen if we could stop near the train station, I would run home and get them delicious steak sandwiches prepared by my mother. I cannot believe that they agreed. I cannot believe that I am not sitting in jail right now!"

We had a good laugh about the story and decided to celebrate by going to a restaurant in Tel Aviv with our girlfriends. It seemed that life in Israel was slowly getting back to normal.

That was the last time I saw Daniel.

In Spanish, they say *"Que en Paz Descanse"* (QEPD), which is the same as the English "Rest in Peace" (RIP). I reflected with bitterness that these words ring empty or even false, in Daniel's case. How do you rest in peace when your life was cut short so early? When your potential to do something valuable, provide love, have family, support your mother, and be a good friend ends so soon and so abruptly?

Maybe the Jewish "Z'L"—translated into "May his Memory be a Blessing"—is slightly better, as we can find some solace in shared memories.

KRYPTONIA – NO LONGER THE SHITHOLE COUNTRY?

(a farce)

It was April 1, 2032. The new country Kryptonia's congress had just approved the new name. It simultaneously declared that the old name, Molgania, and its related history would be archived in a special "Oblivion" file.

The new country requested global recognition through the General Secretary of the United Nations. The request to accept the name change was unanimously approved the next day. A cynical journalist of a famed newspaper casually mentioned that all this transpired on April Fool's Day.

Yes, it was highly abnormal to expedite the vote in this manner, but every UN member wanted to please Kryptonia. In fact, the country's ambassador to the UN was unanimously voted to head the UNDP—the entity overlooking renewable energy developments. This appointment was a token of the world's nations' gratitude for Kryptonia's existence. As if Kryptonians had some kind of vote whether to exist. The island, a small piece of land in the middle of the ocean, was much like J. Maarten Troost's detailed description of Tarawa in *The Sex Lives of Cannibals*—a wonderfully funny book, for sure. Its population was poor, its natural resources meager, its infrastructure underdeveloped, and no real prospects for change. Those statements were the main points of an internal report produced a few months earlier by the US State Department.

Legends are made out of the story that prompted these two formidable changes in a country with only 1.3 million inhabitants and a little over 70 thousand square kilometers. Why was the world so keen on keeping Kryptonia happy?

In June 2031, ten months earlier, a team of physicists, engineers, and agronomists discovered a very unusual plant. Smack in the middle of the small island was a modest mountain rising to almost three thousand feet above sea level; its shape reminded many of Rio de Janeiro's Sugarloaf. At the top of that mountain, hiding in one of its large creases, grew a plant with unique potency. The plant had never been spotted before. Maybe it was because said crease was near the top, and access was difficult. It was by happenstance that some botanists made it there and took a few samples. Soon after that, scientists discovered that the plant could generate enormous amounts of energy when adequately processed. To illustrate the find's magnitude, one of the scientists asserted that as little as two hundred pounds of this plant could provide NYC electricity for about a year. To history aficionados, the discovery reminded one of the discovery of guano (bird and bat shit) off the coast of Peru in the 19th century. That story ended poorly as it culminated in imperialist intervention, war, and economic disaster.

The country's president requested that the plant be named Kryptonita. This wish was totally in line with that president's fascination with all types of myths. Since childhood, Mr. Jonas had been a great fan of comic books, and Superman was a clear favorite. The idea to change the country's name to Kryptonia was a logical consequence of this decision.

Because the population was in a state of total euphoria, they consented. All forty congress members unanimously passed the resolutions about the name change and the symbolic archiving of documentation about the country's prior history. President Jonas wanted his people to imagine a fresh new start.

The Minister of the Interior reportedly erupted in a loud voice,

"We have won the lottery! Let's drink champagne." But when they looked for a bottle of the bubbly, none was found on the island. It was just one more story about the transfiguration of the small island.

Suddenly Kryptonia was inundated by several delegations; they came from the USA, Russia, Germany, Brazil. Everyone wanted to be their friend; everyone wanted access to the unique resource. It was such a tremendous departure from the way the small island country had been treated before. The following story speaks volumes: a few months earlier, the current American president asked for a review of all diplomatic activity. He wanted to replicate what a predecessor had done, even referring to the language that a former president had used. He requested that the State Department compile a list of "shithole countries" that should be totally ignored—little Molgania was ranked third on that list.

Consequently, the small embassy was shut down, its staff requested to return home. There was no need to spend a dime on a diplomatic presence there, it was said. Now, the State Department purchased a large plot of land and applied for permits to build a large compound, including the two largest buildings in Lopalola, the capital.

The President of Kryptonia appointed a committee to further the extraction and production of Kryptonita, this energy plant, its export to other countries, and how the island could best benefit from the unexpected windfall. The decision was taken that any citizen could grow this plant in his garden, land, or rooftop—it was essential to maximize the economic opportunity. Suddenly, many citizens headed to the mountain, some sneaking out at dusk to grab sample species to grow in their garden, even if they had no clear notions about how.

The Ministry of Finance decided on a five-stage plan to benefit from this finding. First, each household would receive a one-time bonus check equivalent to 400 USD with which they could do as they wanted.

Second, the island would launch a modernization plan that would improve infrastructure—the airport and roads were the primary focus.

Third, Kryptonita would seek to set up an industrial park that would produce cheap electronic parts that could be sold to the

"Apples" and "Samsungs" of the world, and a textile plant to make clothing for the domestic market and exports to all of Asia.

Fourth, they would set-up a tourist zone on the north side with beautiful beaches. Only a few foreigners had traveled to the island in the past, but the hotels were subpar, and there were very few restaurants or entertainment venues. The zone would encourage the building of more up-to-date hotels, a casino, a discotheque, and a waterpark to draw tourism and foment that industry.

Fifth, the inflow of money would allow the island to restore the finances of the country. Its bonds were rated CCC. The Moody's report of two years earlier had stated that the expectation that tax revenues and other sources of funding would remain problematic; thus, the low rating would stay in place. Obviously, this analyst had not foreseen what would come.

The promise to all cabinet members that they would receive a handsome $25,000 bonus once the proceeds from the bond's sale came in was, of course, not made public. Needless to say, the President would quietly give himself a special gift of four times that sum.

Highly remarkable were the reactions across the globe. Exceptionally few cast any doubts on the story's veracity; even fewer were circumspect about how long this phenomenon could last. Instead, many started speculating about the impact of the discovery on economies everywhere. This development would affect oil prices and the economies of major oil producers. Indeed, oil prices plummeted 20% within weeks of the discovery. In contrast, the stock price of airlines and other major oil consumers went up a hefty amount. Countries heavily dependent on oil imports—such as Japan—saw their stock markets surge.

At the same time, they established all sorts of entities to exploit the new situation. Some economic historians drew parallels with the opening of Eastern Europe after the fall of the Berlin Wall. Many experts giggled when they saw that a Kryptonia mutual fund was set-up. The fund could only have few investable options— most indigenous companies were not even tradeable in the puny stock market, which had a daily trading value of less than the equivalent of $250k.

The Finance Minister, Puck Balala, was one of the few who had attended university abroad and saw the opportunity. He approached one of the top investment banks on Wall Street with the idea of floating a bond at relatively low-interest rates. It would greatly benefit the island as the current bond, issued five years earlier, had the onerous stated yieldy of 8.75%. The bankers, always keen to strike deals, thought it was a great idea—they explained the island could pay off the expensive bond and finance infrastructure and tourism projects.

When he asked the lead banker, "How big an issue will the markets be willing to absorb?" he was astonished to hear: "How about $1 billion?" Even though Balala claimed to know the American mindset, he was shocked by the astronomical figure. The Minister concealed his surprise and just asked if his counterpart was sure. When that man expressed confidence in his estimate, Balala realized that it was no skin off his—or, in this case—his country's back. Kryptonia would just ride the excitement created by the discovery. Yes, Kryptonia had indeed won the global lottery.

One analyst, working for a smaller firm on Wall Street, wondered if there was certainty in the forecasts regarding this plant's miraculous properties. Would it be possible to assure the potency of the plant's energy emissions forever? In all environments? Would the resource have a finite supply chain? But the general euphoria was too great to give a lending ear to this naysayer. This was "no time for negativity," wrote a rebutting publication.

The first three months after the discovery were as good as could be expected. The plant's processing took place in other countries, but the raw product was bunched together in local facilities—one near the mountain and three in other depots spread around. They shipped it like tobacco plants were: the bales put in bags and sent across the water to faraway places for processing. Huge barges waited outside the only port on the island. Because the port could not provide for adjacent docking, small boats transported the bags to the barges. A small industry of maritime transport sprang to life.

Some disturbing news reached the president's ears about four months after the first discovery. In several plots of land, the plants were simply dying. Overnight, the owners saw the philodendron-like green leaves turn yellow and droop as if in shame, trying to hide their weakness, seeking the ground to be buried away for eternity. As the owners saw this horrific display of decay, their reactions were relatively uniform—they cried, hollered, screamed at the plants in despair. Some tried to revive the plants' vibrancy by pouring more water, caressing the leaves, spraying insecticides and other chemicals—all in vain. The leaves had turned utterly yellow by the next morning, and some were just lying in complete inertia on the ground. Realizing the importance of what had transpired, two of the six owners called the police and, in agitated voices, informed them of the news. In most small countries, this type of story would spread like wildfire. Because there was so much at stake, military police members appeared at the six owners' homes. After inspecting the tragedy, they used the "stick" of possible incarceration if they told anyone about the plant's disease and the "carrot" of the equivalent of one thousand dollars in compensation for their silence. They then reported to their superiors, which was how the developments reached the presidential palace.

The response from the president was swift, if not overly imaginative. He asked his Minister of the interior—an obscure man who was head of the somewhat ruthless secret service—and the Minister of finance to a meeting. They agreed to ask the French scientist who had participated in the original discovery to revisit the country and figure out what had happened in those gardens. They decided that because these were still isolated cases, there was no need to get overly concerned. Nonetheless, because there was so much riding on this plant, it was imperative to keep an absolute lid on the news. The fact that the large bond issue was about to hit the market made it crucial. They did not want to cause any disruptions or delays. The Minister of the interior needed to make sure these six families keep their mouths shut.

The president insisted on getting a daily report to update him on Kryptonita plants crumbling into nothingness. A week passed, and there were no new occurrences, so the palace emitted a sigh of relief. However, the president's forehead showed new lines of worry as the report of three more incidents reached him. They came from a garden near the mountain on Monday, and two more at the far end of the island, where they planned the tourist site, on Tuesday.

"It is a plague!" he screamed. He asked his secretary to convene the cabinet for Thursday afternoon. The ministers were asked to come up with ideas regarding what to do about this worrisome chain of events.

That meeting, one participant told his wife, was dramatic. The president seemed terribly nervous. They decided that until the scientists could discern the reason for the collapse of Kryptonita plants at various private gardens, secrecy had to be maintained about everything. Under no circumstances could the news get out of the island. If the scientists that arrived on the weekend could not discern what was causing plants to die, more scientists should be paid handsome sums to investigate and hopefully find a cure. Too much was at stake.

As the president reportedly said, "We cannot afford for this to collapse. I cannot imagine us going back to the old, poverty-stricken Molgania."

The French scientist arrived on Sunday and was driven to the four sites where the plants had died. He took his glasses off, put them back on, collected a few dead leaves to study, took samples of the dirt, and after three days, came to the conclusion that the sudden death of Kryptonita could not be deciphered and collected $10,000 for his trouble. The president was furious, but there was not much he could do. Disgracing the Frenchman would only risk the word leaking a week before the issuance of the bond. In the meantime, there were reports of twelve more locations with dying plants. He asked his Minister if additional scientists had been identified to resolve the puzzle. Yes, there was a Russian agricultural expert who, it was said, was well trained and could resolve the enigma. He wanted $25,000 for his visit and work. The president frowned unhappily but conceded that the country had no choice but to accept "this blackmail."

By the time the Russian expert came, the number of dying Kryptonita had multiplied. Every day there were reports of ten, fifteen, even more than twenty crumbling plants. The Russian, whose English was limited, asked to go to the dying plants. He also played around with the dirt, collected dead leaves, and then surprised the locals watching him when he lay on the ground and put his ear on the ground as if he wanted to hear some heart palpitations. When the Interior minister reported that strange display, the president yelled, "And we are paying $25,000 for this clownish act?"

Two weeks later, the president's Chief of Staff stormed into the president's office without knocking. "I have terrible news! The word is out! CNN and the BBC have told the world that Kryptonita plants are dying."

The president buried his face in his hands but eventually asked how this had leaked. Apparently, the Russian scientist had made a bundle by passing on the scoop to a BBC journalist in Moscow. The news spread like wildfire.

It only took a few minutes before the voice on the other side of the president's phone announced that the White House was calling—the American president wanted to speak with Jonas. A thunderous and angry voice came across the phone, berating Jonas for not calling the American president to share the news, demanding to know what Kryptonia planned to do, and threatening to suspend all investment plans, including a larger diplomatic presence in the country.

Jonas assured his counterpart that they were trying to get a handle on it. Until this moment, the dead plants had been isolated cases in private gardens and not on the mountain where the plant grew wildly. Kryptonia, he assured the president, would do everything possible to get to the bottom of this matter, and as soon as they did, they would let the American president know first and then inform the rest of the world. Jonas assured the Americans that they wanted to follow full disclosure principles. The American president seemed less animated and ended the conversation by saying: "Let's hope it all works out. For all our sakes!"

Barely thirty minutes passed, and the Wall Street firm called— they were alarmed by the news; they already had several significant cancelations and could only offer a deal for half the original size, at most, and on a "best-effort" basis. Jonas asked the Finance Minister what that meant, and the response was straightforward, if not totally disappointing—there was no assurance of them reaching even the half-billion target. "Maybe we need to suggest to raise the stated interest rate to get enough demand?" Jonas agreed. "Why don't you ask them what impact such improved terms would have on the size of the bond offering," Jonas asked to convene an emergency session of his cabinet. Matters were getting out of hand, and he was afraid that all development and growth plans were at risk.

The cabinet met that afternoon, and Jonas opened by exhorting all members to contact any domestic and global connections these ministers might have. Figuring out what was causing the selective wilting of the plant was critical. It was also crucial to quickly come up with responses/solutions; time was of the essence. They agreed to reconvene in three days.

Two cabinet members told the gathering that they had gotten some ideas about why some Kryptonita plants were dying. One scientist suggested that the soil might not be adequate for the roots to set in properly and absorb the rain—the island did have above-normal rainfall during this, rainy season. Another had a somewhat similar explanation when he said that having too many of these plants in a small plot of land—to reap as great a financial benefit as possible, of course—would cause a similar problem of inability to absorb the rainfall. A third suggested that one should look at the possibility that insects or other diseases killed the plants. Further analysis was needed, but equally obvious was the fact that the clock was ticking as the potential windfall created by a global bond might be voided. President Jonas sent a delegation to visit the various plots and examine whether these hypotheses seemed plausible. He demanded that the report be submitted in forty-eight hours.

Three days later, with the bond issuance coming in two days—it had been delayed for a week awaiting further news about the plants dying—Jonas called the American president. He told him that they had discovered that the plants only died in gardens, plots of land, where greedy owners planted too much Kryptonita. He assured that the government was surveying the whole island to stop this practice. The American president accepted the explanation with much glee. He was looking forward to welcoming Jonas to the White House in about three months. Jonas gracefully accepted the invitation. He knew that such an event would assure his tenure as president of the island for at least a decade.

After he hung up, Jonas told his Minister of the Interior, the man in whom he confided most, that he was surprised how willing the American counterpart had been to receive good news.

He heartily laughed as he said, "I could have told him that we found a miraculous pill that we could feed these plants (as if they were animals), and he would have bought the story. It seems they all live in Disneyland over there." His Minister reminded Jonas that, in fact, he had told the American a half-truth at best. Yes, there were some overly crowded plots, but in other cases, none of the hypotheses panned out, and the enigma was still confounding.

The bond finally launched, and the investment bankers informed the Minister of Finance that it had gone as well as could be expected considering recent developments. The final tally was that $350 million bonds sold, and the interest rate was 5.25%—not as good as initially hoped, but enough to allow for the refinancing of the old bond and pay for some of Kryptonia's projects.

Jonas declared the following Sunday "National Rejuvenation" day. No one would have to go to work; all cities and villages would have parades, and a red carnation—a common flower on the island—would be worn by all in celebration.

Barely three weeks later, many plants on the mountain were turning yellow and dying. And the news spread like wildfire—not just on the island, but across the globe. No one had a clear idea as to what the plague was all about. The island turned somber, as if many had died. They were crying on the streets and not even hiding it. There was a sense of doom for the islanders.

The American president acted angrily and cut diplomatic relations with "that nation of liars and thieves." The plans to set up a sizable representative office were canceled, and the newly appointed ambassador was called back. The invitation to Washington was, of course, rescinded.

The price of the Kryptonia international bond dropped precipitously to something like thirty cents on the dollar.

The United Nations replaced the head of the agency in charge of renewable energy, the UNDP, with a South African diplomat.

A new party emerged in Kryptonia. The party was formed with the sole purpose of unseating Jonas as the call for early elections became more vociferous. Robert Mombi, the man seeking to wrestle power from Jonas, repeatedly said, "We have to stop acting like we are in a Superman movie."

Talking to his best friend, the Interior Minister, Jonas commented that he always wondered how Kryptonite greatly affected Superman. It was not just the quickness of the impact, but the forcefulness—how quickly the hero became powerless.

"It should perhaps have warned me about what might happen with this plant and with us."

THE URN

Ushered in by the beauty of leaves changing color and leaving in the whirlwind of the ghastly and ghostly, that was Rob's October. Moreover, it all got compressed into a couple of hours of shock, memories, and reflection.

Rob was dropped off in front of his house. As he slowly walked toward the front door, his thoughts were immersed in how happy he had been attending his college friends' annual fishing and water-rafting trip. The fall scenery had been so beautiful and calming. When he approached the door, he noticed that it was slightly ajar; he frowned about this unexpected development.

"What the heck!" As of late, he talked to himself out loud, perhaps because he felt lonely. He pushed the door open and dragged his bags in. Once inside, he saw that the place was a mess. Some drawers had been opened, and their contents lay dispersed all over the floor. Two boxes of documents were torn apart.

Lately, when he was upset, he would bump into things. He accidentally kicked the cat's water bowl near the kitchen table. It reminded him he was supposed to pick up his cat. He walked toward the area where his keys were supposed to be. "What are these keys? These are not my Mercedes keys!" He ran over to the garage entrance and hollered, "What's that ugly car doing in my garage? Where is my beautiful blue car?"

What would he do about Monster, the cat? He could not pick him up in this state of mind. He called the neighbors and explained that he had been burglarized. Could they perhaps bring the cat over? He needed to sort out what was going on, what was missing. He did not want to drive right now.

Rob ran back to the garage to look at the strange car. As he pointed at the license plate, which proudly stated that its registration was in Alabama, he thought, "Oh God! It was Cynthia! She must have driven here from Huntsville."

Doris knocked at the door; she had the cat. "Oh my. Are you going to be okay?" She pointed at the mess on the floor, where papers were still dispersed attesting to the trespassing.

"Yes, I will be fine. I need to figure out what happened and how to proceed from here. Thank you for taking care of my cat."

Though he did not want to believe it, he'd never imagined Cynthia would act so violently; he was sure that this had to do with the divorce settlement. The split-up had been the final straw in a relationship that should never have come about and had gone bad quickly. They'd lasted for less than a year.

They had met on a cruise. The Carnival Today ship had left Miami in mid-October and, over seven days, stopped at several touristy Caribbean ports: Philipsburg in St. Maarten, St. Kitts, San Juan, Bahamas. He had been sick and tired of being alone and decided to take a cruise. He even entertained the possibility of meeting a woman on the trip.

The first evening, he'd gone to the bar and seen a woman whose red hair was so provocative, he'd become determined to make a pass at her as long as she was single.

She'd seemed very willing to chat with Rob. She'd said she had boarded the boat with her girlfriend, Margarita. Both lived in Alabama. "Oh! That flight to Miami and the hotel—they were so expensive!" She was looking forward to taking advantage of everything the cruise made available—as long as it was free. She would not take any of the excursions inland—the prices were ridiculous. But "free gin-and-tonics and frozen daiquiris— yummy!"

They had a blast that first night and promised each other to spend as much time as possible together. When Rob had probed about the girlfriend, Cynthia waved it off, "I am not married to my girlfriend; I have a good-looking guy pursuing me, and I need to take advantage of that!"

As he mulled over the early days of his relationship with Cynthia, he kept revisiting the first night they'd spent together. The sex had been so good. He had not been with a woman for nearly two years, ever since his divorce from Maria—the third divorce of his life. He'd wanted it to last forever, and the only way to make it last was to marry the woman. But, he had gotten burned before, so he was reticent. By the time he'd divorced Maria, he'd promised himself he would not rush to the altar ever again. However, we know that some men have a difficult time changing ingrained patterns of behavior. He knew that the words, "Will you marry me?" had great allure; they were as inviting as a double martini at the free bar. He had to bite his lips not to utter that phrase on the sixth night of the cruise.

Instead, he offered Cynthia to come up to Connecticut to see his house. During that visit, he surrendered. He told her, "Let's fly to Las Vegas, hire an Elvis Presley look-alike to preside over our Vegas-style wedding. Quick and efficient."

Two weeks later, he flew to Alabama and helped her move her possessions—neither luxurious nor large—to his house.

It did not take long to be disillusioned by Cynthia; he found her to have limited education, crass manners, and poor taste. He was aghast to find out that she had quit school after two years. Not college, high school, she explained. She neglected the house's upkeep. She stayed indoors, in her pajamas or joggers and a T-shirt, watching sitcoms and game shows, while Rob was at the brokerage firm trying to sell limited partnerships and annuities to less than savvy customers. She preferred to microwave a frozen meal for dinner—grilling a burger or steak was meant for a memorable evening. She confessed that she had never cooked before. "What for?" she'd asked. "Those turkey, gravy, and mashed-potatoes frozen dinners are really very yummy."

Rob, whose original name was Rutherford William, and whose family claimed Mayflower origins, was embarrassed that she was his wife. He found excuses to avoid introducing her to his family—he had five brothers and one sister. They would have made all sorts of nasty comments after seeing her, even if she would have replaced her everyday loungewear and sweatpants.

He showed a strong preference for traveling to isolated places in Maine and Vermont, where no one knew them, and where he could pretend that he was delighted with his situation. To fit in, he even bought some flannel shirts at the local Walmart. Because of the frequent trips, his income at the brokerage house, which solely depended on "production" (i.e., sales commissions), declined.

And as he saw his numbers plummet, he realized that he needed to get yet another divorce. It just was not going to work out. He had made a massive mistake because he felt so lonely; it was time to cut loose and face the consequences.

He told Cynthia he wanted to split up. She screamed, threatened violence and mayhem, told him she had a brother who had already served jail-time because he'd roughed up a former boyfriend of hers. He did not care. He was furious; he told her he would give her $100,000 as a quid pro quo to her departure. She did not understand that term. He told her it was the cost of her leaving. "Go back to Alabama and buy yourself a nice house and a car. This money is plenty."

She complained that she should get more. Maybe about half his wealth. He reminded her that she'd signed a pre-nuptial, and he did not owe her anything. But he understood that she would want something in return. "That's why I offered you this large sum," he rebutted. She said she needed to go to Alabama and speak to her friends and family. While she was away, he changed all the locks and sent a check and the divorce papers to her mother's house.

Now, he ran outside to inspect the doors. Indeed, Cynthia had forced herself into the house by breaking a window and reaching the lock through the hole. She had probably been terribly angry to find a new set of locks. He always left the car keys hanging on a hook near the door—she had seen where he would put them. Stealing his car would not be difficult.

And then it dawned on him: the urn! The urn was sitting in the trunk of the car. He'd intended to do the right thing with its contents at a convenient time, and then Cynthia and the multiple trips with her had gotten in the way.

Rob's brother Alistair had suddenly died while asleep in his home in Martha's Vineyard. He was eight years older and had a weak heart but had not complained about ill-health. No one had told Allistair that it was not good to be alone, but now that he was dead, everyone agreed that their brother had been a bit of a recluse. He never married, and when he'd retired from his job at the New Haven post office, he'd chosen to move to live his last few years in the Vineyard. He loved that island, the solitude it afforded, the people that were there year-round, the beaches.

Rob had helped his brother with the move. They'd packed a small moving truck with all his cherished belongings: his favorite reclining chair, and some kitchen instruments he'd had for years but loved, and brought these to the new place—a quaint small house in the woods near Manuel Correllus State Forest. It had been a house rented to summer visitors, but the owner had died, and the children just wanted to sell it and split the proceeds.

Concerned about his older brother becoming a hermit, Rob had found a neighbor, Mr. Williams, who promised to check on Alistair once in a while and call Rob if there were any issues. Indeed, it had been Mr. Williams, who had called Rob to tell him about his brother's death. He might have been dead for several days. Concerned that he had not seen him roaming around his little garden, the neighbor had gone inside the house and found the body.

Rob had driven up immediately. He first went to the house and made sure it was secure. Then he'd gone to the morgue to confirm this was his brother's body. He hated taking care of all the minutia, but there was no choice. That's how he'd found Alistair's will, carefully placed in a folder that was labeled "Bills and Important Documents." It was as brief as the total estate was limited. He'd wanted all proceeds to be used for two purposes: the cremation of his body with the ashes being dispersed in the ocean and whatever remained to go to a charity dedicated to rooting out poverty in Haiti. That Alistair had any interest in Haiti was a surprise, but Rob had neither the desire nor the time to unravel this mystery.

Rob next contacted all family members. Essentially, these were just the four brothers and one sister. He told them the sad news and asked them to join him for the ceremonies that Alistair had chosen.

Without exception, all of them expressed sorrow and lamented that they could not attend the cremation. They used scheduling and the act's unpleasantness as excuses. In turn, they all promised to participate in the much less stomach-churning event of spreading the ashes to the wind. Since Martha's Vineyard had plenty of access to the sea, it would all be relatively straightforward. Rob told them that he would suggest a couple of days/weekends for this gettogether.

Thus, Rob had been the only one present at the cremation. He had seen a movie on Netflix, where a man had witnessed his abusive father's cremation. It had made him ill to his stomach. Now he stood in front of the oven that was going to decimate his brother's dead body, seeing the orange flames dance with a great appetite as they engaged in the destruction. Because of that movie, he felt ready—a bit insulated. However, when he imagined the actual body, bones, flesh, teeth being destroyed by the fire, he had to look away and finally rushed to vomit in the men's room.

Alistair's family had chosen to assemble in November, about a month after the cremation. Rob would bring the urn, and at about 5 p.m., when the sun was going to sleep on the horizon, they would scatter the ashes upon Alistair's favorite shoreline.

They had agreed to meet in front of Alistair's house. Rob thought that if anyone wanted any furnishings or other items in the place, they could take them. He offered the same to Mr. Williams and also invited him to attend the ceremony. He'd declined, arguing that only family members should attend it. Of course, this was nonsense, but some people don't like alternatives to the proper burial of a coffin in the ground. Lots of people in India might disagree, thought Rob, but that was beside the point.

The family got together at around 4:30 in the afternoon. Some just stayed outside the house, expressing absolutely no interest in roaming inside a dead person's home—no matter whose it was. Two did walk in. Mina, the sister, actually took a couple of kitchen utensils and some "very cute" salt and pepper shakers.

Then they'd driven over to the cliff overlooking the ocean. Martha's Vineyard has several beautiful bluffs; people reaching them could enjoy the island's panoramic view of the sea. It was very colorful—the green of the woods and the sea's blue, along with the brownish-yellow of the dirt and the cliffs that frame them.

Mina, whose long black hair had swirled in the wind, was the first to remark that it might not be possible to spread the ashes. "It is so windy here! If he empties the urn intending that the ashes reach the sea, the ashes will probably swirl around, and fly back in our faces and turn our clothes gray."

Ash, the middle brother whose original name was Ashton and had a very bizarre sense of humor, often bordering the macabre, added that he was not interested in having a burned piece of toenail hit him in the face.

Two brothers expressed disgust by groaning, "Yuck Ash!"

And Chris, who was the "wiseass" brother, added, "Here we go, Ash, being his usual funny self, but this time it's about ashes."

Rob quickly closed the lid on the urn and told everyone how much he appreciated the sacrifice that they all had made in coming. It was useless to ask everyone to assemble again for this matter. In a way, by being there, they had essentially done what poor, lonely, reclusive Alistair would have considered acceptable. He would take the urn with him, find the right moment, and a suitable place to fulfill their brother's last wishes and be done with it.

Luckily, he now commented to himself, he had not committed to informing them when the actual dispersal of ashes was finally performed. One or two of those attending might have inquired why they had not heard from Rob in all these months.

Rob, of course, knew why he had been distracted from taking care of Alistair's ashes. Cynthia had distracted him. First, the courtship, then the multiple trips to seek distance from the crowd that might recognize him, and then, finally, the arguments about separation and divorce. He had forgotten about the urn waiting in the trunk.

Upon arriving home from the ill-fated dispersion-of-ashes event, he'd left the urn in the car. At first, he'd thought of bringing the urn into the house. Perhaps put it on the fireplace's mantle to remind him of an incomplete task requiring his attention. He'd finally decided against that. For one, his cat, Monster, could tip the urn and spread the contents all over the house—what a mess that would be! Besides, he actually felt squeamish about having a dead body, even if in the form of ashes, inside his house. So, he'd left the urn in the trunk.

Now he faced a ridiculous situation: he needed to chase after his former wife and talk to the one person he least wanted to engage with, but he wanted to regain possession of his car.

Then it occurred to him that he might spook her by telling her that the primary reason he needed the car back was that there was a dead body in the trunk. Yes, he would say that, rather than say that these were ashes of a cremated brother. It would scare her to pieces, and everything would become more manageable. That it was late in October, and Halloween was around the corner made it all deliciously suitable.

THE CRASHING OF BRUCE'S WALL

Almost no one knew Bruce Goodman well. Even as a child, he was an introvert; he spoke little and to only a few. He usually kept to himself. In high school, most called him a loner. Later in life, acquaintances described him as a tough man with a grim expression projecting a no-nonsense, perhaps taciturn, personality. Describing him physically, they mentioned his stern face, the muscles around his mouth taut. A couple said they seemed so tight one could imagine him incessantly grinding his teeth. Others, referring to his lips, spoke of thin lines across his face, typically closed and without the slightest hint of a smile. When they curved slightly, it was more the suggestion of a smug smirk than the intent to smile. The veins on his neck protruded thick and blue. His eyes were such a dark brown that one could easily mistake them for black; those very dark eyes would scare and intimidate anyone. As hard as you might try, you could not find any warmth in them. The look was stern, telling of unwavering certainty and a belligerent disposition. His face defied you to confront him, contradict him, challenge his views. He was implicitly daring you to bet against him while exuding calm confidence you would lose.

But there were also a few—Thomas and Sabrina quickly come to mind—who got a glimpse of his soul. For them, Bruce Goodman was sensitive, perhaps even overly sensitive, and intent on hiding that aspect as best he could. Sabrina knew that he could feel hurt, but he would bury the pain deep when he did. Thomas also understood that Bruce would not forget those who caused him pain or why. He always claimed to have the memory of an elephant. Even if locked in his heart, the scars were a burden carried but not shed. Eventually, he once told Thomas, he would get the opportunity to get even and then fully lash back.

He grew up in Brighton, hardly an environment that would toughen you up. It was not the rough neighborhood we might envision in Liverpool or Birmingham—with its lower-middle-class youngsters like those so aptly portrayed in *A Clockwork Orange*. Brighton was a leisure town that catered to endless busloads of tourists. Young men like Bruce undoubtedly benefited from the tourist economy and the seashore setting.

As we well know, much of one's character is shaped by what happens within the walls of the home, rather than the less intimate environment of daily life. There was a stark contrast between the gentle slopes of England's south coast, with its elderly visitors lounging in hotel balconies along the shoreline, and the nastiness Bruce experienced at home.

Bruce Goodman never called the place where he slept his home. Instead, it was the *house*—for this youngster, *the house* meant pain and disdain. When he finally left at eighteen, he tried his utmost to avoid visiting Brighton or bring back youthful memories. The day he left for London, he pledged never to look back.

He had been raised by a stepfather whose excessive drinking nurtured verbal and, sporadically, physical abuse. Intimidated by this man, his mother felt unable to do anything but condone all that violence. In those days, he only shared the pain and fear this elicited with a friend, Thomas Mason. They grew up on the same street, and one day Thomas saw Bruce running out of the house with his stepfather chasing after him. Thomas hid him in his home, and a friendship was born; it would last forever. Later in life, Sabrina also got to hear about his unhappy youth. A few months after the disclosures, however, he told her he regretted having confided in her.

His Brighton years were often dark, but they included one pleasant vignette he remembered with a smile. He would seek refuge in the cellar, lock the doors behind him, sit in a poorly lit room, and read books. These were mostly legends about prisoners escaping remote islands or biblical characters whose heroics involved fighting stronger, better-equipped men. Their stature grew with every act of defiance against cruel kings and ill-intentioned despots. The stories of David slaying Goliath, or the pharaoh's army drowning as Moses lifted his staff, and of the Philistines perishing alongside a vengeful and distraught Samson caused his imagination to fly and his spirits to rise. Written words quickly became pictures in his mind. Even at this early age, he recognized that these heroes had one resource to confront their hostile environment—their inner strength.

At sixteen, he was hardly a naïve boy; he rejected Thomas's attempt to soothe. The friend suggested that this violent period in his life was so unique that it could never recur. He told his friend that he thoroughly entertained the possibility that another person, as ruthless as his stepfather, could victimize him in the future. He told Thomas that he needed to build a wall that would shield him from a recurrence of abuse. "There is only one thing that will protect me in the future. I have to make money, lots of it! It will help me fend off anyone looking to harm me. It would be good to amass it quickly—to put an end to the current pain and give me a sense of security."

"And how are you going to make all that money?"

"Give me a break! I am only sixteen. I have no idea. I will figure it out before I turn eighteen, though. I am sure it will not happen in this dump. I have to get closer to where the money is—probably London."

He began paying attention to stories that discussed money and the wealthy. Many referred to the City, a part of London where most banks had their headquarters. It was good to begin developing a strategy, but first, he needed to do well in school.

For three consecutive summers, he worked at one of the smaller hotels in Hove. He wanted the income, and later, he also wanted to be near people with money. Since he was shy and reclusive by nature, it was hard for him to get close to these Londoners. But he knew he needed to ingratiate himself to those he suspected to be rich. He told Thomas, "These people even smell like money. They spend it easily, and I get good tips. Can you imagine how much better I could do if I were more social?"

In his third year, as he turned eighteen and was ready to finish high school, he developed a sense of urgency. "If I want to get out of here, I have to find someone that can help me," he told his friend.

With that in mind, he began to chat-up some guests. He was choosy in doing so. The selection was purely strategic and practical; he measured up these vacationers on whether they could be instrumental in getting him a job, hopefully in London.

One relatively easy pick was a somewhat rotund man in, he guessed, his late fifties. Bruce concealed a slight smile when he discovered that his interlocutor was a banker. Elliott Gould owned a small merchant bank. Moreover, the older man seemed to take a liking to him.

Bruce was unsure why this older man asked so many questions about what he did, and where he grew up, why he was so friendly, but he did not care. "The City's burgeoning financial district attracts bright young men like you as trainees," the banker told him. If Bruce was interested in such an opportunity, he should give him a call. Bruce was elated; he had found his ticket out of Brighton.

Though still somewhat reluctant, Bruce called Gould in late August. The man appeared to recognize his voice immediately. "I am a man of my word, Mr. Goodman; I can offer you a trainee position at my bank. We will train you to become an assistant-trader on the FX desk, and if you do well, you will be able to become one of my traders on the floor. As a trainee, you will not make a lot of money, but enough to live in London. However, if you do well, you will be able to make a small fortune for yourself."

It all sounded exciting, and Bruce confirmed that he would show up at the bank on the first Monday of September.

"When you arrive," said the older man, "I will make sure that you come to me so we can have a chat and get you going."

~ ~ ~ ~

The Chairman's chambers were what one would expect. The dark mahogany desk, the two large paintings of ships struggling in turbulent waters decorating the walls, and a large portrait of a man whose face closely resembled the man seated behind the desk. But there were also photographs of men in rugby gear, a great many of them. The banker made a point of describing them.

"These are my schoolmates. Men whom I love dearly."

The emphasis on the word *love* seemed odd and made Bruce Goodman squirm, but he did not know if that intuitive sense of dislike was appropriate or just another sign of his general distrust of older men. When the president put his arms around his shoulders, ostensibly as if to guide him on a tour of the banks' premises, Bruce Goodman felt squeamish. He would have preferred to jerk himself free, but he opted to tolerate the man's unusual friendliness and closeness.

Once at the forex desk, he learned from colleagues' gossip that Gould was gay. Bruce concluded that Gould's sexual proclivities were in line with his overly friendly attitude, as were comments about his rugby-playing friends. The notion that he possibly was hired for reasons that had nothing to do with his potential or aptitude made Goodman sick. He now understood why Gould was behaving this way. He was sure he did not invite this behavior. While the gay community in Brighton was significant, Bruce had never had any interest in men. Any casual relationships he had had were with women.

Two months after starting at the forex desk, Gould called Goodman to his office. He put his arms around Goodman and told him how happy he was with his progress—so much so that he wanted to promote him. He also wanted to invite him to his home in the countryside for the upcoming bank holiday weekend.

"You must feel very alone here. Why don't you join a couple of other friends and me?"

Goodman thanked the older man and promised to get back within a week. It was the best he could do without showing how nauseated he felt by the offer.

He called his friend Thomas. "Can you believe it? The bastard has invited me to his house for the bank holiday weekend! What do I do now? I don't want to go back to Brighton."

Thomas suggested he look for another job as quickly as possible and quit. Bruce searched the Financial Times that evening and contacted two entities seeking assistant traders.

A week later, he sent the Chairman his letter of resignation; he thanked him for the opportunity. The resignation was effective immediately because he was joining a foreign bank. He did not explain further. He did not tell him how angry he was that Gould abused his power to make uninvited overtures.

Bruce's stint at the Japanese bank ended up being relatively short. Goodman always expected it would be brief. Two factors made his decision to join that bank easy: he would have an immediate and viable alternative to Gould and his private merchant bank and stay in London. He also imagined the new employer could be a bridge—or better yet, a trampoline—to a larger, better-known bank.

Eventually, he realized that a corporate entity offered him two additional advantages: a more structured organization that could assure propriety and a set of benefits that a private entity was not obligated to provide.

While at the larger bank, he learned critical aspects of his business. They would serve him well in the future. Big banks had bureaucracies that could not react quickly to changing markets and economic news by their nature. Because the management of a section at the bank wanted to boast about profitable results, approaching them with ideas that had the potential for large rewards was a door-opener. If lucky with your vision, you would be well rewarded.

On a late Friday afternoon at the pub after two hours and six pints of Guinness, a somewhat drunk colleague confided in Bruce his mantra: "If your idea was stellar, you get a huge bonus. If your trade scheme is a big flop, but you are known as a good trader, you will always get another chance when you get hired by another company." The implications were obvious: the head of a trading desk was required to get top management approval for any new trading strategy. He would be well-served to highlight the advantages and potential windfall while minimizing any risks. The story was as simple as it was improper. Bruce thought that it all was cynical yet part of his new reality.

Bruce's primary objective was to hone his trading skills. He worked hard, probably harder than any of his counterparts. After four months, he chose to specialize—not too many traded Asian currencies, and that appealed to him. He made it a point to get up early, review Asian and American financial and economic data and trade flows, and see if he could map out a strategy; he would then suggest it to the head trader at the desk. Trading in the yen, the Thai baht, and the Korean won vis-à-vis the dollar would be most appealing because the money flows were large.

With time, he also developed a better sense of market behavior. He learned about herd mentality. It could cause big up and down gyrations. The piling-on when a trend was detected created exaggerated moves. The practical conclusion was that this was exploitable. Suppose one was adept at reading a pattern early enough (when the prices were cheap) and, even more importantly, smart enough to curtail greed and pull-out before the crowd stormed out the profits would be immense.

From one savvy old trader who took him under his wing, Bruce learned another concept: "Always relate the unrelated," the old man told him. This was especially true in foreign currency trading. If, for example, there were skirmishes on the Indo-Chinese border, it was likely to affect the strength of the US dollar.

He used all this knowledge to improve and soon became the head of Asian currency trading at the bank.

Two years later, Bruce was approached by an American bank that offered him to head the FX trading desk handling Asian currencies. A significant signing bonus sweetened his acceptance. He would manage a team of four at a top-line bank, and that was thrilling. Contemplating his meteoric rise—after all, he was only twenty-two and had been trading for only three years—he concluded that he had been quite lucky. Could Fortuna ever run out?

A successful strategy came early in his new job. He was able to ride the wave of a declining euro. It pushed the dollar higher against it, but as expected, also against all Asian currencies. Feeling confident about this trend, he successfully pushed the envelope with the amounts traded.

At about this time, his observation of the FX trading universe concluded that most traders would adopt simplistic strategies— they would invest in the most popular bet by buying "X" and selling "Y." However, some mathematicians were espousing more complex strategies; these were presented at conferences like the one he attended in Frankfurt. They spoke in favor of multiple related trades, employing options, and the use of leverage.

Upon his return from the conference, he sought management

approval to introduce these methods. He argued that he would have a leg-up on the competition: these "traditionalists" with their simplistic approach. They were content looking at charts as predictors of future direction, and their confidence stemmed from being part of a crowd—if they are all making the same bet, a reversal would be difficult. Of course, this was nonsense. The trend is your friend until it suddenly reverses. This historical fact was regularly ignored. When suddenly the pattern collapsed, those in the herd, especially those coming in late, would lick their wounds. They'd stare at the same chart with flushed faces and shrug.

Bruce was afraid he might sound too innovative and dangerous. Thus, in his presentation, Bruce also stated that avarice was a massive problem for the "traditionalists." Because gains were often commensurate with brinkmanship, taking on risk was sometimes rewarded by gains. But, it was necessary to weigh these risks and refrain from carelessness. The kernel of many financial crises was centered right there. Being concerned about risk was wise. He quoted one conference presenter's simple message: "Maybe get on board a bit late, missing the early gains, and get out a bit early, leaving some potential profits on the table, but the fat will be yours."

The management response was positive, but with a caveat: "Implement the new methods, but do so gradually and carefully; we don't want to see big losses."

Using the new tools: multiple strategies that crisscrossed each other, options to minimize risk and guarantee minimal returns, and enhance chances for profitability via leverage whenever possible, he was confident he was ahead of the competition.

These years of growing success were also pleasure-filled years for Bruce Goodman. He had fun in the big city. He did not make close friends—that was hard for him, but he significantly extended his circle of acquaintances. He would usually go to the same neighborhood bar near his flat in Notting Hill. Typically, the Bear Cove was hopping on Thursday nights, when the boys and girls were mapping out their weekend fun. And he often followed this with Friday and Saturday nights clubbing. It was the thing to do for twenty-somethings in those early years of the new millennium.

On one Thursday evening, he noticed a redhead standing in the middle of a crowd of accosting, hungry-looking men. He swiftly made his way over, pushed aside some of these hovering wolves, reached out to take her hand, and pulled her over while saying, "Let me buy you a drink! What would you like?"

She later commented on how she loved his determination and physical presence as he "conquered the territory and liberated" her. For the couple, it was the beginning of a turmoil-filled relationship. There were fantastic highs and heartbreaking lows. In time, Goodman sensed he had little control over the friendship. As could be expected, this bothered him immensely, but he had no wall to protect himself from this tantalizing woman.

Two weeks after meeting her, he told Thomas about her. "She is so sexy! She is the first woman about whom I felt like this. I am willing to go the extra mile for her. But I am nervous. I hope I don't get hurt."

Thomas wished him good luck and just said, "It will be good for you not to be alone."

Sabrina was two years younger, an analyst for a private equity firm, very fit and beautiful. She was quick on her feet, defiant in conversation, and with that beautifully dyed hair, a lightning rod for young men. She also knew of all this—it was a source of her exuding self-confidence. The pair began dating slowly, but a month later, they often were seen together. She had warned him that she was "not always nice," but he ignored it as just talk, maybe a way to test him. In a way, it was a challenge, and as such, her strategy was effective.

One night, they hung out past three in the morning, finished two bottles of St. Julien, and talked about themselves. In her mild stupor, she confessed that dating was "just a game," one in which she excelled. "I am capable of extracting myself from any situation—taking myself out of the picture as if I was a fly on the wall. I contemplate how 'Joe' and I are playing our cards. If he is a push-over, I'd leave him so fast his head would spin."

She seemed to enjoy Goodman's company, his looks, and his relaxed and cocky demeanor. His tough chin was not just a facial feature; it suggested a hard-nosed approach to life she admired. A month later, during an evening of passionate necking, they landed in bed, and after the act, she admitted that she had never experienced an orgasm during intercourse. What timing! Of all things she could have said, this was the one that got Bruce Goodman's attention. He dismissed other statements as perhaps playful, perhaps attention-seeking, but this one rang alarm bells. It was a challenge, and he was adamant about being the first to get her there; it was a huge aphrodisiac. Years later, after many crises, after multiple ups and downs, he admitted defeat—not publicly, mind you, just to himself.

Despite the tension caused by disagreements over seemingly small matters, they grew closer. One evening, Goodman heard how fed up she was with a sloppy, unreliable roommate who did not honor her financial commitments. Bruce immediately suggested that she move in with him.

That weekend he helped her move her belongings. In the next couple of weeks, they grew closer. And as they did and shared carnal desires, they also contemplated what being a couple would be. They talked about what they wanted most. The prevalent idolatry of money and the hedonistic appetite to make every moment as pleasureful as possible were central. They were hardly different from the crowd at the Bear Cove. But travel also was necessary, especially to excitement-seeking Sabrina.

As they plotted trips, she pushed for places with the right mix of "exotic and erotic." He smiled and thought it sounded fantastic. Their first trip, two weeks around Christmas and New Year's, was spent in Barbados. For years, he relived their skinny-dipping to "begin the new year in glorious fashion"—her words as she lured him to join her in the ocean.

In April, they took a week off and went to Koh-Samui. She convinced him to ask a local young woman to join them for dinner and late-night fun in their room. He called Thomas from Thailand and told him the story. He started by saying, "You will never believe this…" Thomas mumbled some words connoting exuberant surprise.

Five months later, they took the Eurostar to Paris. Goodman laid out their plans in meticulous detail. They would stay at a boutique hotel. After dropping off their luggage and visiting Notre Dame—his favorite building in the glorious city—they would head to *Galeries Lafayette*. They would look for the jewelry department, and he would buy her a ring—he specified, "a friendship ring, not a wedding ring." He also noted: "We are not ready for marriage, but we have a special bond, and it needs its symbol." They would buy some unique clothes for that night's outing, he added. She wanted to go to the opera, and though he did not like operas, he complied and bought tickets for some modern opera that ended up being a bore. He also made reservations at a fancy restaurant and a rooftop disco to close the night. He bought her a tuxedo jacket ("You will wear this without a bra, blouse or undershirt," he told her, and she got excited). She looked stunning in black silk pants and the jacket. Any time she leaned over, the opening exposed a partial view of her pink nipples. It drove him wild. It was a splendid night, but when heavy drinking led to him falling asleep before sex, she ridiculed him the next morning. He was annoyed and disturbed—she is dismissing how she had hugged and kissed me outside the Lafayette store yesterday, he thought.

A year after they met, they decided to take a two-week trip to South America. They visited the Iguazu Falls, the Fernando de Noronha archipelago, Buenos Aires, and Rio de Janeiro. During the journey, Sabrina showed no inclination to avoid injudicious, hurtful remarks. One night, she made a sarcastic comment about becoming limp because he drank too much. A couple of evenings later, while dining at the fabulous Belmond Hotel next to *Foz de Iguazu*, she told him she enjoyed exploiting his willingness to spend a lot of money on them. That got him livid, and they went through Rio without saying much to each other. He contained himself from asking her to take an early flight home. However, when they returned to London, he asked her to pack her bags and leave his place; he could not be with someone who enjoyed making hurtful remarks. She shed a couple of tears while packing, then suddenly stopped and, while displaying a grotesque face he had never seen previously, called him a hick from the southern countryside.

He was rather upset and called Thomas in despair. "Can you believe this woman? Her comments are so nasty. It almost seems like she is looking for a fight, for our relationship to explode."

"Why almost, Bruce? She is looking for a breakup. Some women are like that. What have you done about it?"

"I told her to pack her bags and leave."

"Good for you. I would have done the same."

"The problem is, I still have strong feelings for her."

"I hope you get over that, Bruce. She sounds like trouble to me."

It was just the first of several breakups; the sequence repeated itself: first the request to pack her things and leave, then the plea to come back. The love-hate pendulum swung hard in both directions. Three weeks after throwing her out, Goodman called her and apologized for overreacting—he did not mention the cause for his anger or rehash her comments' meanness. He wanted her in his life, he said. She agreed to return. She told him she had moved from one girlfriend's place to the next for those three weeks. She did not say that she had told her friends: "I expect him to call, apologize, and for me to return to his place—that's why I am not looking to rent a flat." She was good at 'playing the game' indeed.

If his love life was tumultuous, Goodman's work continued to be a story of success. His name was circulating in the relevant circles as a very impressive, savvy investor and manager. One spring day in 2006, he got a call from a well-known hedge fund trader, John Wells. Wells told him that he had decided to split from the fund he currently helped manage. He was going to launch his fund and wanted Goodman to join. Wells thought Bruce could manage a sleeve dedicated to "macro" strategies—specifically currencies, gold, and sovereign bonds. He had heard good things about Bruce and had a hunch they might be a good fit.

They met for dinner at *Sartoria* in Mayfair and discovered their trading and hedge funds' views coincided. Bruce agreed that this was an excellent time to launch a new fund. He wanted in. He did not disclose that he was eager to continue building his wall of money—the dream of the Brighton lad that never left him.

While they worked on all aspects of creating a fund, mum was the word. They needed to earn a living. They would meet every two, three weeks to share updates and discuss pertinent issues.

Each partner contributed to the set-up. Wells had friends in the City willing to rent them half the floor in a posh building. Goodman talked to some wealthy investors he knew; he spoke about a new hedge fund looking for seed money without saying it would be under his management. They met with a lawyer to draft legal agreements with each other on the one hand and with potential investors on the other. As they worked consistently and systematically to achieve their goal, they fostered a certain camaraderie.

Finding enough money to seed the fund was the critical piece. Both principals could still rely on their excellent reputation to raise the initial $500m from ultra-high-net-worth individuals. Additional money would flow from a well-known fund of funds (a "feeder fund") that commanded plenty of capital and committed to being involved.

He had no qualms in approaching Gould, the man who originally brought him to London and started his career. Though he loathed Gould forever, he never commented publicly about it. Despite being plagued by illness and old age, the Chairman agreed to hear Goodman's pitch. "You know I am good at exploiting macro trends and making money," he told him. "If you put up some seed-money, we will give you special terms, and you will be handsomely rewarded for putting your faith in me, something you did once, way back."

Whether Gould knew that Goodman would be a good hedge fund manager or not is unclear; regardless, he agreed to be one of the new fund's first investors.

~ ~ ~ ~

The success of the fund in the early days of 2007 was remarkable. The first quarter generated a return of nearly 4.5% (on an annualized basis, that would be almost 18%!). These results spurred inflows of new capital, and the fund surpassed the $700m in total assets under management by the fifth month. The two principals were delighted and began discussing expansionary steps.

But then, seemingly out of nowhere, market volatility jumped while signs of upcoming trouble started popping up. The origins were an incipient crisis in subprime mortgages in the USA; the packaged securities price fell precipitously. Some dismissed it as a little corner of the financial markets. Soon, however. It engulfed many commercial and investment banks, affected their liquidity, and prompted a crisis of confidence in all American and European money centers.

A top financial newspaper described it: critical in any market's complex process is the faith that financial entities have in each other's health. When that erodes, a snowballing effect ensues, and it is deleterious to all. Savvy investors flee, creating problems of illiquidity, which accentuates the panic. Forced selling affects markets. Certain of its components—high-yield bond markets, for example—become illiquid, causing further price declines, and then the avalanche garners more speed, volume, and destructive capabilities.

When Bruce got wind that the credit lines of stalwart big Swiss banks were frozen, he stormed into Well's office and exclaimed: "We are about to experience an earthquake."

For Goodman and Wells, the timing of the crisis was most unfortunate. They were sitting on a lot of cash that had to generate positive returns. But it was hard to navigate these difficult times. If one "bet" materialized as successful, its profits would be cannibalized by two failed investments. "Markets tend to whipsaw you in turbulent times," a seventy-two-year-old advisor at the Japanese bank told him once. The September 2007 results showed a loss of 2.3%, nothing to be proud of.

It is typical for investors to hope, even expect, that normalization follows a crisis. Major central banks like the American Fed would organize a rescue package to bring this about. It would bring about stability and confidence, and markets would respond in kind.

Thinking along these lines, the partners decided to buy cheap assets and make bets in the futures and options markets. The logic was simple enough: they expected a comeback. However, the decision was premature, and on-paper losses multiplied quickly. With the new results, investors demanded to get out.

All hedge and private equity funds fear one development more than anything else—the withdrawal of investors' capital. For one, it forces selling at the most inopportune times—when prices have plummeted already. Furthermore, the selling materializes paper losses, and a vicious cycle garners speed. In late October 2008, large investors were demanding the return of their investments.

Private equity funds like the one employing Sabrina faced other difficulties. They were unable to generate the income to which their investors grew accustomed. Income is closely linked to economic conditions. As the yield of short-term government bonds indicated (they were near zero, or even negative), the world's economies were in tatters. Sabrina's boss told her they might have to dismiss her, and she became extremely anxious.

Bruce and Sabrina were increasingly fidgety; it affected interactions fraught with trouble even in regular times. When a minor disagreement over shared apartment costs came to a boil, it turned nasty. Once again, he suggested that it was best if they did not live together—a veiled attempt to sugarcoat his request for her to leave the apartment one more time. As she was packing, he told her that he did not want to lose her as a friend, but the times were too stressful to have the types of arguments they'd just had. However, he still cared for her and wanted them to stay in touch. Though visibly upset, she agreed and dragged the two suitcases out the door. Her distraught face remained etched in his memory.

The following Thursday, the last one in October 2008, she called sobbing and informed him that she was fired.

"I have sent my resume to three head-hunters, and they have told me that prospects were slim—they are getting swamped with resumes. The industry is spitting out people by the thousands. There are very few outfits that are looking to hire."

She told him that she needed him, his advice, his friendship. He invited her over for some pasta and seafood. They would talk it over.

Sabrina seemed too edgy and unsettled to notice how much her sudden frailty affected Bruce. At moments like this, when she appeared vulnerable, Bruce—the same hard-nosed man who perceived life as nothing but a battle with winners and losers— became a different man. Caring, supportive, dedicated. It was as if he wanted to be her hero. He often admitted to his male friends that he was confused about Sabrina's motivations; still, it was self-evident all he cared about was to help her out in her plight. He spoke to everyone he knew about her skills and smarts. He made sure Sabrina's resume looked as promising as possible. He also discussed other options available to her. "Maybe you get an MBA? Or go into your father's business?"

"And how about you, Bruce? What is going on with the fund? How bad are the losses?" she asked, trying to show that she was not as self-absorbed as he often had accused her of being.

It was difficult for him to talk about the portfolio—particularly when it was not going well. He told her that they had tried to take some protective measures to shield the fund from losses. The articles of incorporation of the fund, however, constrained them. It irritated him no end that he had been handcuffed by the same people who had given him the seed money stating that they trusted him. He told Sabrina that he recently shouted in the office, "If they trust me, why are they limiting me?"

He told her he had "lost it" several times as he sat at his desk and stared at all the telltale signs of declining values. "I was screaming in front of our employees! I had lost control in a way I had never done before. I am so embarrassed. These are terrible times."

How he would have loved to hug and kiss Sabrina at that moment! Maybe he had her sympathy right then, but how long would it last? And could those early times of love be rekindled out of compassion? Bruce was sure that Sabrina only could love a strong man. His strength had been the foremost quality that appealed to her. Now he was being forced to talk about losses, difficulties, and worries; he was telling her about losing control. He clamped down and reverted to talking about her job search and the options available to her.

"Sabrina, have you considered leaving the country to find work? I would hate it, but it is an option, I assume."

Her response was outrageous, but Bruce had learned to expect this much from her—too often, he grudgingly concluded, she said things just to get attention or because they sounded good. For her, they bore no real consequences. Now she told him she had considered moving but could not imagine living far away from him. This was the same person who had insulted him, abused him, and found other ways to irritate him!

When Bruce complained about the inconsistency of her words and actions, she shrugged and told him, "Yeah! that is who I am—temperamental and inconsistent. Everyone is free to choose whom to befriend." Then she lashed out, "Why, do you think you are better?" She continued by pointing out that he often was also hypocritical—that he picked and chose his argumentation. She finally admitted, "I know, I say things that seem right and honest at that moment. I also know you cannot take those to the bank—they are not fungible."

But then he, once more, succumbed to his strong feelings for her and just responded, "I better make sure that I give you all the help you need so that you get to stay around here."

~ ~ ~ ~

It was mid-2008, and despite actions taken by the Fed and other major central banks, the stock and bond markets exuded fear—investors continued to flee. The press said that most hedge funds had activated legal "gates" to delay and prevent withdrawals. Bruce and Wells hesitated for a while but decided to follow the same course.

The fund was then beset by more trouble; it was getting margin calls because they borrowed to leverage their bets of a quick turnaround and produce more massive profits in that fashion.

For a couple of months, Bruce's portion of the fund performance saw some stabilization. But Wells' losses were getting more extensive, and the overall performance continued to hemorrhage. When Bear Stearns collapsed, the fund suffered another significant setback. Wells had purchased cheap Bear Stearns stock, hoping that a rescue package would come about. Instead, that position turned into a total loss. "That was just reckless," Bruce told Wells, "and our reputation has been severely tarnished."

Goodman was nervous, slept poorly, would get up in the middle of the night, trying to figure out things in the quiet of the night, but he could not come up with bright ideas. He felt he was becoming irrational.

Looking for a friendly ear and some support, he called Thomas.

"I have never been this nervous! Markets are dropping. Investors are acting crazy; many are doing things so harmful to the economy and society; it's unconscionable. I even think the quick drop in market prices is engineered by selfish, immoral investors betting on further declines, buying puts, and precipitating further declines. They are disregarding what it will do to the country. These guys don't have any concerns about tipping the global financial system into disarray!"

Thomas encouraged him to stay calm. "You have always been smart and thoughtful. You need to continue in that way. These are difficult times, I grant you that. But you cannot lose your sense of direction—especially now."

The following morning Bruce's mood turned somber once again. The senseless data of bond prices falling below their intrinsic value and company shares trading at near bankruptcy levels caused him to scream, "This is fucking unbelievable!" The fund employees just stared at him in horror.

The dream to accumulate enough personal wealth to erect a fortress was vanishing in front of his eyes, and it terrorized him. He had a fancy apartment in Chelsea and drove an Aston Martin, but his cash levels were sinking, as were his personal account values.

There was no solace coming from his relationship with Sabrina. In the early days of their relationship, he jokingly drew a fake graph with big zig-zagging moves; he'd called it the SVIX and explaining it was the "Sabrina Volatility Index. They both had a good laugh. But he could not forget the good times with her, so he toyed with the idea of having her come back to live with him. He figured that she might become more appreciative of him at this time of financial difficulty; after all, she did not generate income. But he was apprehensive they could be at each other's throats again—snide remarks and outright insults were the last thing he needed now. He had told Thomas, "I seriously doubt she fully understands us. She is bright and has great intuition, but her perspective is clouded by an all-consuming need to be at the center of everything; to see and do things her way. Maybe she is just poisoned by an immense and unwarranted sense of self-worth."

All the same, he decided to invite her for a bite. The conversation turned to the problems in their relationship. "To some extent, I am the product of my upbringing," she confessed. "I am a snob and proud of it. Yes, I am critical, perhaps even hyper-critical of everything and everyone: men dressed poorly, having poor table manners, incapable of spoiling me the way I had grown accustomed."

Indeed, Bruce knew her father was a wealthy Manchester industrialist. She was raised with a silver spoon in her mouth. Her mother was French and fancied herself to be an aristocrat. She made sure Sabrina performed "like a class act" (the mother's favorite phrase). It applied to table manners, cocktail conversations, and how she dressed. Bruce knew from history and other stories that the "class act" did not apply to sexual adventures, of which she had plenty.

She suddenly got up from the dinner table, walked over to his side, extended her arms, and exclaimed, "Please hug me; I need it!" It was apparent this was the first crisis she ever experienced.

His face was flushed, his usually dry hands sweaty. When she rested her head on his chest, she felt that his heart, typically so calm, was pounding agitatedly. He usually was so together, so strong; he always struck her as unfazed by the world's turmoil—whether it was political violence or market turbulence. Not now.

"You know I will always be there for you," she told him. She hoped this sounded honest because, as of late, he had expressed doubts about her sincerity. "Please look at me and tell me that you believe me. Tell me that you know I love you—maybe not the way you want me to love you, but that I am your best friend."

He was too perturbed to decipher what just was said, what it meant, what was real, and what was pure fantasy. What came out of his mouth surprised him. "I want you to move back in with me; I need you to lie next to me at night. Maybe I can get some sleep that way. All I want is your physical proximity and know I am less alone. Yes, lying next to you and not having sex will feel strange. But maybe I can relax this way. I am not doing too well right now."

He knew that in his heart of hearts, he wanted to return their relationship to what it once had been; he was seizing on her momentary weakness to get there. He was opportunistic.

"Let me think about it," she told him. "It is weird, but we are weird. I will get back to you in a day or two."

"Is it that bad?" she asked. She had a good sense of the answer. She was as much a part of the financial industry that saw the worst crisis in decades, maybe as far back as the Great Depression. She admired his perspective on all matters involving the economy, markets, and investments—she knew he had an unconventional view and that he was often prescient about the future.

The look on his face suggested dark humor and anguish. "No, dear, it is actually much worse. But no one seems to know how bad it really will get!" They were reconciling, feeling closer. But then he slipped and provoked her: "Maybe call your dad and tell him to protect his wealth and make room for you in his company."

That last phrase was cynical; Sabrina knew the intent and was not pleased. She always was fast on the trigger: "At least, I did not have an abusive stepfather," she responded. A more painful phrase could not have come out of her mouth. She quickly wanted to restore some warmth. "I might have my father to protect me," she continued, "but you, what are you going to do? You run your fund, and you have obligations to your investors. People who, as you told me so many times, trust you." Before she went home, she promised to let him know her decision about returning to his apartment in a day or two.

The fund had to report performance numbers, and they were not good. The performance was a further decline in asset values. Since inception, they had lost nearly 10%, and for the year, they were down about 16%. The numbers were comparable to other funds, but that was little consolation to investors. Demands for withdrawals increased, and the large investors constantly rang to get updates. Goodman, who always took his responsibility toward investors very seriously, was a nervous wreck.

In mid-2008, two bad trades inflicted more damage on the fund. Wells was sure about the survival of Fannie Mae and bet heavily on that stock. In the meantime, Goodman decided that the Chinese Renminbi would garner strength and that the Chinese would seize on the moment, boost the value of its currency by removing the peg against the dollar. Both bets were logical: Fannie May was too large to fail, and the US government would surely bail it out. Separately, the Chinese economy was the only major economy showing strength. But neither bet panned out.

Furthermore, the outsized purchases seemed frantic and desperate. Both principals bickered about the other's decision. Bruce told his friend, Thomas, "These two ill-fated investments tell me that we are acting haphazardly, we are not principled, and lack discipline."

~ ~ ~ ~

Sabrina agreed to return. After a few weeks of living together, sharing a bed but not having sex, Bruce became uncomfortable with the "neither here nor there" situation he had engineered. He was also perplexed and annoyed by the changes in Sabrina's appearance. Was she trying to look as unappealing as possible? A week after moving in, she had colored her hair pitch black and applied dark eye shadow around her eyes.

"She has become a 'goth,'" he told Thomas—he now was talking to him twice or three times a week. "She wears heavy dark pajamas to bed rather than the usual T-shirt and undies. They feel raw to the occasional touch. I have a stranger in my home and in bed."

Thomas told him he was adding turmoil to his life when he could barely handle market volatility. "This is not sensible," he said.

His outbreaks became more frequent; they seemed unusually childish and very unlike the Bruce Sabrina had known. Instead of the easygoing man, was this irritated, intolerant, and demanding person. At one point, he told her he wanted more consideration, more sensitivity, and more attentiveness. To Sabrina, it all seemed like a ploy to renew their sex. The more erratic his behavior, however, the less likely she was to acquiesce. It was an uncomfortable status-quo, it was about to gush over.

Then came the ultimate strike. Sabrina told him to decide if he could accept her dating someone else and not sleeping with him some nights, coming back late others, or not at all. It was not a hypothetical question, she added. She had met "this darling boy, Peter, who is a bit younger." She liked him, and better yet, was sexually attracted to him. She intended to, at least, have a fling with this guy.

He felt sick to his stomach. So much cynicism! He had pledged his friendship to her, and denying what she wanted was wrong. On the other hand, he thought she was highly insensitive by taking advantage of him at this crisis moment. He told her he had to think about it.

The next day, she called him at work. He thought she wanted to show remorse, and that's why she was calling during working hours. Instead, she said, "I really like Peter! He is perfect: gallant, smart, wealthy, and so smooth. I want you to tell me what you think of him. Can you please join us for dinner? Maybe tonight?"

So smooth? What had she meant by that? Here he'd thought she was trying to make up for her indiscretion; instead, she was asking him to validate her judgment about this guy. She should know Bruce well enough to admit that this would hurt.

They sat down for dinner—Sabrina sat between both men. The young man seemed pleasant and smart. He was a financial journalist and still had a job, which was a good thing these days. He also could see why Sabrina wanted to go to bed with him. He looked like a young Troy Donahue.

Peter asked him if he liked his job. Goodman responded thoughtfully, "Do I still like the financial world? I never liked the people orbiting in this industry. Many are much too arrogant—they flaunt their wealth instead of being thankful or embarrassed by it. After all, their richness is not commensurate with their intelligence, integrity, or morality. Many are too self-centered and callous about society. It is so evident lately," he added. "On the other hand, I like puzzles. Every day I am facing a myriad of puzzles. In shorthand: what to invest? And how to do it—outright? Leveraged? Employing options? That is the greatest appeal. It is intellectual. To be perfectly honest, I need the work and income. Not too many other options are available to me."

Why was he so honest? Why had he bothered responding at all? For one, it helped him sort out his thoughts. Because times were tough, his mind did not function well. Besides, Sabrina had pitted them in the same arena—like two fighting cocks to duel over her; he wanted to come across as smart, tough, and relaxed. Inside, however, he was shaking, his chest ached, he was anxious and angry.

The two dominant factors in his life were spiraling out of control. He replayed in his mind the news of the day. The story about the probable collapse of Lehman was most disturbing. September started poorly for the fund, and these recent shockwaves would weaken the performance further. He and Wells could expect more withdrawal demands. Could they perhaps, decide to dismiss some staff to reduce the fund's expenses?

The next day her theoretical question became a reality. Bruce chose to think he was being tested. She did not show up by the time he went to bed. He locked his bedroom and tried to sleep but could not—he was waiting for the sounds of Sabrina "coming home." The ridiculousness of it all did not escape him. He decided that he needed to put an end to the mess—once and for all.

As he attempted to sleep, during the sort of night when you don't know if you are dreaming or imagining things, his mind flashed scenes of the storybook he had read as a child: Samson and Delilah's story. He saw Samson bringing down the temple on himself and the Philistines. Delilah was standing on the side and laughing as the walls of the temple were collapsing. Delilah had Sabrina's face.

The next morning, he waited for her to get up and told her he could not handle this weird situation. He was still in love with her, and it was too painful.

She told him she understood, and she would, once again, pack her things and move out that morning. She turned around and moved to the guest bedroom, where she had slept that night.

~ ~ ~ ~

It was about eight in the morning, but he chose to call Thomas, anyway. He needed some way to let out the accumulated pressure. He told his friend that the world around him was collapsing at the speed of light. Markets had been tumbling for some time, but now commodities were in free fall; he had bought exposure to gold and oil to bring stability to the fund, but to no avail. Thomas asked if there was no help from governments—he had heard something in that regard in the news.

"So far, nothing has worked, Thomas. The Americans are squabbling whether to produce a bailout package. In the meantime, the major central banks have lowered interest rates to near-zero without achieving much of anything. Heck, in Germany, the yields are negative; you need to pay them money to hold their bonds—how ridiculous is that?

"But here is the terrible news: some people are being kicked out of houses they should never have bought and cannot afford. Some older men and women work as cashiers in supermarkets because their high-wages jobs are no longer available, and they are suddenly destitute.

"And in the meantime, some bastards are getting filthy rich as they bet against anything of value. As they do that, they sink more and more people into poverty.

"I have concerns about my financial future. Never mind my hopes for a monetary fortress. Investors are threatening me with suits, and even my partner wants to sue me for malfeasance. Even if I can survive their threats, I will have to spend money on lawyers. Can you believe that some, presumably sophisticated, investors are calling me several times a week? They know what's going on! I am no magician.

"And as to Sabrina. She is now out again. She is packing her things as we speak. I don't want to get into the gory details."

Thomas told him how sorry he was. He did not have great words of wisdom. But he was sure that Bruce needed to make sure to stay healthy and keep his cool—even if it was too complicated right now. It was good that the crisis evoked a social conscience in his friend. He was sorry if these words hurt a bit, but they were a positive statement.

Two days later, Sabrina called to tell Bruce how happy she was with Peter. It seemed like she wanted to hurt him. When they reverted to talking about the markets, he relayed he was under a lot of pressure. She responded coldly, "I can't help you, Bruce. I know it's tough, but it is tough for everyone. I just hope you do not get thrown out of the apartment the way I was."

That same evening Bruce called Thomas once more. Yes, he had gone back to the office, and yes, he knew it was past 9 p.m. "I am trying to figure out what to do," he said. "It has taken years to build up a well-respected professional standing. It has taken years of hard work to reach a financial status that seemed protective, allowing me to forget childhood pains. But now, the ground is wobbly under my feet and threatening all of it."

He ended the conversation with Thomas, saying that he felt he needed to break the vicious cycle and the downward spiral. Thomas made him promise he would not do anything too silly or harmful. He was worried about him.

Bruce did not respond.

He went home, had a shot of whiskey, and another night of poor sleep.

He reminisced about the Samson and Delilah picture book when he decided to act that morning. He was fed up. He walked into his office at about 7:15, well ahead of anyone else. He went through all the investments under his management and reversed them. He instructed to sell all the holdings the fund had, and, instead, bought puts betting on their decline—all the put options held by the fund he sold and gave orders to buy the shares instead. He essentially turned the fund on its head. The pluses became minuses and the minuses, pluses. Everything would get executed two hours later. He would be a hero or a goat. He was willing to go out in style.

He then emailed Sabrina. "I have reversed all my positions in the fund. These will get executed when the markets open. Maybe I am swimming against the tide, and maybe I will lose the battle. Goodbye, Sabrina. Have a good life. You have finally brought me to the point that I am now. I despise you."

It was the end. He knew he had nowhere to go. Like Samson, he was taking down the walls with him. He stood in front of the mirror and slowly lifted the shiny Beretta to put finality to his voyage. His heart was pounding fast, and his hands were unsteady as one large tear rolled down his face. He put the barrel in his mouth and slowly pulled the trigger.

He was surprised that he did not hear a bang. He was still standing. He had not collapsed. He touched his mouth and temple, and there was no blood.

What had happened? Why was he not dead? He sat on the edge of his bed and searched his memory. The night before, back at home, he had called Thomas, his good friend, one more time. He told him about his despair. Everything was collapsing around him. He did not want to live anymore. Thomas begged him not to do something stupid. He had achieved so much in such a short time. He needed to forget about Sabrina; she was no good for him. But he should not cut short anything else, let alone his life.

After that conversation, Bruce had emptied the revolver of its deadly bullets. He told himself that Thomas was right and that committing suicide was just cowardice.

He had a terrible night. It caused a whirlwind and much confusion. In a frenzy, he had run to his office, put in those orders reversing all positions. He then rushed back home and reached for a gun without bullets.

He looked at the watch and saw he still had time to undo the damage. He got up, dusted off his clothes, and ran back to his office. He undid all the trades that were were meant to be executed twenty minutes later. He had just beaten the clock. He felt great relief.

He'd thought he would never talk to Sabrina again; after all, he had written a finite email. But his phone rang, and it was her.

"What happened, Bruce? Why did you do what you did? Are you okay?"

Bruce responded in a somewhat incoherent way. "I had a nightmare. It was a comic book about Samson. Remember what he did?"

She sounded confused. "You mean Samson and Delilah?"

"Yes. After they cut his hair, they displayed him in his weakness in front of all the Philistines. In his anger, he pushed the pillars of that temple and caused the walls to collapse on his enemies and himself—he was going under, but he was taking everyone along with him."

She told him she was afraid he had gone insane, to which he simply responded, "Maybe I have, and you have plenty to do with it. I have to go."

He called Wells and told him that they better get themselves ready for the period after global market turmoil ends. They needed to think conceptually first and be poised to act smartly, not like they had done lately—with desperation.

VILDE CHAYE*

●*A Yiddish phrase that literally translates to Wild Animal but is primarily used when referring to people. The derisive term suggests that a person, or persons (*chayes* is the plural), does not behave according to some preconceived norms.

Marta was brilliant, unexpectedly so. She finished first in her graduating high school class. She also excelled for the first two years at university. While not fully crystallized, she leaned toward a focus on biology, though she was disinclined to be a doctor. No one in her family had ever made it past high school; her father, one of seven, had been asked to work at the family clothing store. When he'd asked, "But, what about school?" he was told that only his brother David—who was considered the brightest—would have that luxury.

The youngest of three, Marta had her mother's features, dark brown eyes—so dark one mistook them for black—thick eyebrows, a pointed nose, and broad, full lips. She was not a big woman. On the contrary, her 5'4' frame could have been described as fragile.

Like most teenagers, she seemed to exhibit the usual inner conflict between wanting to be appreciated and loved at home and desiring to be accepted by the larger society, which was in turmoil.

She liked being praised and spoiled at home, but she was also cognizant that there was poverty, conflict, and violence on Buenos Aires' streets. Would her social consciousness conflict with the way her parents saw her?

Marta was resolute, even stubborn, and definitely not shy. Despite her frail body, she never showed weakness or fear. She faced altercations at school and on the streets of the Flores neighborhood. Often, only girls were involved in the melee. She punched back whenever someone hit her. She never ran away from a challenge. She was not the one to start trouble, but she was not fearful when it was thrust upon her.

Back at home, she was told she was special. Eventually, she developed a sense of entitlement. She would approach her mother and ask her to buy pretty clothes for her or request her father to go to the movies. Usually, they would humor her.

Her parents were also very intent on making Marta reject the dangerous society around them. While her parents usually doted her with compliments, they were also strict. They wanted to make sure, they said in unison, that the "craziness of the times (the '70s) does not infiltrate her and send her future asunder."

After reading some story in *La Prensa* or seeing something terrible on TV, they would express their grave concerns. "Your generation is too involved in illicit drugs, revolutionaries wanting to overturn the government, the Cuba of Fidel and Che Guevara spreading communist fervor among the poor all over the continent."

They were projecting their own worries, of course, and Marta knew it. These trends threatened their recent economic ascendancy to the middle class. The years of financial struggle had been difficult; now, they could finally afford to buy a second apartment and rent it out, get a fancier car and drive around Palermo, maybe even a vacation in Mar del Plata. They also had high expectations for a better life for their three children, especially brilliant Marta.

Once at university, Marta got swept up in the currents flowing through the university's halls. This, despite still living at home. Years later, she would reminisce and say, "I was the 'radical' wearing Gucci shoes. I was the anti-government demonstrator that marched down Corrientes towards the obelisk at *Plaza de la Republica*. Still, I conveniently drove a brand new Peugeot to join the demonstrators at the convening location."

All that hypocrisy did not escape her—she was too smart for that. But she explained it away. Personal conveniences did not necessarily clash with her social perspective and her emotional support for just causes. She saw poverty in the working-class areas of the capital and heard from friends about even worse conditions outside the city and the farther-away provinces like Mendoza and Salta. She was distressed by the news that students, some she knew, had been arrested in the middle of the night or beaten up by paramilitary troops in broad daylight. When her cousin Daniel, who was active in the student union, vanished, the whole family was in an uproar. Marta expressed her opinion forcefully, and it upset her father tremendously.

"What happened to my brilliant Marta?" he said. "Why have you turned into a *vilde chaye*, a wild animal? What will we do if you also are kidnapped and your body surfaces in the waters of the Mar del Plata? Do you think my parents escaped the pogroms in Russia to set up a better life for their family so that we lose our daughter to this? Can't you just concentrate on your studies and not be involved? I understand feeling sympathetic in your heart, but why act on it?"

She had heard those words—*"vilde chaye"*—a few times in the past. Most often, when either her mom or dad watched acts of vandalism or brutality on TV, they showed their disdain, shrugged, and just said, *"vilde chayes."* She considered the derisive term vulgar and racist. It highlighted a certain arrogance toward the general population, some non-whites, mostly not Jewish. Suddenly she felt scorn for her parents; they clearly did not understand. They just cared about their money and comfort.

She was so distraught and felt she was facing a no-win situation; she decided to quit attending university. She told her parents that she was placating them this way. she no longer would be exposed to ideas rampant on campus. She will not be identifiable as a sympathizer of the cause of the left by the police. As frustrated as her parents were by the decision, they could not counter it—she had used their concerns and turned the tables on them. But she insisted that while living at home, she would have her own living space and negotiated to turn the family room into hers to decorate and furnish as she saw fit. Over time, she often reflected on that momentous decision. What if she had stayed enrolled in the "Uni"?

She agreed to work in the store the parents owned in the *Once*—the area with many Jewish clothing workshops and stores. But she was not happy there. There was no intellectual challenge, no use of her knowledge or talents. She was bored to tears. Her father quickly recognized the source of her unhappiness. He called an old friend, a *Boca Juniors* fan who often joined him in *La Bombonera* to attend matches, and told him about his problem. Would he possibly be interested in having Marta work with him? In the evening, he proposed it to his daughter.

"Luis Enrique is a skillful architect, and he is very willing to have you work with him. You have the math skills, and you are smart. You also have good taste; look at that dress you are wearing. I think you would enjoy it."

Marta was thrilled by the opportunity to do something different, away from the *Once*. She would no longer go to the drab store in the dowdy area of the city with its narrow streets and multitudes of people hustling back and forth, where they indiscriminately used elbows and hands to push their way forward.

About three months later, her father called the architect to find out how she was doing. Luis Enrique was full of praise. "She is terrific! So smart, so intent on finding things to do. She wants to help with the business administration while learning everything concerning architecture. She sees her future in this realm. I am sure she is pleased to be here. Can't you see it in her face?"

"To be honest, my good friend," the father responded, "I barely see her. When she comes home, she goes to her living area. She reorganized the apartment to take over the den as her room—it is full of posters I disagree with, calling for revolution, declaring Che a martyr, and whatever. She goes out most nights, and I do not know where she goes. I assume, and hope, it is just coffee shops and bars where the young hang out. Maybe discotheques. I do not ask; I do not want to upset her, and, with my heart issues, I do not want to get disturbed myself. She no longer is the little girl I doted over."

Four months later, Marta asked to have her parents' attention; she had a big announcement. Would Friday night be a good time?

They sat around the dining room table, and she told them that she'd met a man she intended to marry. She thought they should know. She had met Sergio at her workplace.

"He is a great guy, smart, good-looking, and a good person."

"What is his last name?" asked the father.

"Boren. His last name is Boren."

"He is not even Jewish!" screamed her father.

"Yes, he is. From Borenstein, it is an abbreviated name adopted by his father when they came over from Poland."

"I do not believe it for a moment! You are just a *vilde chaye!*"

Marta's mother tried to be more understanding. "How long have you known this boy? Isn't it too early? You are still so young. How old is he?"

When Marta said she'd known Sergio for about five months, her father resumed his accusations. "You are just wild! How are you two going to support yourselves? Or do you expect us to maintain you?"

Marta stormed toward her room as she put her hands over her tearful eyes.

Years later, after both her parents were long dead, Marta would tell her closest friends that the tag "*vilde chaye*" stayed branded in her mind forever. Even when considering a professional move or facing a personal decision about where to live, she would reflect and ask herself whether it was a "crazy decision." She rejected the notion that she was "wild," but it always made her wonder if she was not.

She married Sergio one month later and had to attend her father's funeral three weeks later. She always worried about whether the two events were connected. Her father had died of a massive heart attack. Unspoken remained the fear that she contributed to her father's death.

Marta and Sergio continued working at the same firm and seemed happy enough. About a year later, Marta's cousin Miriam invited her to come to Florida for a visit.

Miriam, who had anglicized the spelling of her name to Myriam, suggested she bring empty suitcases. "You will fill the suitcases with clothes that you buy at substantial discounts at the Daytona outlet mall and then sell them in Buenos Aires at much higher prices; I have done it. You will be able to make a decent amount of money and even pay for your trip that way."

Marta was amazed at how easy it was to pass customs at Ezeiza airport, these trips became frequent, and the side business turned routine. Yet, she always remembered the Wild Animal tag father gave her on every trip she took. But the money was so easy and plentiful. Eventually, she brought back some Ecstasy. That was even more profitable.

Four or five times a year, she came to the Florida area. After three years of travel, she began looking around for a gig as an architect—there was so much construction going up. She was always concerned about the economic ups and downs at home, and during recessions, she often thought about moving to the US. When she posed the idea to her husband, he rejected it immediately. "They were Argentinian through and through," he argued, and "they belonged here." It was yet another sign of the growing rift between the two. They seemed to be at odds on important matters and petty issues like the storage space in their apartment. Sergio did not like her trips and the risk of getting caught with contraband. She disapproved of him spending their money betting on anything from horse-races to stocks in the local, corruption-filled market. They chose to divorce after six years.

Years later, she would reflect that this was an inflection point. She sought out psychiatric help because, too often, she was depressed and nearly emotionally paralyzed. She would refuse to leave her apartment, having to wear street clothes rather than her pajamas, to engage with friends and family. It took a good six months to gain some semblance of her old self, go out, and see a few close friends. She had lost a lot of weight—some had a hard time recognizing her.

Fifteen months later, she met a man that piqued her curiosity. Nearly seven-foot-tall, with a muscular build and a broad smile, he was a mover and a shaker, organizing events of all sorts, often concerts by rock bands and Latin music favorites. But he also sought involvement in a variety of construction projects, a shopping mall here, a new housing development there. Those who hired him knew that he had a decent ability to round up the money to fund these businesses' launching. He was not a banker or a lawyer; he was neither a treasurer nor an administrator, but he was good at selling an idea. You would be silly to rely on him to provide the legal documents stipulating the project's terms. But he knocked on doors, sweet-talked himself into boardrooms, and got the monetary commitment that would make reality out of an idea. He was very charismatic. His smile had many, especially women, smiling at him in return.

Their first encounter was pure happenstance. Marta had been hired to be the interior designer for a new shopping mall in one of the new suburbs outside the capital. It would have many of the features that drew so many to the malls in the USA. Because she often had a keen eye for such matters, her visits to Florida became a source for Argentinian innovations. He was touring the mall with a group of potential investors he was trying to entice into investing in a second mall on the other side of town.

Marta was transfixed by the force of this man's smile, his demeanor, his gait. The energy that emanated from him—that same power that would impress her time and time again—was so persuasive. She was sure that he would be the tonic that she needed to lift herself up. For the first time in many months, she was interested in a man. For the first time in her whole life, she was adamant about having a meaningful relationship and would do anything to make it happen. Until then, she was always the one to be chased, the object of adulating reverence.

She approached him and suggested they have coffee. It was the beginning of many years of turbulence. Carlos was a charming man with a beautiful way of making you feel at ease, protected, and cared for. He was captivating, and yet it all seemed so effortless, so normal, so genuine. Marta was smart enough to see through any man who was faking it; she was certain Carlos was not of the same ilk.

That first meeting over coffee was replete with laughter and good conversation. A couple of dinners followed, and by the third date, they were rolling in bed. Later in life, she would comment that she'd never imagined she would sleep with a man that early in the relationship.

A month later, Carlos had an idea he wanted to share with her. They could put together something unique and exciting. He had been to Europe the previous summer and saw youngsters rushing to nightclubs and dance the night away. What if they put together a combination hotel, spa, nightclub, and casino in a hot location frequented by wealthy young Latin jet-setters looking for excitement, fun, and luxury. A "Latin American Ibiza of sorts," he remarked, and since she had only heard of that island of excess, she just raised her eyebrows. He insisted, "Where would one place such a pleasure paradise in the Southern Cone?"

She suggested Mar del Plata; he shook his head. "It is beautiful, but only Argentinians frequent that city these days—they are all beggars," he exclaimed, and they both laughed. It needed to be a place with an international appeal.

"How about Bariloche?" she pondered.

"Excellent idea," he responded. "The problem is the busy season is in winter when people come to ski. It is not surprising that Ibiza is as hot as it is. It is a summer resort."

"Punta del Este in Uruguay," she said excitedly while pointing to the sky as if the idea had descended from the heavens.

"Yes! That's it! Perfect. It has been a resort frequented mostly by older Argentinians for a long time, but I heard that Brazilians are getting interested. If we develop this attraction, youngsters will come from all over the continent and maybe the USA and Europe too! Let's put together the specific pieces of this."

The thrill of a new project was a tremendous aphrodisiac. Soon after that, she told him she was pregnant.

Her older brother told her he was happy; she would have a child and did not care that she was not married to this man.

"How are you going to raise the child? As a Jew? Your partner is not."

Her response should not have surprised her brother. "I will raise him to be a good man."

The family was not thrilled to find out that she had chosen to name her son Ismael. Her contrarian spirit was shining through once more.

Two years later, a daughter was born, and appropriately she chose to name her Fatima, once again, poking at her family and heritage. The family gossiped: "She better stop having children; otherwise, we will have an Abdul and an Ibrahim in the family."

Carlos and Marta still did not wear wedding bands. She was quite adamant that marriage was nothing more than "a piece of paper."

The birth of a second child closely coincided with the opening of the *Fiesta Celeste* Resort. It had everything that Carlos had imagined. It was opulent; the hotel rooms had large balconies overlooking the peninsula's ocean side; the casino sprawled through a large area and offered all the table games and machines of a Vegas establishment. They made sure that the nightclub's music did not affect the sleep of the elderly. Crowds flocked to the nightclub; young and not so young men with mostly unbuttoned shirts showing hairless chests; women and girls barely of age whose short skirts allowed a peek, occasionally revealing that some had forgotten their thongs at home. You could find them banging on the tables to the music's rhythm and dancing on those tables when, later into the night, the liquor had had its effect.

Marta, who had been in charge of all the interior design, commented that only with this project did she fully understand her profession.

After a tremendous success in the first year of the complex, Marta's eyes opened up to a fact that was difficult to absorb— Carlos was terrific at setting up things but was a horrendous administrator. Notwithstanding that there were two young children at home, she decided she better take full control of this establishment's finances. She feared he might object—she was a woman, after all. On the contrary, he was happy to surrender the reins. He preferred to plot events to stage at the Fiesta Celeste club—the mambo band he found, the salsa teacher getting everyone to line dance on top of the tables. She also noticed that he was thrilled to be the darling of young women as he doled out free tickets. The promoter in him showed little restraint when he offered free drinks and food to a large group of pretty, barely clothed twenty-year-olds.

Catching him in the act, Marta protested loudly. "We are here to make money. We have two children under our care. We have high maintenance costs, including a payroll that is now in the order of almost two hundred people, and you are being Mr. Charming and giving out freebies and kissing many girls on the lips—I saw you!"

The possibility that this man, very much the "macho man," might fool around with another woman was a secret concern she'd harbored from the first morning she'd gotten up from the shared bed. She'd decided to take the chance. She never was deterred by risk.

New dangers of a different kind came about when the local

police approached her. "Ms. Marta, are you the one in charge of this establishment?"

She nodded and asked how she could help.

"We have clear indications that illicit drugs are consumed inside the club."

She vehemently denied and explained that all guests are frisked before entering the club.

"Trust us, Ms. Marta, tomorrow night, we will find a pouch of cocaine in your VIP area, and your establishment will be closed. But there is a way to make sure that this does not happen. We will guarantee that nothing of the sort occurs for a reasonable weekly fee of five thousand dollars. We would collect from you every Monday. We know you will be able to make that and a lot more on the busy weekends."

Marta called her husband as soon as they left. She sounded agitated. "We now are in the hands of the police mafia. I want out of this place. They will keep on pressing for more once they see how easy it is. It's always the same on this continent!"

Carlos agreed to sell the establishment and started looking for buyers. Over the last few years, Brazilians had turned Punta del Este into their top destination for summer vacations. Many had gotten rich during the recent economic boom and flocked to the famous place. Thus, it was not surprising that a group of wealthy *Paolista* men made a bid that exceeded the sellers' expectations. The original investors in the project would get an excellent return. Marta and Carlos, who had contributed with the initial idea, the planning, and their administrative work —though no seed money— would be well-rewarded by a significant minority stake in the business.

"What are we going to do with all this cash?" Marta asked. "I suppose we could invest in income-producing properties. I think I will visit my cousin Myriam in Florida and see what we can find there. The police mafia will not interfere there," she added with bitter sarcasm.

Carlos suggested that they travel to Ibiza to search for investment opportunities.

Marta was incensed and showed it by glaring at him. "Are you eager to kiss some young women, Carlos?" She felt that she was losing it and decided to return to the psychiatrist who had seen her before meeting Carlos.

Nonetheless, she agreed to go to Ibiza. At that time, it was the hotspot of global hedonism. She could feel the sensuality of the place. Maybe it was because of the drug consumption rampant among most visitors. Perhaps it was because of the nightclubs' underlying sexual overtones. The nearly naked dancers animating excitable visitors were part of the atmospherics; even she could sense the pull. All the same, she told Carlos she would not move there—the children would not be brought up in such an environment. She would object to investing there because such business needed monitoring, and they would be incapable of doing so from afar. She convinced him that buying a property in the US was a much better idea.

They purchased a two-bedroom apartment on Collins Avenue. "So close to the water, it will always have great value," she told him. The other investment was in a smaller one-bedroom near Las Olas. She was happy to have established a foothold in the US.

Back in Buenos Aires, they bought another apartment—a rental unit. Every Argentinian, after coming into some money, acquires an apartment for rental income, he observed. She asked to use some remaining funds to renovate their house in the suburbs. She had insisted on buying a home in the closed community because it allowed for safety when it was precarious to live in the capital. People were robbed in broad daylight, even while walking through the best neighborhoods. The assailants used motorcycles in the assaults. The back rider would pull out a gun and threaten pedestrians. The victims surrendered money and jewelry, and the heist would end when the accomplice driving the motorcycle would return to pick up his partner criminal.

Difficult economic times also caused Carlos to lie low for a while. Once the new government triggered a turnaround, however, he was eager to get involved in a new project—the development of what had been a neglected area near the city's old harbor. Puerto Madero was going to be a zone with many high-rise apartment buildings selling at much higher prices than the rest of the metropolis. He expected the wealthy to migrate to this area because it was much safer—the police's extra care and the security outfit hired to secure that area made sure of that.

Carlos told Marta that the only way to seize on the new

opportunity was by promoting her abilities as an interior designer. Her exquisite taste could attract wealthy clients who would want their kitchens outfitted with Italian marble and German technology, the living rooms decorated with the best in French home-furnishings, the living room furniture displaying smooth Scandinavian lines. She knew so much more about all these things than he did, but he would hunt down potential buyers and negotiate the project's cost with them.

So, she thought to herself, *he will be the hustler, and I will be doing the work*. It was part of her disenchantment with the man she lived with, the father of her children. He did not show much interest in the kids' welfare, even though he was a good deal of fun when he played and kidded around with them—typical of a *bon vivant*, Marta thought. He did not seem to care much about Marta's depressive episodes, which became more frequent. When these happened, he would close the door behind him and head to a *'boliche'* (the Argentinian name for a nightclub) like "New York City" and hang out with his male friends and whatever women came over to their table for a free drink. She felt alone, abandoned, and even more despondent.

In a way, her favorite refuge was to travel to see her cousin in Miami. Her excuse was to look over the properties. Eventually, she decided to stay longer and undertake some small steps toward possible immigration to the US. She garnered information about becoming a real estate agent and joining a mid-sized company of architects and interior designers; investigate what schools the now-teenaged children could attend. This last trip took about two months. The children were with her as it was summertime at home. They were excited to attend school in Florida and suggested that they eventually could also attend college there. Marta told Myriam that it seemed like a confluence of factors were conspiring to make her move.

Once back home, Marta discovered that the decision had been made for her. Carlos, she found, had been sleeping with a close friend of hers for months. He'd taken full advantage of her absence and did not even hide it too much. He was seen kissing and holding this woman close to him. It happened at the nightclub he frequented and in plain daylight at the coffee shops and restaurants of Puerto Madero. Marta was angry. She went straight to the woman she'd once thought to be a good friend.

"How could you do this to me!" she screamed.

"Well, you know how charming and good looking he is," was the response made with a mocking smirk.

Marta was surprised by her reaction and spat in the woman's face before turning around and heading home.

She packed her bags and drove to her brother's home. She needed to get the kids and head to the US, but all of that would take some time. In the meantime, she had to start divorce proceedings; did her brother know a good lawyer for such matters? But wait, they'd never officially gotten officially married. Was she losing her mind amid her bout of rage? There were multiple assets held jointly, and a need to make sure she did not lose them. Did her brother know a lawyer that could help with that? Maybe her brother could sit by her side at a meeting with Carlos. It was absolutely essential to have such a meeting as early as possible. Her brother agreed that this needed to happen.

They gathered at the brother's office. She could barely look at Carlos—she felt betrayed, disrespected, insulted, and dishonored. Carlos acted like this was another negotiation for some project. He would take full possession of all that was happening in Puerto Madero, even though she might have contributed mightily through actual work. Marta protested, but Carlos pulled out a ream of papers that, he said, would constitute the legal grounds for his grab. Marta and her brother were welcome to review them right there.

"The bastard," she said to herself. "He was laying the groundwork all along, and I was an idiot for not going through the contracts and agreements stipulating the rewards for my work."

As soon as the meeting was over, Marta made two phone calls. She told Myriam she was going to be coming to Florida and settling down. She gave an abbreviated version of what had transpired between sobs but told her cousin she did not want to expand on it further. The second call was to her therapist; there was an urgent need to see her as soon as possible.

At night, while alone in her brother's guest room, she made one more phone call to an old friend from university. Pedro had always lived on the margins of what can be considered the law-abiding civil society. For a long period during the military attack on left-wing activists, he'd lived clandestinely and engaged in petty thievery to survive. But he was not a wanton criminal, nor was he unkind to friends. She'd always had a soft spot for him, and he was still thankful for what she did for him. They would talk from time to time on the phone, or he would come over for coffee. She was careful not to meet him in public; he understood why and never voiced a complaint. On a few occasions, she'd lent him a bundle of cash when he was on the brink of homelessness and starvation. She did so without ever expecting to get the money back. She saw it as an obligation and, in her own words, "To pay homage to those I abandoned when I stopped attending the university."

She needed a big favor, she told him. "Pedro, you have connections. Maybe a couple of these guys can find Carlos and break his legs…"

There was silence on the other side.

Pedro was pondering what Marta just had said to him. He did not confirm or deny. He told her to take care of herself and be a good mother to her two kids.

As she hung up, she mumbled to herself, "Am I a *vilde chaye* again?"

Three weeks later, she found out through the grapevine—Carlos was in the hospital. He had just exited "New York City," the nightclub, when two men attacked him, broke one arm and his collarbone. They also broke his nose and left him with a deep knife slash across his left cheek. Because nothing was stolen, the police concluded that this was not another robbery case.

Marta evicted the renters of one of her apartments—she had to pay a hefty fee for them to leave, but she wanted to take possession of one of the apartments purchased after the Punta property sale. She moved her children to this apartment and told them to get ready to move to the USA. Because they knew about the parents' strife, they did not object.

Marta used her brother's connections to find a lawyer with the reputation of being tough and very successful in divorce cases— her brother said he was the top lawyer for this type of work in the capital. She told the lawyer she would give him 10% of the value of any property he could wrestle away from Carlos's hands. The lawyer took on the job but warned that it would take time, and because of the unique circumstances, the probability of success was not good.

Marta and the children took off to Miami; she tried to look serene for no other reason than to prevent them from seeing how sad she was. But they were seventeen and sixteen and had a good sense of how the separation was affecting her. She did not know that Carlos had called them before their departure and told them about the assault, the hospital stay and that he thought their mother had something to do with the men that had ambushed him.

The two kids discussed it among themselves and began to harbor a measure of resentment toward their mother. She made it sound like it was all his fault, but maybe she was culpable as well. They discussed what she might have done to contribute to the split. Fatima talked about the frequent trips to Florida and the extended stay-overs, the lack of interest in him, and what he wanted out of life. Ismael chimed in, speaking about the few activities they engaged in as a family, most often because she claimed to be too busy with the Puerto Madero projects. Finally, they concluded that she probably was no longer interested in being with him. That's what happens when children witness a marital split-up—they act as lawyer, judge, and jury.

Once in Florida, they told Marta that they would be better off attending a private boarding school that was academically strong and offered them excellent preparation for university. Marta managed to convince them to stay home but commute to the North Broward Prep School, which would meet their academic needs. Myriam was the one to suggest the school; she had begun the research as soon as she'd heard that Marta was coming.

Marta, the once spunky, vibrant, elegant woman, looked and acted desolate, uninterested, and morose. She continued her therapy sessions with her Argentinian counselor via the phone. She took long walks along the ocean and wondered what would become of her life. Myriam insisted she register on a dating internet site.

"Maybe you can meet someone exciting and find a man who will honor and respect you the way you deserve."

Marta acquiesced but grudgingly and did not show much interest in the goings-on taking place on that site.

She got an email from a man that seemed to have matching characteristics—he had grown up in South America, had Jewish origins, and was an architect. He piqued her interest. They spoke on the phone, and he claimed that he was about to build an important building in Barcelona and had to travel to that city. He would call her from there.

Two days later, he called and sounded distressed. He told her they had stolen his bags and all his money. He urgently needed some cash to survive. Would she please wire him five hundred dollars? Perhaps recent history had caused her to lose some of her edge, but she would not fall into this trap. She asked him to call back three hours later. Together with her cousin, they investigated his name on the internet. They found out that, indeed, there had been an architect with that name. He had done some great work in that Spanish city…in the '50s! He died about seven years earlier. This man was an impostor. The sequence of events only justified and augmented her displeasure. Men were just not trustworthy.

"I am going to build a life around my persona and my children. I do not need a man near me."

A new low in Marta's animus came about when her daughter declared that she did not want to see her mother anymore. All this turmoil, she said, had been imposed upon the family by Marta's crazy ideas. She also had received new information from Carlos that confirmed that Marta had plotted to cause him harm. In fact, Marta had received notice that Carlos was suing her for conspiring against him. Her lawyer told her it would be best if she did not return to Argentina anytime soon.

The following day, Myriam called Marta. Myriam was unaware of all that had transpired but intended to find out why she had not heard from her cousin. When her call went unanswered, she drove over to the nearby apartment. The doorman rang through the intercom, and there was no answer. Using the spare key held by the building, they entered the apartment.

Myriam's heart galloped as she feared something terrible had happened. Indeed, she found an unconscious Marta lying on the living room floor. She called the emergency services, and they worked hard on reviving her. The first responders found a bottle of sleeping pills on the bedroom floor. It seemed like she wanted to go to sleep forever. They moved her to the nearby hospital, where they pumped her stomach to empty all the drug remnants.

Marta stayed at the hospital for observation.

Myriam insisted she sees a psychiatrist in the area. "You need someone here, not in Argentina." The new counselor told her she needed antidepressants and something to calm down the rattled nerves. She also suggested that Marta see her on, at least, a weekly basis for the forthcoming future.

A few weeks later, while having an afternoon tea with her cousin, Marta observed that *Lorazepam and Prozac* now subdued the *vilde chaye*. She made a face that was hard to interpret. Was she sarcastic? Perhaps just self-deprecating? She was resigned to her new reality.

BON DIA, SENHOR ANDREAS

Andreas Wurmli sat in his Swissair economy seat and nervously fastened his seatbelt. Barely a month ago, he had attempted to perpetrate a horrendous murder. Terribly ashamed, he decided that it was time to take distance from Zurich, from his liquor consumption, from his depressed mental state, and seek help. He thought it was best to do so in a place that he remembered with fondness, a country that embraced him in his youth. With its beautiful beaches, pretty women, happy samba music, Brazil would be an excellent location to attempt recovery. People were warm, friendly, helpful, and even loving. So different from austere Switzerland.

Traveling with him in the belly of the plane were two bags containing clothes he would need for an extended stay. He thought he would be away for at least three months. However, he did not need too many clothes; Brazil has a hot climate, and the dress is casual. He'd taken on board a backpack holding some notes with the names of people he would want to contact; these were names related to his childhood. The three friends he remembered fondly. Because he did not fully trust his memory, he wanted to review these at some point during the long flight. There were also a couple of rehabilitation places that curiously, he thought, had English names. And he took along two small flasks of whiskey that would help him survive the inevitable stress of the nearly 12-hour flight. He was relieved to learn that Swissair had a direct flight to Sao Paulo. He would not lose his way at JFK or another airport during a stop-over.

He had promised his daughter he would look for a facility that would help him overcome his alcoholism, and he intended to keep the promise. He guessed that one could not remove such dependence with some minor surgery, so he imagined spending a month or two in some luscious Brazilian location—maybe a place like Buzios.

But secretly, there was a more dreamlike element to this trip. Andreas wanted to find the Brazil he'd dreamed about the Brazil he was yearning for and the Brazilians he imagined encountering every step of the way. Who knows? Maybe he could relocate and set-up a new home. He would be around people who would like him, people who, unlike his Zurich neighbors, would not disparage him for his prior misdeeds.

Because he was not wholly deranged, he understood that the expectations about Brazil and Brazilians might be exaggerated. But, though he was an alcoholic, he could swear that his strong feelings for these people were genuine and deserving. He had to make sure not to tell them about his recent madness when he'd plotted a crazy plan to shoot a world-renowned figure. That, at the time, he imagined that the ensuing uproar—an earthquake of sorts—would get him the attention of all those that had ignored and dismissed him over the last few years.

He had carefully scribbled some information ahead of his trip. Flight information, hotel reservations, and the names of his friends from yesteryear, when he'd been a youngster—Humberto Soares, Mario Neto, and Laura Carvalho. Would he be able to find them? Did they still live in Sao Paulo? When, as a 17-year-old, he'd followed his parents back to Zurich, he exchanged letters with all three, especially with Laura. But, as time passed, those exchanges became less frequent, until his only correspondent was Laura—the girl for whom he had a secret crush. But then he'd gotten married, and because his wife was the jealous type, and he'd worried she might have a fit should she find out about the correspondence. He'd informed Laura that he would discontinue writing and hoped she understood. He had not gotten a response. He'd been so willing to be a good husband at that time; little did he know, years later, his infidelity would derail that marriage and his life.

The border police greeted him with a smile. *"Bom dia Senhor Andreas, seja bem-vindo!"*

He felt wonderful. He had booked a room in a small hotel in Sao Paulo's Nova Centro. The hotel was inexpensive, which suited his thrifty personality. Since this could be an extended trip, some frugality made sense, he said to himself. He found the room was modest but clean. It did have a small table and a chair that he could use as he engaged in the quest to find his old friends.

He asked the front desk if he could borrow the local phonebook and took it to his room. He was mildly surprised to find that it listed twelve Humberto Soareses, eighteen Mario Netos, and eight Laura Carvalhos. Even though he had time on his hands, it would not be comfortable calling all these strangers. The project's immensity scared him; he would have to call each number and hope to get lucky with an early find. His Portuguese was rudimentary, and he was sure that few in this country spoke German, not to mention Swiss-German. He would try English, but he guessed, and quickly learned, that it was not commonly spoken here either. He dimly remembered that only a few had spoken English when he'd lived here a good thirty years earlier; it had not meaningfully improved since then.

He was somewhat taken aback by some reactions to his phone calls. Several said something along the lines of "I don't know you" and hung up. Others said they did not understand him. A third group said they did not recognize his name. There were even a few that hung up without any explanation. That shocked him as he'd never imagined Brazilians being this rude or unfriendly. After thirteen frustrating calls, sad and confused, he decided he needed a break. He walked out to see if he could find in this neighborhood the Brazil he'd always glorified.

It was about 3 p.m., and he felt hungry and thirsty—mostly the latter. Alcohol would surely help him feel better. He was amused and appreciative that there were seven restaurants spread over a two-block radius. He passed over a couple that did not seem too busy and entered a third that was well-visited (he knew the adage that a busy place was a good sign). He ordered a ham and cheese sandwich. He deftly found the more interesting page on the menu—the one listing alcoholic beverages. He'd been too young to have any when he'd lived in Brazil previously, and some of these names were anathema to him. What were *Caipiroshkas* and *Caipirinhas*? It so happened that the waiter attending him spoke pretty good English; this place was really a great find! The waiter explained that they first used vodka alongside the typical components of a *caipirinha*: sugarcane liquor—called *cachaça*—lime, and sugar. He ordered a *caipirinha* first and then a *caipiroshka*. He thought they were just delightful and light drinks, so he repeated the second, which he liked a bit better. Once he got to his room, however, the three drinks showed their effect, and he quickly fell into a deep sleep. As his eyes closed, he mumbled something about these drinks being terrific.

When he woke up, he concluded that his love for the country was reinstated despite the string of disastrous phone calls. At this moment, he wilfully ignored the fact that he was there to get better, not finding new ways to perpetuate his addiction. He was supposed to be in an environment that was less conducive to liquor consumption, so all those bars in the neighborhood were hardly ideal.

Once he got up and washed his face to regain some clarity, he switched his phone search from the Netos to the Soares list. Maybe he would get lucky with this one and find Humberto. Indeed, his second call hit the jackpot. Yes, this number corresponded to his childhood friend, and more importantly, he remembered Andreas, their trip to Petropolis, the mischief they'd gotten up to as young boys with much idle time on their hands. His friend suggested that they get together for lunch the next day. No, dinner would not be possible since he had a family and needed to be with them. But lunch would be great. Around 1:15 p.m., he would meet Andreas at the hotel entrance. He knew a decent fish restaurant in the area.

Andreas was tremendously happy with his quick find. In his excitement, he forgot to ask about the other two friends. He would do so when they met for lunch. He wondered how Humberto had changed—would he even recognize him? Humberto told him he would wear a white shirt and blue jeans to make the recognition easier. In any case, he doubted too many people would be looking for another person in the hotel lobby.

That night's sleep was difficult—the caipirinhas gave him a headache, and he was excited about the rendezvous with his erstwhile friend. He stayed awake for much of the night, speculating about a variety of possible developments. In his agitated state, he did not consider a potential disappointment, a less positive reaction by his friend—a let-down.

He got a late start to the new day as he'd finally succumbed to exhaustion and some sleep. His body clock was still adjusting to jet lag, which might have contributed to him sleeping from 3:30 to about 9:15 a.m. Breakfast was not a reason to get up—it was unusual for him to feel hungry in the morning, and recently, his appetite had diminished, anyway. But he had the urge to have a drink.

He shook his head, thinking that a change of location had not, as if by magic, changed his habits and stopped his alcoholism. "At some point in time, you will brush your teeth with whiskey," he murmured, but there was no sadness in the mirror's reflection. He was too embarrassed to look for a coffee shop that would sell him a shot of liquor; instead, he reached for the Johnny Walker bottle he'd brought on the flight. He made himself a mental note to search for a liquor store that would allow him to replenish his stock.

He was in the lobby about ten minutes before the agreed-upon time and impatiently waited for a good forty minutes. He knew that Brazilians were not punctual, but this was hard on him because he was punctilious as all Swiss. A man with a white shirt, jeans, and sporting a black beard came in and looked around. He also carried a broad smile, which convinced Andreas it was Humberto. Andreas swiftly moved toward him and stretched out both arms. His friend reached out to shake Andreas's hand; he was not ready for the offered, friendlier, embrace.

They walked about four blocks and found the fish restaurant, *Coco Bambu*. Humberto told Andreas that he worked at a foundation, doing all sorts of political and sociological research. He'd received his Ph.D. from Yale, where he'd met his wife, Liliana—also Brazilian, of course. He had two daughters, ages seventeen and fifteen—yes, he'd had a late start; academic work and economic uncertainty had delayed the decision to have a family.

Andreas also provided a biographical sketch that carefully bypassed the reason for his divorce and made no mention of the recent ill-fated plot. He elliptically mentioned that after the divorce, he'd been very disillusioned and developed a drinking habit. With that, he called the waiter and asked for a *caipiroshka*.

Evoking hazy memories of past camaraderie, Andreas concluded Humberto was careful and correct; but, disappointingly not more. Significant gaps in a long-term relationship are not easily bridged. Frustration could ensue after both sides tread carefully. It may not be the reason for a seismic tremor, but a subconscious foreboding that yesteryear's friendship might never be revived and evoke the same levels of empathy and devotion.

Perhaps because of his annoyance, Andreas shifted attention away from Humberto—did he know anything about the other two friends from the old days? What was with Mario and Laura? Had he kept in touch? Could Humberto find them and help Andreas reconnect?

Andreas thought he saw Humberto produce a savvy smile that suggested he understood Andreas's mood shift. It was not castigating, Andreas thought, but neither did it show empathy. Humberto told him that Mario's tracks were lost. The last he'd heard, Mario had moved to Natal. He was heavily involved in the construction spree that gripped the Brazilian Northeast. Humberto did have casual contact with Laura, now a physician living in Leblon, a pleasant Rio area. He would be happy to give Andreas her phone number.

Andreas told him about the phonebook ordeal. The search for Mario had led to many disappointments. He was glad he'd found Humberto quickly.

Humberto laughed as he shook his head. "Yes," he said, "we Brazilians, come in all shades and colors. Not of our skin, mind you—although that is also the case—but when it comes to how friendly we are, how kind, how willing to help a stranger. Just like any society."

Andreas did not tell him about his admiration of all things Brazilian—first and foremost, its people. Humberto could not possibly understand Andreas's perspective without having lived in

Switzerland. That thought prompted him to ask if his friend had had the chance to visit Zurich, Geneva, or the Alps. Humberto once again produced the same smile—apparently, he smiled anytime he had to say something slightly tricky. He had spent six years in the USA. He'd also gone to several conferences in England and other European cities like Frankfurt and Milan, but he had not had the opportunity to visit Switzerland. He was sorry about that, he added. Andreas tried to sound sarcastic as he told him not to worry. "It was no big loss, even though the land's scenery is beautiful."

Humberto sensed the negativity his friend had toward his home country. He looked at his watch and told him that he had an appointment with a colleague at the foundation and better leave. But they should get together again—hopefully, sometime soon.

Anyone who saw Andreas walking down the street would have noted his hanging head and his uncertain gait. Indeed, Andreas was quite disappointed with what had just happened. He was even more discouraged about what had not occurred. He'd hoped for more warmth, more enthusiasm about the encounter. He even thought it possible to be invited to his friend's house, introduced to his wife and children. And maybe Humberto might have even suggested that Andreas relocate to Brazil if he was so unhappy in Zurich. It was not that Humberto had been unfriendly or curt but that Andreas had expected so much more than this polite correctness.

He was so flustered by the luncheon that he spent the rest of the afternoon in his hotel room watching Brazilian TV and sipping whiskey. He saw that the TV offerings were home productions, a soccer match between *Botafogo* and the local *Corinthians*. Two other channels showed what seemed to be Brazilian movies—later he discovered that these were *telenovelas* (soap operas) and were very popular in the country. One of the shows portrayed people during the 18th century; and told the story of the main character—a woman called Gabriela. The other was more contemporary and purposefully farcical. His Portuguese was too rudimentary to make heads or tails of these stories, and he did not care much about soccer either, but he decided to watch the game. He knew that Brazilians were tops in that sport. Soon exhaustion took over; he closed his eyes and dozed off.

When he awoke, he felt depressed; Andreas began wondering

about the purpose of his trip and whether he had done the right thing in coming here at all.

He sat at the desk, grabbed one of those hotel letterheads, and with a reflective effort that was almost painful, wrote:

> *Damn the delirious mind that sets me up,*
> *The heartaches when reality usurps*
> *My consciousness checked at the door,*
> *Like an old coat at the "Escape Bar."*

He was surprised that he'd mastered this. Sometimes he was quite clear about what was going on in his head. He looked at the paper and decided that there was little sense in staying in Sao Paulo. Humberto had been a disappointment, and there was no purpose in hanging around, hoping to see him again. Laura was in Rio; maybe he should arrange a hotel and move there. But first, he had to make sure that she would be willing to see him. After what he had just experienced, he was more circumspect.

The next morning, he waited for his watch to strike ten, then called Laura's office. The doctor did not answer. Instead, it was a receptionist whose English was poor. But Andreas was prepared for the occasion. At dinnertime, he'd discussed with the English-speaking waiter how one would say in Portuguese: "I am an old friend of Dr. Carvalho; may I please speak to her?"

The receptionist said something he did not understand but added, "*Um momentinho, por favor.*" And so, Andreas waited.

The voice that came to the phone was unmistakably Laura's. Half-tripping over his own words in excitement, he quickly told her that he had gotten her number from Humberto, whom he saw the day before, yes, in Sao Paulo. He remembered her with great affection and asked if she would be willing to meet him. If so, he would fly down to Rio the next day and set up a time to rendezvous whenever it would suit her.

The momentary silence that ensued almost caused Andreas's heart to stop. Ultimately, Laura said, "Dear Andreas, you came all the way to Brazil to see your old friends! How can I refuse to see you? Today is Thursday, and the weekend is coming up. Let us plan to meet over one of those days."

Andreas was euphoric, and his words came out staccato. "Of course! That sounds wonderful. I leave it up to you to choose the date, time, and place, and I will be there. I will fly down tomorrow and call you in the afternoon to hear about your choice."

He barely could sleep, so great was his excitement. He looked at an old picture, Laura's black hair blowing in the wind, her smile broad and pleasant, and her shorts shorter than most Swiss girls would ever wear. She looked vivacious and self-assured in her posture; no wonder he liked her so much! He recited to himself the words he had heard on the phone a bit earlier and looked up where Leblon was on the Rio map. He noted that it was close to the *Dois Irmaos* rock formation protruding into the water—like so much of Rio's geography, this gave it the natural beauty so many admired. He had checked out hotels in the Leblon area, and nothing was to Andreas' liking. Even though the Cesar Park Hotel in nearby Ipanema was expensive, he decided to book a room for a week. He did not want to leave the impression of being destitute. Besides, Ipanema was well known to be a tourist mecca, and he might well have an enjoyable time.

They agreed to meet Saturday at around 11 in the morning. She would pass by the hotel; they could walk along the beach and grab some lunch. She clarified that it was going to be a sunny day but not excessively hot. Multitudes would crowd the famous walk with its legendary black and white wave-like mosaic design. Notwithstanding, they could still talk and converse over lunch. A bit tongue-tied, he only was able to say that he could not wait.

He was in the lobby a good fifteen minutes before the set time. Laura might arrive early, and he did not want her to wait. Eventually, a woman entered the lobby. He spotted her immediately but was unsure it was Laura, for she looked different. That woman's hair was black but cut short; her face was a light brown like Laura's, but it had aged.

He approached her and timidly asked, "Laura?"

She smiled and nodded. "Good to see you again, Andreas."

They crossed the chaotic traffic toward the beach and tried to have a conversation despite the many people crisscrossing around them while noisily chatting away.

"Tell me about yourself; I understand you are a doctor?"

She told him that she headed the university hospital's oncology department. She also taught at the medical school and had a small private practice. She had studied at the same medical school where she now worked. "It is one of the best in the country—in South

America in general," she remarked with manifest pride.

"I was busy with my studies and had little time for finding a boyfriend, marriage, and having children. Eventually, I married another doctor; we had a daughter, Joanna, who is now getting her degree at the same university. She will be an epidemiologist. I am no longer married—we divorced five years ago when I found out that he was having a fling with a nurse that worked in the same hospital."

"That's terrible!" he proclaimed, showing Laura a lot of empathy but forgetting his misdeeds that culminated in divorce.

He felt he needed to reciprocate and tell about himself. He started by saying that he too was divorced but just attributed it to diverging paths—" a common thing these days, as you know," he observed. He did not tell Laura about losing his job, but he was candid when he said to her that he had a drinking problem. Like with Humberto, he avoided mentioning the recent plot derailed by a malfunctioning gun.

"I have often thought about my times in Brazil, you and the other friends. I missed all of it. I decided to see if I could find you, Humberto, and Mario; find out if my idyllic memories were just a fantasy or had solid grounding."

Laura smiled and reacted positively. "That's wonderful!"

It triggered his excitement—he garnered courage and asked if he could see her that evening. His hopes were quickly dashed. No, that would not be possible. She would spend the time with a man she had been seeing for about fifteen months. Sensing his sadness, she suggested that she would pick him up the following day—they could go to the Corcovado and the Botanical Gardens.

"These two are among the most wonderful things to see in Rio, and I want to be the one to show them to you."

The next morning, they went up the Corcovado where a statue of Jesus, with stretched-out arms, sought to bless the city. The view from up there was stunning, and Andreas was effusive about it.

Laura remarked, "We Brazilians are a mixed-up people. On the one hand, most are devout Catholics; on the other hand, maybe because of the African heritage, we have a strong strand of beliefs closer to voodoo and black magic. Nothing that Rome preaches or condones. We generally are also naïve and gullible."

Andreas interpreted that as if Laura was simultaneously distancing herself from the masses and their ignorance while embracing them and their uninformed cultural traits. When she saw his eyebrows lift, she added, "Yes, I know that sounds snobbish. Let me explain. It's wonderful to be surrounded by loving, nice people, and yet, terribly frustrating having to deal with their ignorance, their stupid actions, the inability to follow basic rules of hygiene."

Laura and Andreas did not say much more as they looked down at the sprawling *Cidade Maravilhosa* underneath.

Laura told him that they were off to the Botanical Garden because it was one of her favorite spots. "It was founded in 1808 by the then king of Portugal. It is good to see how well the place has been preserved. It reflects the horticultural diversity of Brazil but also has monkeys, toucans, and other animals. I hope you are not too hungry yet. I promise a nice meal after we leave that place."

For lunch, they headed to *Lagoa*. "It may look confusing to you, Andreas. This neighborhood around a lake is in the middle of Rio, between Leblon, Ipanema, and the *Jardim Botânico,* where we were. Isn't it pretty?"

Though the restaurant was attractively situated with a lake so near the ocean, and though the food was quite good, for Andreas, the most critical aspect of their visit was the personal conversation with Laura. He told her that he had been smitten with her when they had been mere sixteen-year-olds. He had hoped that those feelings would sprout again when they met. He understood that she was seeing another man, but he needed to tell her this. She shrugged and said nothing. He then asked if she could do him a favor, though. He'd heard there was a place in Brazil that could help him with his addiction. He had written down the name—did she know anything about it?

She looked at the piece of paper, put her hand on his forearm, and said, "My dear friend, that place is in the United States!"

He started saying, "But—" When she cut him short.

"There actually is a place called Brazil in the State of Indiana—in the region they call the Midwest—in the middle of that country."

He was so embarrassed—he closed his eyes and shook his head.

He then let out a strange laugh that made Laura's eyes get larger; it was so full of cynicism and self-disdain. The laughter reminded her of *The Joker* in a movie she recently saw. Andreas looked strange, even scary.

She chose to continue discussing the matter as an empathetic clinician would. "Brazil is still behind in its treatment of addictions of all kinds. The young love to drink; the warm weather is conducive to drinking. It starts with beer and eventually glides to more potent mixed drinks, and ultimately drugs. There is little federal or state activity we would describe as public health services. It all is kind of sad. I understand why you thought that this might be an excellent place to seek recovery. With its pleasant climate and friendly people, Brazil may give you the best environment to regain a psychological balance. That would be so helpful for anyone—it really could be an ideal place. However, I am so sorry to give you this piece of bad news: Brazil can offer you little to nothing."

He looked at her with eyes that were hard to interpret, perhaps a mix of frustration, pain, and admiration.

She added, "Wherever you go to seek treatment, you need to know that this is not something that you cure with a shot, like penicillin, and then you are done. It is a process with possibly a lifelong dedication and the building of a crucial support system that helps you stay sober. Just that alone suggests that maybe it would be best to go back to Switzerland. They have world-renowned sanatoriums. Some are expensive, but I am sure there are some affordable places as well. Maybe a health insurance scheme would cover at least part of the cost. Why don't you try that?"

They gave each other a warm hug in front of the hotel, and Andreas headed to his room. A glass of scotch in his hand, he reflected on the conversation. Laura was so smart and so honest. No, there was no hope in rekindling yesteryear's relationship, but she spoke as a caring friend, and what she said made sense. He should go back to Switzerland and see if he could find a clinic in the mountains—a place with the pastoral beauty of low-lying hills, a lake providing the calmness of blue and springtime green trees making his eyes smile.

The following morning, he got up early. He needed to expedite certain chores. He told the lobby that due to unforeseen circumstances, he would cut his stay short. He then called Swissair and wondered if he could re-book for an earlier return home. Both entities accepted his requests without much trouble. He would fly back on Tuesday evening—two days later. He then called his daughter to tell her the news.

"Hello, my dear. I have decided to head home earlier than expected. It would be wonderful if you could pick me up at Kloten and spend some time with me. I need to discuss something with you."

The silence at the other end indicated that the call had come as a total surprise; maybe his request was a bit inconvenient. Eventually, his daughter told him that she would be happy to fetch him at the airport, and she would take a couple of hours off from work to talk to him.

Having completed these steps, he went to a nearby store, bought a cheap swim trunk and flip flops. As he was leaving, the attendant pointed to a bottle of sun-screen. He smiled; yes, indeed, his fair skin needed protection from the intense Brazilian sun. He grabbed a beach towel offered by the hotel and crossed the busy road toward the beach's nearly white and smooth sand.

He planned to take it easy for the next two days—admire the people playing soccer and volleyball, look at the women in their skimpy bathing suits, drinking his *caipiroshkas* at the nearby restaurants. He would try the coconut milk straight from the fruit peddled by young men walking barefoot up and down the hot beach sand.

There still was much to like about Brazil. Even if his experience with his erstwhile friends had not been as good as expected, he still had good feelings about the country. Laura had opened his eyes to some of the more problematic social and cultural aspects, facts about which he knew little to nothing. Nonetheless, he still liked looking at these people who were refreshingly uncomplicated and unabashedly pleasant. Many people on the beach were young; they were not wealthy or highly educated. A significant number of them came down from the *favelas*—the shantytown neighborhoods in the mountains surrounding the beautiful city. He had heard that occasionally, they caused the better off, mostly white, people to fear them. But he just saw them enjoying themselves as they kicked balls around. Yes, he had heard of rampant crime and was cautioned not to wear expensive watches or flash a pricey cell phone. But for the brief time he was in Rio, there was no apparent cause for fear.

Once on board the plane back to Zurich, he took out a block of paper and a pen with the hotel's logo; he had taken both to jot down what he wanted to tell his daughter. It was imperative to come across as coherent and clear as possible. He would keep this paper in front of him while talking to her. He would not discuss the incident a month back, but he wanted to explain to her what he needed to treat his alcoholism. He wanted her to acknowledge this and provide him with emotional support because, as Laura stated, he needed his daughter during this long odyssey to recovery.

He would tell her that Brazil had been a disappointment but also an eye-opener. He would share his disillusionment from the meetings with Humberto and Laura and the enlightenment that had made him conclude that home might provide a better environment for him.

He found his luggage quickly and headed to the exit doors. Once outside, he tried to locate his daughter, but there was a large crowd of villagers with Alpen horns and cowbells waiting for one of their own. His senses were thrown into confusion by the racket the villagers created. Finally, he saw arms waving at him; he recognized his daughter smiling at him. He rushed over, gave her a big hug, and they headed to her car.

"Let's go to the lake and find a place outside to grab some lunch," he suggested. "It's a sunny day, and I will be able to thank you for your willingness to come and hear me out by buying you lunch."

He thought that *Quai 61* would be perfect. It was not particularly fancy but had a large deck on the water and offered the quiet environment needed for a heart-to-heart talk. As they drove down Banhoffstrasse, he briefly thought of the malfunctioning gun he had thrown into the nearby canal; had anyone found it, he wondered.

They ordered a salad and, at her suggestion, a chicken sandwich to split. She started the conversation, indicating that she was surprised he'd come back so soon.

He pulled out his folded piece of paper, opened it up, and responded, "I have put my thoughts on paper because I want to make sure I get to tell you all that is on my mind. I did not want to miss anything and regret it later."

She nodded, understanding.

"I went to Brazil with several purposes in mind—I wanted to see again the country that I liked so much. I still love it, and its sincere, simple, and nice people. I never had any concerns about them being hypocritical. I also went to seek out the friends I made when I lived there as a teenager. You have heard me mentioning their names before. Finally, I thought that maybe I could find a place to help me overcome my alcoholism. It is messing up my health, and worse, it is damaging my mind."

He proceeded to tell her how unhappy he was with his search for Mario, how Humberto had come across as polite but distant, and how he'd had some excellent conversations with Laura. She was such a success story, and he was most impressed with her, proud to know her. She was friendly and caring and was the one that suggested that he go back to Switzerland and begin the long process of recovery. "Laura told me that it was not enough to go to some clinic and detoxify. But, because an addict always has the urge to go back to his old habits, I will need to develop a support network that could include family, friends, and the organizations set up for that purpose. "I decided to contact you, my dear daughter, because I need you. It seems that my son, your brother, has divorced me alongside your mother. Could I ask you to be part of that support group? I do not have many friends left in Zurich and even fewer family members. Could I count on you?"

The response was immediate. "Of course, you can count on me, Papa! Look, about your trip; it is often the case—I would say almost always—that strong feelings of love or friendship one may have felt decades earlier fade with the passage of time. People change, conditions change, needs change, and time erases happy memories. Suddenly inserting yourself anew into Humberto or Laura's life may have been a natural offshoot of your warm sentiments. You probably can admit that you suddenly showing up took them totally by surprise. Maybe your expectations were just set too high.

"I will help you search for a good place to get rid of your condition. Just be aware that Switzerland is now struggling with much more dangerous addictions. Heavy drugs, such as heroin, are causing deadly overdoses. In attempts to get these drugs, people commit crimes and have unleashed a dangerous wave. You may find that your issues are not getting the priority or the care you may want. Still, we need to look for the right place, a facility, and a location that will satisfy you emotionally. Laura was right, of course, that you need social and community support. I will look together with you for some organizations that may help. I will be there for you, and I will speak to my brother and see if he will join me. You will also need to start looking for some daily work and other ways to keep yourself busy. You need to change to a healthy lifestyle."

Back in his apartment, Andreas mulled over the last thing his daughter had said. So, she thought he was a bum. That was painful. But was it on point? He had been out of work for a few years; it had left him staring at his TV or the walls of his living room for endless hours. Yes, it was conducive to drinking, and she was right in connecting the two. But it still was hurtful. The analytical mind exposes facts in distressing ways.

A tear rolled down his red, rosacea mottled cheek, and he reached for the bottle of Johnny Walker.

NOW WHAT, TATIANA GRISHKOVA?

She met Boris in the hotel lobby. Just before approaching him, she tightened her expression and narrowed her eyes. She had to make sure she reflected firmness and toughness. She was aware of his past, and she had to make sure he would not do to her what he had done to others he had perceived as enemies.

He offered her a chair near him, but she refused; she wanted to come across as tough, stand tall. She was afraid her knees would buckle, but they did fine. She told him that she was leaving the empire. She expected to get paid through the end of the month; she did not expect any further payments after that. She would not accept his apologies. He should be happy she was not suing him— all she wanted in return was that he leave her alone for good. "No contact, no mafia-style vendettas, no reprisals, and no violence," she specified.

When she stormed out of the building—"To catch some air," she told him—she ran across the road, perilously avoiding taxis and cars, which, as always, rushed through the heavy NYC traffic. She continued running when in Central Park—roughly through the same area she had been ambushed before. She turned back, but no one was following her. She felt very lonely, something she rarely had felt in the past. Even when she had been alone before, she had not been bothered or saddened by it. She was also afraid; fear was not something that she experienced often, but now she was scared. Yes, she was worried about her physical well-being. Who knew what a nasty former Russian-mafia guy might do to her?

She'd researched and found out that some believed that on two separate occasions, he'd killed a man. He, the articles said, was the executioner of orders from his bosses. She also was nervous because of the incertitude of what lay ahead in her future. The strong sense of direction, of next steps to take, which had been the hallmark of her existence since adolescence, had vanished. There just was no obvious professional path, and she had no clear idea of what lay ahead in her future.

Despite what she had told Boris, she was apprehensive about any repercussions, gossip, and maybe even vendettas. In the last month, the situation had turned uglier. Her suspicions were heightened when the team's physical therapist—a woman with connections and plenty of inside information—had warned her about real physical danger. Ever since that conversation, all she could think about was finding a smooth way out.

She went back to her room and packed her bags. Maybe Los Angeles would be suitable for her after all. Over the years, ever since getting some exposure to the freedoms on the other side of the Urals, she'd gradually converted toward the belief that the West offered clear advantages—a refuge from despotic rulers and arbitrary lawlessness. At this particular moment in her life, those were significant attributes—she was hungry for that type of freedom.

~ ~ ~ ~

Her father had been a military man, essentially most of his adult life. First as an officer in the Red Army and later as a General in the Russian Federation army. Toward the end of the Brezhnev era, he was appointed to head all infantry regiments in Siberia. As much as his family disliked it, he'd been forced to move his wife and three relatively young children—to remote Yakutsk, where the Lena River was iced-over for the better half of the year. For the remaining few months, the weak sun only provided some semblance of beauty.

The youngest of three, Tatiana, had shown distinct personality traits from early on. At age five, her strong will came across when she rejected foods she didn't like, willing to go to bed hungry rather than eat another version of Pelmeni. Later in life, she became a foodie; she'd delight in Georgia's spicy food served in the finer Moscow restaurants, enjoy French haute cuisine in Paris, or marvel at Peter Luger's steaks when in Manhattan. At the age of nine, she argued with her mother at home and with her teachers at school. Russian women needed to be less willing to follow their husbands to distant places with no culture, like Siberia. Her mother was not too happy about the feistiness and the antics.

"Why is she so rebellious?" she'd complained to her husband.

He'd smirked while suggesting that they should just let her be.

On the other hand, the school director did not take kindly to these outbursts. He punished the girl by having her write one hundred times: "I will not disparage Siberia ever again."

She was strong-willed and argumentative, but also cute, charming, and very smart. The smile of that child turned into a magnificent weapon when she blossomed into a young woman. The blue eyes that seemed to invite you to play hide and seek at age ten turned a more intense blue-green, which disarmed the men trying to figure her out and conquer her heart eight or ten years later.

Above all, Tatiana was determined to succeed, make a name for herself, and defy the terrible odds in a country so unwilling to give a woman the path to wealth, power, and status. She knew it would be hard and against the ironclad rules of the male-dominated society. Nonetheless, this dream kept popping up, especially at times of reflective solitude. She liked these moments because she could appraise her life and what her future would be. She felt she needed to review and ascertain whether everything was going according to plan, whether she was on the right path, and if not, to *regain her compass*, as she liked to say.

Whether she was playing a "second fiddle" role, the resourceful organizer, or the elegant emissary, she always kept her ultimate goals in mind. She would say to herself, "One day, they will honor me, send me gifts, and translate my Russian words into French or Spanish."

~ ~ ~ ~

Her upbringing took place in a distant region—far from the Russian epicenter of all economic success and political power. Moscow was more than three thousand miles away. Just as every Russian knew, with different degrees of consciousness and at varying points in life, Tatiana understood that being geographically far away from the capital was not smart. Success would primarily be found in Moscow or—perhaps to a lesser extent—in St. Petersburg. Moving to either one of those two cities seemed essential.

However, there was another geographical concept that simmered in her mind. Even as a teenager, she had the intellectual curiosity and the much less common belief that her path to success would involve knowledge, expertise, openness to the world outside Russia, beyond Moscow, on the other side of the Urals. She immersed herself in every aspect of European and American culture, art, music. These were not always accessible, and her English was not good enough to understand everything, but she gave all possible effort into getting Western exposure.

Before the Soviet Union dissolved and the Iron Curtain collapsed, such acts were considered treasonous, so they were secret, aspirational, and limited—more dreamlike than concrete, more speculative than specific. She was not alone in that quest. There were others—bright members of her generation who often sought the same information, secretly sharing it with like-minded friends. But none of this was easy. Even in the early 80s, when Western European and American culture infiltrated more copiously, it reached only those hungry to know more that gathered clandestinely. Getting more than a superficial glimpse of music, literature, culture, and fashion 'over there' remained complicated. Gradually, it became more feasible under Glasnost. In effect, Tatiana became a product of that era, and she exploited the new openness more than most others in her age-group. She was aware of being unique in her pursuits, and that made her proud. She always wanted to stand out.

At the age of seventeen, she fell in lust with Piotr. He was about her age, good-looking, tall, with a pronounced nose and muscular biceps. They would spend a lot of time in the gym, hiking, engaging in all sorts of sports, and because she wanted to develop strength, she began lifting weights. To show him how much she cared about sports, she joined a basketball squad, even though she was a bit shorter than most. She developed into a good guard because she could dribble, run, and shoot the ball accurately from a fair distance.

However, she also wanted physical intimacy. Her mother told her that boys mature later than girls, but she did not want to believe this. She discovered that Piotr was not only a novice and timid but plain disinterested in sex. She felt distraught and rejected. For many months following their split, she wanted to see no one. It was difficult to admit, but a measure of disdain for the other sex set in at that time.

Later in life, she would tell her friends that Piotr was only the first in a long string of disappointments.

As she was finishing high school and with Piotr out of her mind, she reverted to thinking about her next steps and decided that her career had to have an international bent—she was too fascinated by the world outside Russia.

It was clear as water—only a few Russians spoke other languages, and she could seize on the opportunity by learning a couple. She would study English (of course!), but another language would make her that more special. She applied and got accepted to the Moscow State Linguistic University; as a sign of the times, It had just changed its name from Maurice Thorez, the former French Communist leader. She had good grades, and her father's connections smoothed the acceptance process.

She was rather surprised that so many students attended the university. Somehow, she'd imagined that only a few would be there, and she would instantly become a member of the elite. Not so! Thousands were there. Later she learned that they were not all in competition with her. Several were foreigners, even black people, which she had never seen before—all there to learn Russian and about her country.

But some were like her, seizing on the opportunity of the new opening produced by Gorbachev's policies. With that realization, she decided that it would be smart to choose a less common additional language and picked Arabic. Once again, she sought differentiation. At home, she heard her father discuss how the area extending from Russia's southern border and to North Africa—where Arabic was commonly spoken—would become a center of international disputes as superpowers vied for control over oil, territory, and political influence. Those discussions left a strong impression on her, but more than anything, she thought it would be cool to pick a language that only a few others cared to know. Her drive to singularity came to the fore once again.

Two weeks after arriving in the big city and marveling at its relative opulence, she met Dima. He was also a university student, but he'd picked German as his language of expertise. He felt that Russia and Germany had much in common—going as far back as the Romanovs. He was a philosophy major in college, and they had lots of animated conversations about Marxism (which they both disliked) and existentialism. She loved those discussions because they were so intellectually stimulating. Still, she also was eager to have a boyfriend to put her arms around. She wanted a male companion to wake up next to in the morning and admire his strong back—she always had a thing about male backs and lower backs. She made some moves because she was not about to waste time. Dima's response was very puzzling; he'd smile and quickly change the subject.

Soon after, she challenged him. "Dima, why don't you kiss me? Am I not attractive to you? I have given you indications I like you—not just as a friend, I mean."

And then it came out, so shocking to Tatiana, so strident, she felt actual chest pains. "Yes. Of course, Tatiana, I have noticed. But it seems like *you* have not noticed that I am gay, that I like men. You have seen me hang out with some and us showing affection to each other. I am surprised."

She got up from the living room sofa, put on her coat, and ran out. She did not stop running for five blocks, running and crying. Years later, she told Maria, her best friend, "How could I have been so blind and so dumb? There were signs. He was trying to send a clear message—he did so at least a couple of times."

Because she was smart, had an excellent ear, and worked diligently on her language studies, her grades were excellent. Fifteen months after she began, she got a government scholarship to spend six months in Tunisia. She was elated! She would travel abroad. Her first trip. She was getting recognized. She belonged to the cream of the crop! She would have preferred Paris or New York, of course, but she had chosen Arabic. Perhaps she could meet a wealthy young prince from the Emirates—a man who would buy her fancy clothes and possibly allow her to drive his Ferrari, she kidded with Maria.

She wound up giving a mixed review of her experience in Tunisia—it was an exciting place, more exotic than she'd expected, but less urban and less cosmopolitan than she'd imagined. The country was visited by wealthy sheiks when they did not want to go to the more distant favorites such as London, Paris, or New York. Some of these visitors pursued her overtly. She mostly ignored them, as she could not imagine herself living in their countries.

In terms of her professional development and expertise, the stint was a grand disappointment—those who spoke Arabic spoke a slang that she did not fully understand. Those who could speak *High Arabic,* the language she learned in school, the language of journalists and diplomats, were also educated in French and preferred to show their elite status by speaking that instead. She concluded that this scholarship was a prime example of Russian bureaucratic idiocy. Like many of her age group, she saw the government bureaucracy as well deserving all the criticism.

Upon her return from Tunisia, she continued to focus on English at the university, French?—*rien de tout.* Arabic?—no longer interesting after the Tunisia disappointment. Tatiana decided that the path to happiness would have to involve economic success and enlisted for a two-year program focused on business and economics. She entered Plekhanov University. While that school always had been linked to the government's economic activity, the program chosen concentrated on practical aspects rather than economic theory. It would give her the knowledge she needed to move forward.

Consistent with her desire to direct attention to Russia's international affairs, Tatiana wanted to learn about international business. Her selective courses focused on trade and commerce— she was sure they would help her in the future. Her strong math and statistics skills made the required classes easy. But the place of Russia in global commerce intrigued her. How could she be a part of that new construct? And how could she profit from it? She saw herself as a burgeoning capitalist, even though she knew that her specific knowledge was rudimentary at best. She took a course in business English and another class that taught her conversational English. It was clear to her that the keys to success would involve English-speaking countries, especially the USA.

After finishing her course-work, she found a position in a smaller company striving to export fur coats to Europe. She saw this position as a small window into Russian international trade. It made her happy.

Convinced that a sophisticated, worldly image would be helpful, she became very fashion-conscious. She spent hours looking at foreign magazines that enlightened her about the most recent developments in haute-couture. She was very aware that she was beautiful, that her high cheekbones and green-blue eyes attracted men. She could fix her blonde hair to look elegant, sexy, or wild depending on mood or circumstance and the image to portray. All she needed was some beautiful clothes and shoes to be a showstopper. However, she did not have the deep pockets necessary to purchase these. Those, she would say to herself, would eventually come. In the meantime, she needed to learn a lot more about fashion.

Self-confidence remained high throughout these times of change. When men attracted by her looks approached her, she often dismissed them as not measuring up to her standards. She wanted a handsome, intelligent, and successful man; she was sure she deserved that.

It was a period when Moscow started emulating other big European and American cities. Young women and men went to nightclubs and discotheques, most turning lively only well after midnight. She discovered that she enjoyed the club scene, primarily because of her love of music and dancing and because she saw so many attractive people. Eventually, she found that some men were gay and could not be her boyfriend; many others did not qualify because they seemed so entrenched in the old Soviet system. She did not think they could see eye-to-eye about a future together. She was quite frustrated by the dearth of potential mates.

On a Friday summer night, she met Sasha. Just like her, he was fascinated by the new opportunities of a more capitalist Russia. He also wanted to make a lot of money. He was handsome, tall, and well-toned. She decided to give the relationship a meaningful chance; they started dating seriously soon after that.

Sasha was the son of a high-level bureaucrat in the foreign ministry and had spent several years of his young adulthood in Paris and London. Tatiana was fascinated by that and continuously asked him when he would show her those two cities—she was mesmerized by the idea of visiting them.

The following spring, she got her wish, and they spent two weeks in London and Paris. They visited every place a first-time tourist would, but also, at her insistence, went looking for hip clothing stores—she was determined to spend every euro and sterling on fun clothes she could afford. She was intent on making her girlfriends jealous.

For years, she spoke of those two weeks as the best in her life. It was not only due to Sasha or lovemaking but because she was thrilled by the sites and her shopping cart's size. She called her friend Maria to tell her that she had finally fallen in love.

However, Sasha's relationship lasted only a couple of months following their return One Saturday night, while dining at one of Moscow's new, fancy restaurants in the Krasny Oktyabr area, Sasha told her he was no longer in love with her. He was still in lust, but he was sure that that would not be enough for her. She was devastated—it came as a total surprise. Nonetheless, she did not sob or create a scene. She got up and left. Only her pillow witnessed the crying.

The short relationship with Sasha triggered a lot of thinking, a revolution inside her head. She asked herself whether the pain and unhappiness she felt was worthwhile; she concluded that it was not. She said, "You should not fall in love with a man quickly." She promised herself not to repeat that mistake.

She gave little consideration to what might have precipitated the collapse of their relationship. She did not want to sink into a bout of self-doubt and uncertainty. She did not want to wonder why her relationships with men were so complicated. She decided that she would weigh the real benefits of a relationship in the future rather than whether she could fall in love. It was much more about material success than love—there were no fairy tales, she concluded.

She decided that already established, successful, and wealthy men were a better prospect than those just starting out, even if they were a bit older. She had seen the pictures of wealthy Russian magnates posing in Ibiza, St. Tropez, and Puerto Banus; they were mostly older and pudgy, their arms embraced young, gorgeous women twenty to thirty years younger. She understood that this was part of modern Russia, and she was okay with all of it. She had no interest in passing judgment on either the men or the women in those pictures.

Until now, she maintained the belief that hard work and intelligence would bring her to the pinnacle of society—to a beautiful life with power, wealth, and prestige. She had hit the walls of communist Russia—bureaucracies—and was keenly aware of the high barriers set up by men in power to prevent others' access and success, especially women.

In the Russia of those days, Moscow not being an exception, people were either struggling laborers or lower echelon bureaucrats. You heard rumors about extremely wealthy men who acted much like the Italian mafia as they secured their privileged position. You could also hear grisly stories of blackmail and murder launched by the newly rising upper class as they fomented their climb. Stories that could easily feature in a Mario Puzo's Godfather-like novel. Tatiana became a lot less naïve about paths to success.

There were times she would tell you that she still believed that applying yourself smartly, learning about the world, learning languages, developing skills were the keys to success. The two weeks in Europe, and the relationship with Sasha in general, prompted new question marks.

Maybe she could exploit readily available shortcuts instead. She was pretty and smart, and men were so willing to please her in hopes of conquering her heart. In a way, a scheming, calculating mode was so much easier than working your tail off. She did not share these thoughts with anyone, but when she was alone, in bed, and half asleep, her pensive mood revolved around these thoughts.

With time, shrewdness became her new mantra. She focused on her presentation's attractive features—the physique, the clothes, the walk, and the smile. As she practiced in front of a mirror, the idea was to become more suggestive and inviting. She went to a tailor and had her skirts trimmed a few centimeters; she bought slightly lower-cut blouses to reveal more cleavage. She bought shirts with buttons that allowed her to unbutton one more hole. She bought pants that were rather tight to a body that she had kept trim since her days with Piotr. She went to nightclubs and smiled in a coquette manner to men that seemed rich. She made sure to stay choosy in the men she sought to attract—she delicately dismissed older men who she thought were too fat.

She made sure to escape attempts to engulf her in a sexual embrace, to say no to drunken men who might have lost control. She wanted to believe and worked hard at convincing herself that she would never be in danger. She made sure she never drank so much that she would be at risk of losing it. To some of her friends, that kind of certainty was a source of concern, but she rejected their warnings.

It was around the same time that, quite by coincidence, she was offered the job of managing a highly ranked tennis player's international business. Vladimir Cherenkov had risen to prominence, and he needed someone with business acumen and languages. Igor, Vladimir's manager, thought Tatiana fit the needs and would not be too expensive, so they offered her the job.

She immediately saw this as an opportunity to do lots of travel and be at the top of the sports segment of society—athletes always well regarded in Russia. She quit her current position, whose exports were not making huge strides anyway, and joined the tight group of trainers, medics, fitness coaches, and money managers who were part of Vladimir's entourage. He had ascended quickly from the low hundreds to the top ten after making the quarter-finals in Melbourne and Wimbledon. Soon, commentators voiced their excitement: they expected him to be a contender for the top five world rankings.

The money flowed from tournament prizes, endorsements, and commercials. It came in multiple currencies; it needed tough negotiations; it needed to be administered smartly to avoid excessive taxes, overspending on staff, and other indulgences. That's what the head of the management team told Tatiana; she needed to help him with all these matters. She would get a good salary and spending money. Yes, she needed to look the part. Of course, she was athletic and beautiful, but the clothes had to match her position. She loved that aspect of her compensation!

It soon became apparent that the tennis player himself had had no input in hiring her and cared little about what she was doing. Still, she needed to perform to ensure the team's head, the entourage leader, would be satisfied.

Igor Soborov was almost fifty years old; he did not appear to want sexual favors in return for hiring her—a common concern for many Russian women. Nor did he seem eager to belittle her when she excelled at transactions or events that would further Vladimir's fortune—power plays being another issue about which Russian women had to worry. She commented to Nadja, a close friend, "He is an unusual Russian—he minds his business and makes sure everyone else does the same."

Tatiana was happy not to feel threatened in any way. Friends had warned her:

"They will take advantage of you."

"You will be asked to do things you do not want to do."

"You will get intoxicated by the jet-set lifestyle and lose your principles."

As she saw it, she could handle Igor's demands just fine. She knew to be strict and disciplined. It seemed a perfect match, and both seemingly recognized it as such.

But the tennis circuit was challenging, and the physical demands on the sportsman were high. There were concerns that Vladimir would become physically weaker. He needed to find a way to maintain his vitality. Everyone knew that Olympians dabbled in a variety of prohibited drugs to retain their strength. In the 80s and 90s, Igor had procured pills, infusions, and whatnot for Russian (earlier Soviet) Olympic gymnasts, weightlifters, and track and field stars. But, if he'd managed to save his skin then (he had been removed from the Russian Olympic Committee—a meaningless, symbolic punishment), he also knew that he was being watched closely by those seeking to clamp down on violators of the code. There was only one person who could do the deed without causing suspicion or creating problems for Vladimir.

They asked Tatiana to travel to Turkey, meet with a certain doctor Yakub, get a vital flask containing potent medication, and bring it back to Moscow. Because of her desire to travel to new places, her heart almost skipped. She asked if she could be in danger if she would be safe. They promised her a local bodyguard to make sure that she would not suffer any harm. She asked if, upon her return, she could take four days off and travel to Nice for the film festival; she wanted to do this. Igor promised her that she would not only have those days free, but he would also pay for her travel and a stay at the fancy Negresco Hotel. Strangely, she was infused with youthful naivete and never wondered about this significant and expensive gesture.

And this was how Tatiana—the tough girl from Siberia, the straight-arrow student that believed in hard work and excellence — was co-opted and tainted for life. The woman who did not look for favors to get ahead, the one who often rejected sexual overtures because she wanted to make it on merit, was willing to engage in nefarious activities.

The amazing thing was that the lure of fancy trips and alluring places had such an intoxicating effect on her that this significant deviation from rules and norms occurred smoothly, no questions asked, not even the lift of a puzzled eyebrow. Instead, she got the thrill of telling her friends about the luxurious trips, showed off her new beautiful clothes, and told the world about the exciting people with whom she hob-nobbed.

When social media platforms developed, her pictures and news items spread broader and faster, and she made sure everyone knew she was living a thrilling life. Suddenly there were pictures of her showing off her flat tummy, blowing kisses, displaying cutting-edge fashion, and hugging famous Brazilian soccer players in Barcelona. She seemed insatiable in her pursuit of fame and adulation. Maybe it was just an endless effort to gain popularity and trigger the jealousy of her Moscow girlfriends?

Months passed, and she had to go back to Istanbul to contact Dr. Yakub once more. Knowing what was at stake, she put a price-tag on her voyage. She wanted a $10,000 spending spree in return. By then, Vladimir's prize money surpassed $2 million, and another large sum resulted from advertising, which Tatiana had helped organize. Her demand seemed like "small change" to her bosses. Behind her back, the managing group laughed at the request. They were willing to pay ten times that. As savvy as she was about business, she did not know how to squeeze the best deals for herself. No one knew whether she was just playing it safe— wanting to enjoy this opportunity for as long as possible.

The trips to Istanbul became a recurring event—every three to four months, she would get on a plane, seek out the doctor, get the flask, and fly back a couple of days later. The routine always included a bodyguard, a special bonus, and the usual cautionary moves. However, Tatiana did not realize or did not want to accept it as a risk—with every trip, she set herself up for extortion and related trouble.

In the meantime, she continued to be obsessed with social media. It was an essential element in her daily life. On the one hand, it allowed her to do some useful research about everything involving the tennis circuit, the players, their indulgences, the gossip, and everything else that could be useful to her boss. On the other hand, she kept posting pictures and comments about all the beautiful components of her evolving private and public life—the nightclubs, the music events, the museums and shows she attended. Her girlfriends back home always reacted with great excitement, and that gave her a rush.

The frequent travel to tournaments in Europe, Asia, Australia, and the USA was not very accommodating for a serious relationship, but Tatiana did not care. She enjoyed the club scenes at night, the flow of money, the ability to buy expensive clothes, and the envy of her friends—most friendships had originated at the university, and many did not become such exciting globetrotters. She had a few flings while on tour—a good looking "Australian boy" (that's what she called him) who had a tremendous sexual appetite, lacked manners (but at night, at the clubs, she did not care much); he taught her about *meat on the barbie* and other Aussie expressions. There was an Argentinian, Juan-Jose, a tennis player whose ranking was in the thirties but whose black hair and blue eyes made him look like a movie star. He made romantic overtures as she had never experienced before—she would recount to her girlfriends and end the story by saying, "Ah, those Latin men."

During one of those rare periods when the annual circuit went into a brief hiatus, she spent many hours with her Moscow girlfriends. She confided with them that she might be getting a bit tired of the "circus," the constant packing and moving from city to city. She regretted the inability to have a serious relationship with a man instead of those short flings. She pretended to like these interludes while they happened, but once they were over because of travel or anything else, she disdained them. Probably, her best friend guessed, because she realized she would spend the following nights alone again.

Suddenly, during a very hot Australian Open, while watching Vladimir in a last sixteen match, Igor collapsed at court ringside. Eventually, the doctors told the group that he had suffered a heart attack, needed to get urgent bypass surgery, and probably could not continue living a stressful life. The group decided that it was essential to replace him with someone younger, and Boris Petrovsky took his place.

Petrovsky was in his early thirties. He used to play tennis professionally, but a back ailment had forced him into retirement. Knowing little else, he started teaching the game to young kids. Most relevant, Vladimir insisted on hiring Boris because he was his cousin. This even though he knew that Boris had engaged in underworld activities in St. Petersburg.

Within a few weeks, Boris started coming on to Tatiana. She pushed back; she did not find him attractive—not at all. She told her girlfriends that he reminded her of the boorish men she had encountered in Siberia. They were appalling, she thought. After landing in New York ahead of the US Open, Boris suggested they could share a room at the Hilton, or perhaps a different hotel to make it less conspicuous. She laughed at him, and he turned red. Later that evening, when the group finished dinner at posh TAO, he pulled her over with some force and murmured, "You better be nice to me. We all know about your trips to Turkey."

She had a sleepless night wondering what his threat meant. Was it just bluster? She decided she needed to do a little research into his past. She asked a close friend to help. Three days later, she discovered that he had been accused of roughing up a competitor for his previous employer—a man owning a taxi business in St. Petersburg. He also had been accused of groping a woman at one of the nightclubs in London. Was there more, she asked the acquaintance.

In quick succession, Tatiana experienced great unpleasantness that made her more anxious. One late night, while in NY, she found herself with Boris in a hotel elevator. They were alone. Soon enough, he was pushing himself onto her, trying to kiss her. Two nights later, during a team dinner at Le Cirque, she caught him attempting to pour some powder into her drink. She was savvy enough not to confront him while others, including the tennis star, were present. Instead, she purposely acted clumsy and had the glass fall and spill its content. She looked at him angrily and whispered, "Never try that shit on me again!"

That evening she got an email from her Moscow contact about Petrovsky's presumed involvement in two mafia-style murders. The details were gruesome. She called her friend Maria, who was surprised about the odd hour. Tatiana said she needed to confide in someone; she was about to make significant changes. She wanted to quit her job and move—at least temporarily—to the USA. Los Angeles, she specified. Maria pleaded with her to think twice before taking such a big step.

"You told me, yourself, Tati"—Maria was the only one to call her that—"that you thought Americans were such big hypocrites, that you never felt sure about anyone making statements, pledging, pleading, anything. Do you really think you will be happy there? What will you do? How long do you think you will last over there? And what will you do if you decide to come back?"

Tatiana listened without interrupting, without feeling the need to argue, to counter all these intelligent objections. She knew her friend had presented cogent arguments against her move. But Tatiana was increasingly adamant that, with all its faults, America and Americans had two fantastic embedded qualities—it was a much freer society, and it was less misogynistic than Russia. These two factors were decisive.

In any case, she liked the adventure, the challenge, the desire to try something new in a place that was almost virgin territory for her. Yes, she had spent a couple of weeks in the area during the Indian Wells tournament, but that, and whatever she had read, were the sole sources of information.

The following morning, as she went for her routine run in Central Park, a biker wearing a wool hat covering much of his face hit her side-wise, causing her to fall and badly scrape her skin. Luckily, at the very last moment, she was able to see the impending attack. She also heard a loud "Watch it!" from another runner heading in the opposite direction. She managed to partially move out of his way—enough to avoid full impact and suffer broken bones. It might have been just some maniac trying to cause mayhem or abuse a woman physically, but the events' timing made her highly suspicious that these were linked.

She was trembling when she reached her room at the Essex House. She thought that this had not been a random accident. She was sure that Boris stood behind it, and she needed to figure out what to do next. She called the physical therapist and told him that she would not go to Forest Hill to see the tennis match—she had a terrible headache and would stay in bed.

She then called Vladimir and told him she needed to have a private conversation with him. They agreed to meet in the lobby at 5:30 p.m.; they would find a quiet corner and talk. She wished him good luck in his match that early afternoon.

Later in the day, around three, Tatiana was pleased to see that Vladimir had won his match. It would put him in a good mood, and the conversation would be easier, she thought. She decided she would be better off not telling Vladimir about Boris-related recent events, any of the ugly developments.

She applied as much makeup as she could, but her face still showed the effects of her fall in the park. She told Vladimir that she had tripped over a branch that might have fallen during the rainstorm the night before. He accepted the story at face value. Then, she told him that she was resigning from her position and moving to LA. She made up a story about wanting to be involved in the music industry and promoting shows. She knew someone that might help her find a career-path over there. She also told him that she was getting older, wanted to settle down, marry, and have children.

Her employer looked at her with surprise. "You never seemed to have a serious relationship going on." But he voiced the adage that women could change their minds—that was what his father had told him many times.

Vladimir was never too possessive or demanding—it was not in his nature. He accepted her resignation and wished her good luck; there were no reservations or attempts to change her mind. She was very thankful for that, more than she let on. She expressed her appreciation for all the opportunities Vladimir had given her—the personal growth, all she learned about advertising, the trips, the gifts, the roses, and the dresses that made her smile. She just could not do it any longer. She begged him not to be angry at her and to let her go in peace. He gave her a friendly but unsentimental hug.

BEING LIKE WOODY
THE TORMENTS OF ASYMMETRIC RUPTURE

How do we deal with issues of the heart? Are these different from other psychological ailments? What do we tell our patients? Do we explain to them that they may have contributed to their desolation? Are we supposed to deal with their issues with empathy or with analytical objectivity? I was thinking about these issues as I was compiling the stories presented here. I have not decided whether I will deliver them at a conference or write a paper. Many speak derisively about case presentation at conferences that I am leary to do so.

My name is Dr. Aminci. Because I want to protect my name and that of my clients, it is a pseudonym. I am sixty-five and about to retire from psychiatric counseling. I have had a successful practice in Manhattan. Most of my patients, it so happens, were men in their forties, fifties, and sixties. About twenty years ago, the word spread that I provided sound advice, and more men flocked to me. I do not know how helpful I was. I made a good living listening to people presenting their grievances and telling their stories. Their most frequent complaint revolved around some major disappointment in their romantic relationships, eventual breakups, frustrations with their dating women. I was always a good listener, and maybe that was why these men were pleased. Here and there, certainly not ever, I came up with good ideas. In doing so, I often talked about things my patients were familiar with, either from daily life or perhaps from a book they'd read or a movie they'd seen.

I feel that sharing some stories will help a wider audience. These stories do not appear idiosyncratic to me; they have a commonality that makes them valuable for introspection and self-assessment. Maybe we can all learn from them.

Some time ago, I got an email that prompted the title of this compilation.

Peter B wrote:

I am writing to you because writing is a better way for me to organize my thoughts. I want to tell you what haunts me when I am alone in bed and longing for a woman. I know I am not good-looking; I wear glasses, have almost no hair, am a bit chubby, a bit clumsy. But others are not hunks either—they are not walking off the silver screen into our lives. Not everyone is a DiCaprio, a Beatty, a James Dean, or a John Wayne.

I am having such a hard time finding a long-term, fulfilling relationship with a woman. I am afraid I am losing it. It just makes no sense to me. After all, I am not worse-looking than Woody.

As I frowned, trying to figure out the reference, Woody, who? He resolved the puzzle in the next paragraph:

He looks frail, pale, bespectacled. With his high-pitched voice, and his neurotic persona, he could hardly be considered a heartthrob, and yet… Whether a character in a movie and, I guess, in real life, he has relationships that seem to be lasting and indeed very sexually satisfying with gorgeous women who strike you as intelligent, charming, and entertaining. Diane Keaton, for example. Yes, that Woody—the director, the actor, the jazz player. Why can't I get lucky like him even once? Please help me figure it out!

I wonder if my client is even aware of all the allegations against this guy? His relationship with his adopted daughter has turned off many people, totally nauseated others. And there are more

155

allegations about his misbehavior that have been trashed around in public. The next sentence clarified his adulation.

Of course, I know that he is not everyone's cup of tea! In a way, though, Woody is just a fictional character for me. The combination of his "nothing special" diminutive physical persona with a high intellect and (I am guessing here) great passion and his apparent success with "his ladies" is so intriguing. Why? Because I can see the physical similarities. I believe I have some of the intellect, the passion, perhaps even a bit of the neurosis. Maybe I am not as funny as he is; maybe my humor does not plunge into the ridiculousness as he does? Have you read "The Metterling Lists"?

On the other hand, without a doubt, I am unattractive physically. I am indeed hopelessly unsuccessful in my relationships with the women I have been courting for over two decades. I am not passing judgment on him, on the complete individual with his strengths and weaknesses. It is about the disturbing discrepancy between us when it comes to a female companion.

If we were sitting in my office, I would say, "But you surely agree that the better situations involving 'Woody' are from the movies—fantasyland. His personal life may not have been anywhere close to this idyllic." I suspect he would answer thus:

Woody is, for me, a symbol rather than a real person. He is what could be happening to me but stubbornly refuses to occur. I keep on having decent take-offs, like a large plane heading off to some distant and wonderful place. These are smooth moments, full of promise. But soon enough, there is plenty of turbulence, and I start feeling nauseated, fearing the imminent crash, wondering what may go wrong. Did I read the manual properly? Is there a mechanical problem? Did I communicate correctly with the person co-piloting this voyage?

Lately, my relationships' absurdity sent me into a state of such confusion and despair that I lost my appetite. I could not sleep. I could not understand what was happening here. Why can I not have Woody's success?

His email made me reflect not just on this patient and his somewhat childish diatribe. It made me think about a significant number of clients who have similar issues. Maybe the common features are just in my mind—a place so infused with psychological theory. Perhaps I am right. In any case, the plight of these men should not be ignored or dismissed offhand. That they spent hundreds and thousands of dollars on counseling—on someone, me—listening to them, not necessarily helping a lot, just points to the solitude and despair they felt.

As a movie buff, I often use film characters to get the point across. So, this man's parallelism was meaningful to me. I will come back to "Woody" from time to time.

~ ~ ~ ~

Can I deal with dumb and nasty?

The story told by Henry M. will illustrate that asymmetry can go both ways and prompt questions about fairness in both directions. While I see a commonality in my clients' complaints, Henry's issues point to the complexity of human relations.

I, of course, tape all conversations, and this is a word for word transcript of the relevant parts:

-   **"I have to confess to it; I am drawn to beauty and sexuality. To a large extent, Lolita matched these needs. Those legs, oh, those legs! We were in our fifties. Neither one a spring chicken, for sure. But her legs were young and beautiful. She knew it and exploited it. She wore short skirts that, at some point, especially later in our relationship, when I was used to their existence, made me blush a bit. Walking into a restaurant and having so many people turn their heads (and hearing some snicker!) produced mixed feelings at best."**

-   **"We were in bed fairly soon after we started going out, and it was quite good. Lolita was loud, which aroused me. She was willing to do things that others did not. Do I need to specify?"**

-

-   *"No, you don't."*

-

- "I can say that I enjoyed that. We also had fun otherwise. We went to restaurants. To the Bronx Zoo (I love animals, especially those funny monkeys.) We saw a couple of Broadway shows."

-

- *"So, Henry, that all sounds good."*

-

- "It does. But and here comes the rub I eventually discovered that Lolita was neither too smart nor too well-read. She had come to New York from Europe. From France. Originally, she was from Venezuela. But she was not fleeing Chavez when she came here. She had been in France for at least 10-15 years (I don't remember when exactly; something like that.) When her marriage fell apart, she chose to come to the US. Her brother lives here, and it would allow her to be closer to her old mother, that had moved to Miami to be with her sister. Maybe she wanted distance from her daughters. I have not decided. During a dinner with my friends, I realized that her English was limited (we spoke Spanish when alone). Right or wrong, I felt a bit embarrassed. Then we got together with her brother and his wife and daughter, and I realized that her intellect, knowledge of world affairs, politics, and literature was limited."

- "I started asking myself if a person with that profile would eventually cause dissatisfaction."

-

- *"Did you start wondering whether you could get fulfillment from other aspects of joint life, other than just sex?"*

-

- "Exactly! I was pondering whether well-known cases of intellectual mismatch worked and concluded that most didn't. But I was just secretly waffling. I did not voice any concerns to her."

- There were two occasions when my internal alarm bells went off. One time, she came to my place while my friend Fred and I watched a basketball game. Later that night, she wanted to head back to her home (she did not stay with me every night) but realized she did not have her car keys. We looked all over the place. I had this crazy idea that maybe she put the keys in my friend's bag (yes, he carries a small black bag that may have looked similar) instead of her own. I called Fred. Indeed, he found them there. I had to drive her to Fred's place to retrieve them. I thought to myself:' how dumb can you be?!' The other occasion was when she told me she had made a big mistake but was afraid I would get angry. I asked what it was. She repeated the same accusation: you will get outraged! "What is it?" I asked again. She told me she wanted to do something useful and throw away the garbage, but she also sent the apartment key set down the chute. I laughed but was steaming that she attacked my personality as the best way to tell me the disturbing news. I said to her that resorting to attacking as the best defense was what irritated me most."

-

- "While struggling with these issues, I suddenly had to confront—better say, witness—a much more disconcerting fact. Lolita was mean to her somewhat troubled daughter. The young woman had just come to visit her Mom. The daughter had quit a practical training job that would have forwarded her career in the hospitality industry. A rift with her boss caused so much unhappiness the daughter decided to leave. But according to Lolita, she had some real psychological issues before. Regardless, her daughter was morose at this point. I saw that with my own eyes. I invited her to join her mother and me at a nice restaurant on the Upper East Side, and this young woman stared at her plate the whole evening. She was possibly trying to hide her acne-filled face. Or, more likely, she was finding this to be a good way to elude any conversation. I was stupefied when Lolita acted nastily towards her. I do not want to go through the gory details; do I have to?"

-

- *"Not unless you think I would miss out on important information."*

-

- **"I concluded, doctor, that Lola was not for me and cut-off the relationship. Was I too abrupt? Was I too stubborn? Was I just being a snob? Would a Freud or an Einstein accept a partial ignoramus as a partner/wife? Not that I equate myself with them—I am not that full of myself! But...You know what I mean?"**

"I can confirm to you that it is not easy to find a partner that fulfills your biological, sensory, call them 'animalistic' if you wish, needs, as well as your intellectual and spiritual preferences. I can also confirm that some individuals have found it possible to live a significant part of their lives with someone less gifted, less intelligent, less articulate, or otherwise a mismatch. At the end of the day, this is a very personal decision—there is no right or wrong."

And this is where the commonality emerges. In Peter's eyes, Woody, the idol, gets what he wants despite his limited physical appeal. On the other hand, Henry is mesmerized by physical beauty and later discovers that the person lacks intellect or character. He gets disenchanted by that 'glass half empty' observation and decides to punt.

"Henry," I said, "you feel despondent or frustrated by another relationship falling apart. You have some notions of who you want as your companion, and that is good. But when the smoke clears, and there is no complete match, you cut it off. You have to understand that you will need to compromise, and you will need to get a better sense of the person as a whole--not just her looks."

~ ~ ~ ~

The Big Poodle

Paul T. is another patient who decided to punt. At least, to not pursue further the woman in this story. He came to me seeking help. You might find the story amusing or ridiculous. This is what he told me:

"Helen was tall, intelligent, successful, beautiful, and elegant. At one point, she had been a top manager at a major retail chain. But then she got demoted. She sued for sexual discrimination and obtained a pre-trial settlement that was large enough to allow her to stop working altogether and purchase a gorgeous duplex on the Upper West Side."

"We connected through a dating site. Before we ever shook hands, Helen informed me that she had this beautiful white poodle she adored. When scheduling a get-together, we would have to consider the poodle. The hour and location of a restaurant, for example, had to include consideration of the restaurant's distance from her home and the hour. The dog had to be taken out before and after a possible dinner date."

"I was smitten by her looks. She had dark hair, tanned beautiful brown skin, long legs, and a slim figure. Her face had lovely features that made her striking. She was smart; I always was a big fan of bright women. I needed to sense the challenge and abhorred relationships forcing me to explain the obvious. Alongside the attractive physique came a personality trait that I liked a lot less; she was fond of making little snide remarks that would belittle me. They came for no good reason and without provocation. A way, I thought, to maintain the upper hand in the 'battle of sexes,' a battle I never declared nor intended to join. I said to myself, "you can't expect perfection, and there is a cost to dating a woman who is financially well-off, bright, and beautiful."

On a Spring Friday evening, I crossed over to her side of Manhattan, went to her place on the way to the restaurant she chose. This mediocre restaurant's foremost advantage was that we could be back quickly to let the dog out. I did not care about the quality of the dishes; I was much more interested in her. As we bid goodbye in front of her building, I asked if I could see her the following day or on Sunday. She smiled, "No, no, maybe next weekend; I will let you know."

As was customary for me, I wrote an email to thank her for spending some time with me, told her how impressed I was, and declared that I would be happy to see her the following weekend. There was no response. I tried again on Thursday; I texted: "Could we get together sometime?" Her answer came by email and surprised me: "You told me you like cereal and blueberries for breakfast; I bought some and am looking forward to seeing you Saturday for early dinner at someplace nearby. Two blocks away from my place is a great pizza place, and many say they have the best pizza on the UWS (which for the non-cognoscenti is the Upper West Side). Let us go there". I was elated; breakfast meant staying over. This woman was direct, and I loved it!

I could hardly wait for the weekend to come around. On Friday, I went to get my hair cut and bought a new shirt that would look good. I took a long shower and applied some fancy eau-de-cologne. I gave myself enough time to hop on the bus, cross Central Park and walk the two blocks to her place—I wanted to do so at a moderate pace, not to appear overheated.

We gave each other a quick peck on the lips, nothing too romantic but promising, and went over to the pizza joint. We shared a salad and a small pepper, anchovies, and mushrooms pizza, which was quite delicious. On the way back, she made one of her hallmark little snide remarks along the lines of:" I see you bought a new shirt for the special occasion" (how on earth did she know?!). I ignored it.

We went into her duplex, and Peter, the white poodle, was eagerly waiting to be taken out. Peter was not your typical small, cute, full of himself poodle. He was huge. He looked at me with disdain, growled until Ellen sweetly told him to calm down, and we went for a quick walk so he could eliminate. We did not say much during that walk.

Inside the apartment, we sat in the living room, listened to soft rock, and had a glass of cognac. Eventually, she took me by the hand and guided me to her nicely appointed bedroom. We quickly took off our clothes, and I started covering her body with small kisses.

I was surprised at the sight of a significant anal prolapse, suggesting that Helen may have engaged in that type of sex. I was kissing her labia when suddenly Peter burst into the room and started barking and growling loudly. I looked at Helen and asked if the dog usually slept in her bed. She replied that sometimes, and if not, he had his bed in the bedroom we were.

It is difficult to describe the barrage of thoughts that flooded my mind at that moment, but I will try. I admit to a slight panic that the dog might bite off a piece of my backside. As a child, I visited my "girlfriend" (how ridiculous were the parent-induced notions that upgraded a friendship between two kids to something more special--we were not even thirteen years old!). She had a mean dog that ran after me and took a bite that mostly damaged a pair of pants; it did leave some teeth marks on my butt as well. The flashback of that occasion did not help. I also wondered how the night would progress with the dog barking away, and my love-making became compromised. As I turned limp, she turned to her side of the bed, which was the end of the night.

It was quite difficult for me to fall asleep. How does one handle something like this? What should I say to her the next morning? Both of us are in our fifties and are supposed to act like adults. Still, it is hard to have a sensible conversation on the first, second, or third day of being together, with a beloved dog barking while having sex for the first time (maybe even at any time).

Cereal and blueberries, coffee, and silence. I could not find a way to approach the subject and thought that it was best to wait for her to discuss the incident. Not a chance! She went about business as if nothing happened. She put the dishes on the table, the cereal and blueberry boxes, and made coffee. When she finally said something, it was to propose that perhaps it would be good to go to the park—it was such a beautifully sunny day.

Okay. I can play it cool too. As it is, the first date may be awkward in most cases. "Where shall we go for dinner tonight? Maybe we can pick a more luxurious place?" She suggested a French restaurant La Boite en Bois. "The fish stew is great; I have had it. But that may be for a colder winter day." Instead of the dog incident, we talked about my work and her previous employer (she did not disclose the rift's reason, but I googled it). We talked about politics since she thought this was a subject I am keenly interested in and could have some original insights. From time to time, she would make a sarcastic remark that was slowly getting to me. For example, she said: "So, famous political science professor emeritus, what do you think about the Iraq war?" or "As a portfolio manager, maybe you can tell me the direction of interest rates in the next six months." She was, I estimated, too bright not to understand that the questions were thorny rather than innocent, not seeking answers as much as testing the reaction of the person quizzed.

After a quick break for a shared quiche and some lemonade, we headed to the Guggenheim. She wanted to see a new exhibit presenting the works of young ex-Russian painters who moved to the New York area over the last 20 years. I would have instead revisited the Monet, Kandinsky, and Pollocks. The nice thing about walking through a museum is that it is natural to hold hands without saying much or even walking alone. My mind, I must confess, was still busy with "Peter issues" and what the forthcoming night may bring.

I do not want to bother you with repetitive details of a delicious dinner (I had a veal dish), many sweet light kisses, admiring her nude body, and more arousing efforts that were affecting. But, just as the night before, Peter showed up with a big thud. He came in with such force that the door made a big noise. He accentuated his entrance by barking loudly, growling, and jumping on the bed.

I instantly stopped whatever I was doing and looked at Helen with eyes that may have suggested to her what my mouth wanted to say: "Again? Are you going to do something about this?". She looked coldly at me and uttered an unexpected response: "Don't you dare say anything!".

I moved away from her, grabbed the clothes spread out on the floor near "my" side of the bed, put them on, and told her it seemed apparent she preferred Peter's company to mine, and I would see myself out. She could stay with the poodle.

I ask you, my dear shrink, would you have handled matters differently? Would anyone have done anything else? Maybe someone else would have turned to Helen and, in an excited voice, argued that this was wrong. Perhaps showing some level of neurosis, say that this was untenable, that in a large duplex like this one, a dog could stay downstairs in his quarters, and if he did not have his room, maybe it was time to set one up. Possibly another person would have argued that loving an animal does not extend to sharing a love-nest with it; that this was just too weird. In other words, I could have hung out in that room and argue this point of view while Peter menacingly growled, barked, and jumped up and down the bed. I do not have the patience, nor do I trust that people can change their set ways. So, I often rush to conclusions and cut my losses.

The issue of "feeling disrespected" by the presumptive partner is a recurring theme in the cases brought forward here. It is something worth addressing further.

~ ~ ~ ~

I do not like your smoking

Rober U. was quite bewildered as he told me his story; he just could not understand the hypocrisy.

Sonia was a beautiful woman exuding so much sexuality, and because of it, she had a dramatic charismatic pull. She was from Colombia; her Andean accents gave her a unique exotic profile-- a significant component of her beauty. She also came across as a fully committed professional--hard working and looking to excel in her field. She had moved to the US in her early 20's. She spent a couple of decades in LA, where she worked for a company that set up and organized significant musical events. There were concerts of every genre in venues like the Rose Bowl or the Hollywood Bowl. She told me that she had moved to NYC a few months back. She felt a great need to leave California after discovering that her husband was cheating on her with a woman who worked in the same office Sonia managed. She had hired that woman a couple of years earlier. To Sonia, she seemed hardworking and willing to give a hand when needed. "Yes, she also was young and pretty, Sonia said, But I was too trusting to think that she might be fucking my husband behind my back." Yes, on most occasion, Sonia was not overly delicate with her expressions. I did not mind that.

The first time we met, she told me about a small bar near the restaurant we would be dining our first meal. It was on a side street in the '70s off 2nd Avenue. She would know how to get there, and if we wanted to, we could stop there after dinner. The bar usually had a live band playing jazz or soft-rock, and the crowd was friendly. I liked her entrepreneurial drive, her smile, her very red lips, and her sexy attire. From the first moment we met, I was very attracted to her physically.

As we walked out of the restaurant, I could not resist but grab her and kiss that beautiful red mouth. Because of how we touched each other's hands and sought to touch knees under the table, I felt she would respond positively when I drew her closer for that first kiss. Almost like teenagers, I mused to myself.

She guided us well to find the bar she had mentioned before. We were shown to a small table not too close to the stage, a good thing since we still were learning about each other, and the music could drown our voices. She said: "I liked your kiss, but I really don't like the taste of cigarettes, so I am a bit conflicted." "I hear you, dear, I said. What can I do? I have been smoking since my late teens, and, as you well know, it is an addiction, and getting rid of it is not easy. Yes, I have attempted the patch and other ways to stop, "cold turkey," gradually, everything. I stop for a while and gain a bunch of pounds because I am so hungry. I want to occupy my mouth with something other than inhaling smoke, and then a crisis comes, or something else pushes me back to the habit. I am healthy, though; you need to know that."

Notwithstanding that comment, we kissed a good number of times that night. The kisses were passionate and provocative. When she hailed a taxi to take her back to the Village area where she lived, it was hard to say goodbye. But we promised to see each other the following weekend.

When we spoke mid-week, I suggested Saturday. We could go for dinner in the Village, to a sweet, cozy Italian restaurant on Mulberry Street I like. After that, we could go to the Blue Note for some jazz, a woman vocalist of some fame will be performing. It was a beautiful night. We seemed to have a lot in common in terms of tastes, interests, outlook on life. As you know, the Blue Note serves food and drinks while the concert is going on. Many consider the large venue a 'tourist trap. 'All this did not bother us; we concluded that you need to take the good with the bad. As the waiters passed around the dishes, seemingly oblivious about the noise they made, we just shrugged our shoulders. We chose to ignore." It was part of this outing," she commented philosophically, and I nodded in agreement.

As we exited the place, she grabbed my arm and just said," this way." I knew she was guiding me to her 3rd-floor apartment on Bleeker. The night was as passionate as two middle-aged people could make it. Eventually, we turned to opposite sides and fell asleep. In the morning, she told me she did not have much to offer as food. She apologized for not having planned better; the idea to bring me to her place was just a 'spur of the moment' decision. I offered to treat her for breakfast at some cafe nearby. Because she had important work to do later, the weekend get-together was cut short, but we knew we would continue the romance the following weekend.

Sometime during the week, she called me all excited. The following Saturday, one show that she was bringing to the stage was being performed at an off-off-Broadway theatre. I was happy for her and wanted to share this incredible moment. "Should we have dinner before or after?" She would be busy with last-minute arrangements, she said. It would be better to go after the play— probably it would be over by 9.15 or so."

When I arrived at the theatre I spotted her almost immediately; the distinctive features were easily recognizable. But, if in the past she would practically run towards me, this time she seemed a lot more deliberate in her approach. If previously she gave me an unabashed sexual kiss, that evening, she gave me a small peck that tasted like nothing. I was perplexed. Maybe, I thought, it was because she was nervous about the play's success, the number of tickets sold, or whatever minutia she may have ignored.

When the show ended, I congratulated her, hugged her, and sought to kiss her, but she gave me her cheek. I hailed a taxi, and we headed to the restaurant. On other occasions, we would sit close we'd almost be on top of each other. This time she sat further apart, and I looked at her quizzically. She did not say anything but "later." We got a corner table at the French restaurant. When I made the reservation, I told them it was a special occasion, and the corner table would be terrific. I told her that I wanted her to feel special and asked for this table. She gave me a shy smile that was oddly different from anything I had seen coming from her before. In typical fashion, I pressed for tabling whatever was irritating her: "Okay. You have behaved weirdly tonight—first, the peck, then keeping distance in the car. Something is going on, and I would like to know what is bothering you. Have I said something? Done something that you did not like?" She looked down at her plate and asked that we wait to discuss it later; she did not want to 'create a scene' in public at this charming restaurant. Honestly, I had a difficult time enjoying the meal. Efforts to pass the time and chit-chatting about this or that was never a strength of mine; it was particularly tough when something unsettling was about to be sprung on me. But I had no choice, Sonia would not disclose what was bothering her, and she gave no indications that she would surrender to any pressure.

We finally made it to her walk-up apartment. We sat down. She took my hands into hers and solemnly said, "I like you. I like you a lot. I want us to be lovers. Maybe even more. But I have not been totally candid with you. When I was in LA, just before I left, my husband told me that he contracted an STD, you know, gonorrhea. We had had sex after that, and when I got tested, it came out positive. I should have told you before we had sex last week. I am so sorry."

Of all things, this one never crossed my mind. It would not have made the top-fifty list. I do not like to have protection during sex and did not the week before. I may well have contracted the disease myself. I was livid. These words came from the same woman that had told me that she hated my smoking?! I got up and left without saying goodbye.

I took a taxi home but asked the driver to drop me off a couple of blocks before my address; I needed to take a walk. I saw some young men in front of a bar; they were smoking. I asked them if I could buy a cigarette from them. I had not had a cigarette for a few days to placate Sonia and carried none with me. One offered a Marlboro at no cost and said: "You look all shook-up; everything okay?" I told him what just happened, and he, philosophically, answered: "well, it could have been worst, she could have hidden it from you for much longer--be happy! But you probably should get tested first thing Monday morning.

I tested and was very nervous during the five days it took to get the results back. They came in as "Negative," which was a great relief.

Maybe an existentialist would have been more liberal about the whole story—something along the lines of "shit happens, and you need to move on and make the best out of the situation; yes, she could have been honest and considerate about it, but she didn't. Often enough, people are just like that. No sense sinking into despair."

~ ~ ~ ~

That evening, going over my notes, I wondered if those thoughts were said earnestly. Would Robert be less cavalier if the tests would have come out positive and facing Sonia under such circumstances? Philosophical ruminations are cheap when there is no skin in the game.

Does honesty equate or emanate from respect for the partner? While rereading these stories, I concluded that the expectations for decency, honesty, and respect were often unmet by these men's partners.

~ ~ ~ ~

Manipulation

Jack S. lives in Florida. Consequently, our sessions were via conference-call. Sometimes we exchanged emails. This is his story:

I was elated. Penny was sweet, amenable, loving, and sexy. Better yet, she was willing to push the limits of regular activity and taboos when in bed, the sort of things that cause a full body-tremor, acts that bring sheer ecstasy. She came from a lower-middle-class background, and as far as I could tell (based on what she told me), she opted for an early climb to a higher social stratum via marriage. It precluded her from finishing college.

Nonetheless, in her self-description, she had claimed to be a graduate of McGill. Profiles on dating sites are often a beehive of smaller and bigger lies: the age of a member miraculously comes down, success and achievements get magically inflated. I was willing to overlook this for the sake of companionship, sharing, and sex. Eventually, she married for a second time; the man was successful in his business, she told me. He also was abusive—not physically, mind you, but verbally. She lasted for about twenty years with him. Trips all over the world were fun. They lived in a large Ft. Lauderdale apartment during winter, and a beautiful house in Montreal, the rest of the year. Life was comfortable and made the negative aspects more tolerable. Eventually, she could not take it anymore and left him.

She moved to Florida for good, even though her two sons lived in Montreal. She told me that one son was much brighter than the other. He was married and had a small child. The other was often out of work, had not gone to college, and currently helped manage a sports-equipment store. Penny told me she was worried about him: "He drinks too much and maybe takes drugs also." I asked her why she does not talk to him. "You say he loves you and was very sympathetic when you divorced his father, so why not talk to him?". She switched topics, and I had no interest in escalating the conversation further.

She claimed to be good at bridge, a card game I love. At our first get together—a dinner near where she lived—she tested my "honeymoon bridge" skills--a two-person variation of the game. She said she was eager to go to the local club and show off her game. I was quite willing to demonstrate my abilities, so we went to the local club and revisited that place several times after that. It did not take long for me to conclude that she vastly exaggerated her abilities; she tended to overbid but then underplayed the cards. Nonetheless, because many mediocre players attended the club, including some in their eighties with poor eyesight and a slower mind, we frequently finished among the top three.

Despite the divorce from a wealthy man, which presumably left her comfortably placed, she claimed that she had a hard time "making the month." She did some work as a seamstress, but that did not generate much income. She thought that maybe she could reduce her costs by moving in with me. I told her that it was something worth considering, but, thinking it was premature, left it there and did not go into details or the steps to make it a reality. For the time being, I was hoping she would be content with me paying for all our outings, whether these were movies, dinners, or bars.

We had been dating for about seven weeks when she told me she had to go to Montreal; a family member had suddenly died. During those five days away, she called at strange times—often past midnight. The main topic was her sons. She told me that she had spoken to "the good son" and pleaded with him to talk to his brother and influence him to stop drinking and, perhaps, cut his relationship with this "no good woman" living with him. I did not know he lived with someone; she had never mentioned her. She thought that this was a relationship that caused her son to become a bum of sorts. "She is also the one that has caused him to drink." I asked what" the good son" responded, and she claimed she was suddenly exhausted and needed to sleep. I thought this was all very strange; it bothered me.

Upon her return from Montreal, we arranged that I would spend the night at her place. She insisted it would be an excellent way to strike a balance between us—after all, it always was my invitation, treating her to shows and dinners, my bed. She thought she needed to give back, and I appreciated the gesture. I came to her apartment in an old building with a wall-to-wall mirror in the living room to make it look larger (I always thought that gimmick was ridiculous).

I arrived, as planned, in the late morning, and we headed to the bridge club. I was incredulous! I was stunned by her mistreatment of these, mostly older women that afternoon; it was appalling. I had never seen her act like that. Her behavior instantly created a wall between us-- in my heart and mind. I did not say anything. Once done, we headed, as we tended to do, to a bar that played soft rock or jazz. The band was playing; some people were dancing on the small dancefloor devoted to it. I was still bewildered by what had just happened, and that made me a mute.

We turned back to her apartment and planned to hang out there for a short while before heading to dinner. What ensued was another shocker:

"You have misled me, she said. You told me you loved me, but you did not offer to marry me. You told me you wanted to be with me, but you are heading to a bridge tournament in Italy and not taking me with you. You just threw some candy in my direction, 'got the best sex of your life,' those were your words, to me. You did not act on all this; I now realize that those were empty promises you heaved in my direction."

The bottom line: she was asking me to fund the presumed blank check, except that I had never written such a check. I was shocked and angry. I felt she was manipulating me the same way she managed her sons. I could have said a lot. I could have responded to her charges. I could have countered with other reproaches. Instead, I just said, "I am sorry,"; I said so three times as I was collecting the items I brought in to use while overnighting there. The third time I said, "I am sorry, "I

opened the door and headed out.

I reflected on what just happened on the way home. I heard his voice, the unusually sad, excited, unbelieving, yet argumentative sound of a man, too often frustrated by a relationship gone bad. It was my alter ego talking. Manipulation is not uncommon; on the contrary, many may say, as does that strident voice, that manipulation is rampant and too often used as a convenient, acceptable device. It also showed me that asymmetry is not an objective measure. In this story, the woman also had her feelings of being "used" and suffering from an asymmetric relationship.

~ ~ ~ ~

Mi Rey

Robert P. told me this sad story; he said he was exploited, taken advantage of. But what about him? What role did he play in this debacle?. He sat down in my office and looked relaxed as I described his story with plenty of detail; some information was unnecessary, but I do not like to interrupt.

I was again single and a bit sad. I took off to Vegas, as I had done before when I felt down. During the day, I would spend time at one of those European Style pools where the action was a bit more hedonistic, the blackjack tables, and some fantastic restaurants for dinner. Late at night, I would hang out at one of the clubs. I probably was raising the average age of the attendees by a significant percentage. Still, I did not care—I enjoyed the young men and women having a good time and behaving in an edgy manner.

I would usually stand in a somewhat elevated area, say a balcony, that allowed me to look over the scenery underneath. Such was the case on that Friday night. Near me stood a younger woman, and I was not sure if she was alone or not. She looked quite attractive. Maybe, I thought, she was of Latin descent as she had dark hair. I had never dated a Latina, I said to myself. Despite living in New York City with its large population from that corner of the earth.

I asked her if she could save my spot as I had to use the restroom and get a second glass of vodka. I offered to buy her a drink in exchange and was surprised to hear her decline. In any case, I was happy I made the connection. When I resumed my place on that balcony, she told me she was a local girl; she was finishing her coursework to become a social worker and still had to do months of practical training. She asked where I was staying (an adjacent hotel) and whether I would like to go to the bar downstairs, away from the club's noise, so we can talk a bit more. Usually, I would not leave before 2 a.m., but this looked so much more promising than ogling over some youngsters carrying on that I gave her a quick "let's go."

I will not surprise you when I tell you that we spent many hours together for the next two days (I was there for a long weekend). What may surprise you is that what followed was a romance period involving us shuttling back and forth –me heading to Las Vegas, Maria coming to New York. I offered to pay for her flights, and of course, I covered the restaurant, shows, and events we attended during these trips. I got rewarded with lots of platitudes that were supposed to make me feel good. "You are my man, 'Mi Rey' (My King), my excellent companion." But when we were in bed together, she would be adamant that it was premature to have sexual relationships.

I was, in the language of those younger than me, "totally into her." I wanted to do everything to turn her into my lover, my partner, my spouse. So, I kept on splurging, spending hours helping her with her coursework (her English was not at a level that would allow her to write cogent reports about the clients she visited), and planning more trips to possibly far-away places.

And so, it is that I planned a trip to Vietnam. I told her we would be spending my "round-number" birthday touring the marvelous beauty of Halong Bay. And subsequently, we would go to China to see Shanghai, Beijing, Chengdu, and other places. I had planned to make this trip before I met her, and there was no reason to spend a few more dollars and enjoy the journey together. She was so excited about the news; she expressed this in a high-pitched voice: "You are mi king, more than that, mi emperor, mi hombre." Obviously, in her excitement, "my" was replaced by the Spanish "mi." I sidestepped the ignorance, focusing instead on her bust.

According to the plan, we would take off from JFK on a Sunday night. I suggested that we spend a couple of days having fun in New York before departing. An erotic, sultry event, I came to accidentally, was making waves in the "having fun in the Apple" press. Held in a building that was once a theatre, it featured semi-nude, men and women dancing around the guests and evoking the imagination that this was Caligula's Rome. When I mentioned the historical antecedent, she looked at me like I was speaking a foreign language. I let it go. We attended, she got all excited about the event's sensual nature, but it never spilled over to any action in bed. I found it odd but said nothing. I was frustrated. However, since I do not believe in coercing or extracting unwanted activity, I just hoped that things turn around in the future.

After a long flight to Hong Kong, we headed to Hanoi. Because jet lag turns night into day and day into night, the first two days were weird. The most memorable event was a "foody tour," We skipped between hordes of bicycle riders, cooked our pancakes, enjoyed sitting on small plastic chairs, and enjoyed a variety of tasty, spicy foods. On the third day, we headed to the cruise boat that would tour Halong Bay. We would also visit nearby pagodas, take a smaller boat to tour the shallow waters flowing between massive cliffs, visit the famous caves, and enjoy the ships culinary treats at night.

The birthday arrived, and I was eager to see what the woman who repeatedly called me "Mi Rey" would do to celebrate me. I was distraught. More than that, I was decimated. She did not even have the intelligence of getting a greeting card. She kissed me on the cheek and wished me a happy birthday. I got a better deal from the boat crew who prepared a typical for Vietnam, I was later told, special birthday cake, and organized the full dining room crowd to sing the traditional 'happy birthday.' There was a large group of Australians who were genuinely kind to come over and shake hands. Deep down, I was despondent, nonetheless.

Knowing that there were still two weeks of joint traveling

was a profoundly troubling fact. I decided to make the most out of the trip by remaining calm and collected, focusing on the sites explored, the novelties, and the unusual sites we visited. I did not act out angrily; instead, I was cold towards this stranger. Sharing a bed does not require physical contact, and that's what happened--for nearly two weeks!

Time and again, she only addressed me to take pictures of her--dozens of them! When we said goodbye at the Hong Kong airport (thankfully, she was flying home through LA), I told her not to contact me again.

The notion that a woman, any woman, would address you as "My King" is already fraught with all sorts of controversy—primarily because of sex equality with all its ramifications and variations. Beyond that, what does it mean when it is just a manner of speaking devoid of any value? What does it say about both the speaker and the listener when words are the cheapest of currencies? What happens when such accolades have no further consequences?

My hunch is that a savvy man schooled enough after who knows what experiences would know to devalue and dismiss. Maybe I was just very naïve. Another man may hesitate to fall into the trap the way I did. I need guidance, and that is why I am here, doctor.

~ ~ ~ ~

I told Robert that it was understandable that he was so angry. That he probably was as mad at himself as with the woman. After all, he got lots of warning signals that she was exploiting him. He had ample opportunities to confront her about what was going on but always kept quiet and continued. He hoped she would turnaround. It is crucial to be cautious about self-deception.

Years later, I got a letter from the same Robert. He had moved to the Miami area. He wrote: "Remember the story of Maria who always said "Mi Rey"? I moved south and am still single. I have dated several women down here; many are Latinas. The "Mi Rey syndrome" has repeated itself twice already. Quite amazing, come to think of it. I just laugh it off these days. At least I learned that lesson.

~ ~ ~ ~

Deceitful silence

"What can I tell you, Doctor? Sometimes silence can be as deceitful as the spoken word." That was how George C. started his session with me.

To move things along in my relationship with a woman Loretta, I had proposed that we take a trip to New Mexico. I encouraged her to agree by describing how many find it a wonderfully charming place. I never had been down there and was excited to get to know its rich culture. She nodded but did not respond, which I found curious.

Later that day, I restarted the conversation about the trip. "It will allow us to spend continuous time together and find out if we are comfortable with each other," I said. I probably had in mind a glitch we experienced during our first run at this relationship. "Why don't we decide on a date?"

The answer hit me as if I just got hit by a bomb. It was destructive in its power. "You know I am going with my girlfriends on a weeklong trip; we are all photography buffs, and we are going down to the Florida Keys," I confirmed being aware of that. As soon as I return, two days later, I am heading to Spain to stay with my daughter and her family. I plan to move there for good. I am staying there for two months before coming back, selling my place here, and migrating to Madrid."

I was stupefied and incensed. For about five weeks, we had spent a lot of time together, at least three-four times per week, and she never saw the necessity to mention her desire to emigrate. She could have suggested that her plans could rock our relationship or cause it to come to sudden death. At the very least, it would involve significant changes in one life— mine! How does one behave like that? How little regard for the companion, the lover, the friend, the whatever!

I was upset, and the recourse was to tell her to go not to Spain but hell. I wanted nothing to do with her anymore. I asked her to take back whatever clothes she had left in my apartment.

Though the relationship was dead, my state of mind was unsettled. My bewilderment, my lack of understanding of why such things would be happening to me, kept me wondering whether my unfortunate lot was unique.

Loretta was a relatively new immigrant from Venezuela, pushed out by the circumstances that followed the Chavez election and the country's economic collapse. In Venezuela, she was a dentist, and she still had patients coming to get treatments after his ascendancy to the presidency. But often enough, they had to pay by installments or by way of barter for other services or goods. The whole situation seemed too threatening to her. She also had a daughter in New York and wanted to be near the two grandchildren.

We met when a friend suggested I should meet this woman she knew from back home. She was pretty. She had a somewhat unremarkable face, but I liked her big brown eyes and those full lips that invited a kiss. We had a few outings; the regular stuff: lunches, dinners, movies (she was a big movie buff, she said).

Eventually, we made it to bed, but that did not go too well. It may have had something to do with my anxiety about being a good lover. I do not know for sure. She was good about it as she told me that sometimes the first time is often problematic. "We are adults and can handle this," she added.

Two days later, we planned to go to a movie. It started at 7:15 and was about ten minutes' walking distance from her place. When I arrived, she was on the phone. I told her I would wait in the lobby to give her privacy. When she came down, she looked upset. I asked what happened, and she burst into inconsolable tears. I wondered what was wrong, and she told me that I was rude to storm out and yell that I would be waiting in the lobby as if she owed me to stop the phone conversation and come down. She had a husband that was a bully, and she would not have another man like that. I was puzzled and outraged. I did not yell. I removed myself to the lobby to enable her to finish her conversation in a relaxed manner. I had intended to be the least intrusive and avoid coming across as a bully.

Maybe it all had to do with the unsuccessful sex a few days earlier.

As I went home after the movie, I decided that this lady had huge baggage that may make our relationship difficult. I was better off taking some distance from her.

Weeks passed, and I felt lonely. I also had to settle a matter of my own "sexual ego" after the disappointment of the last time we had sex. I told her that I missed her and wanted to see if we can patch up disagreements and hurt feelings. She accepted the invitation. We started going out together, and things went smoothly. Our second sexual encounter went reasonably well. Everything seemed to be heading to a much better place. But then I was hit by the bombshell news. I could not understand how a relationship between two people in their late fifties could be anything but open and straightforward.

I told him that though logical, his theory was unreal. It would be nice if mature people would be less deceitful, more overt about uncomfortable facts, be more open about what they like and dislike. At least it was not borne by what I had learned, read, and experienced by my other patients. It was possible that the older we get, the more adept we are at hiding things that we would not want the other one to know. I am sure that this did not provide any sort of comfort. I also told him that my best suggestion was to take things slower and learn more about the partner. This way, by not "going all in," we may be able to protect our emotional wellbeing and even avoid making exaggerated financial or other commitments.

~ ~ ~ ~

Stradivarius

Henry K., one of my Miami clients, told me this story; throughout, he smiled, though I suspected that he just tried to disguise his anguish:

She identified me in her search as a potential candidate, and

I felt good about it. All the same, we limped towards each other like two iguanas missing a leg lost in previous dating forays. We texted a couple of times, emailed each other with significant interludes of silence in between. Finally, we agreed to have a get-together at a restaurant—just a drink and an appetizer as she had something else scheduled an hour later.

Brenda was unlike anyone I had dated before—a real celebrity with her own Wikipedia page, a website, and the immediate name recognition when mentioned to friends.

From our first restaurant outing, it became apparent that many, strangers to me, sought to greet her and appeared pleased when she acknowledged their presence with a bow, a wave. They were elated when, often enough, she exchanged a few pleasantries, a casual statement about the weather or what-have-you-just like the Queen of England would do.

While many in modern society may ascend to notoriety because of some circumspect achievements that may invite a turn-up of the nose, or perhaps a sneer, for all I could surmise, Brenda had accomplished much through hard work, intelligent management, and political skill. There was no parent, brother, husband paving the way, greasing the wheels, helping climb the ladder. No one assisted in opening the doors of coveted establishments. So, I concluded, no one was justified to look with askance at her surge to the top. On the contrary: a woman, and Jewish on top of it, surely would have invited the occasional mix of racial and sexist antagonism common in this Southern society.

I was flattered to have been "discovered" by her (she picked me from a hodge-podge of individuals subscribing to the popular dating site). I was happy: she was bright and a leader, and I assumed she could pick among many contenders. I dismissed as minor her confessions about her intolerance of those coming up with excuses and explanations to halt any criticism about an incomplete task or a poorly executed assignment; I was eager to make this work.

I had an opportunity to accompany her to a cocktail party preceding a performance at the institution she headed. As I watched her with a great deal of acuity, I realized how much she enjoyed her status. It produced the after-the-fact imagery described to a friend: "She plays her role like a Stradivarius--she relishes the act of strutting from table to table, from one group of attendees to the next, greeting and being greeted, self-assured and conscious of her power despite a short stature and a fairly conventional appearance." She plays these situations like a virtuoso violinist, and strutting conjures well with Stradivarius, but you could also liken it to a Prima Donna singing her aria. She did not mind exchanging little kisses on the cheek or even a formal hug, knowing well that it would not diminish her political status. She was clearly in her métier, loving every moment of it. She delighted in the "tour de force" performances and made sure not to miss any of them."

It became clear with time; she even was willing to get out of her sickbed, ignore the virus afflicting her, just not to miss such an opportunity.

Listening in while she conversed with a group of people that had achieved their notoriety, their accredited social status, I noted with a measure of surprise that Brenda was more the listener than the talker-if she felt less brainy, she hid it well. On two occasions, when she did voice an opinion, it seemed that her statements were somewhat trite and non-controversial, so I wondered why these were voiced at all. I concluded from that interlude that the answers were embedded in two facts: she was not as smart and intellectually gifted as the others. But at the same time, she was blessed with political skills and adamant about keeping everyone happy and not cause any ill feelings or animosity. She knew how to play it safe and was obviously too risk-averse to leave an opening that could rock the boat.

Her website was replete with pictures of her attending all these events; the cult of personality was elaborate. Like a politician, I concluded, as I took an excursion into her social media exposure. Another important conclusion was suddenly in front of me: I was transfixed and blinded by her status and titles--indeed achievements that should be recognized. Scratching the surface, I surmised that she was a woman that was much more average than I first thought.

In the meantime, our interpersonal relationship was hardly a cause for celebration. I was affected by the lack of warmth and bothered by the lack of effort. Eventually, more aspects irked me: the lack of femininity in her appearance, choice of clothing (to this day, I can only guess what her knees look like), her walk, her voice. The words coming out of her mouth, as intelligent as they may have been, sounded cold and strident. She came across as harsh; the guttural sounds reminded me of my brother Boe. On such occasions, I am a bit ashamed to say, I focused, perhaps too much, on her small teeth. The picture of a piranha popping into my overly active mind.

I am self-conscious enough to be auto-critical of these last statements. Why should a woman sound different than a man? Have I not been bothered by excessively sweet or high-pitched female voices before? Why was I expecting sweetness and smiles? Little coquette gestures? Why was I applying such shameful bias? My only excuse is that her behavior, the totality of it, made me feel extremely uncomfortable. In fact, on our first brief get-together (as usual, she had to attend yet another function), I felt more like I was going through a job interview. I told her as much at one point, and she did not like my description. I thought she was smart enough to understand that a series of questions rifled across the table would suggest such an interpretation, so I was puzzled she took offense.

I am unsure whether all these incidents would have had such a deleterious impact if the rest had been more positive. Would the content of the interactions be colored in brighter tones? Would I have felt more satisfied emotionally?

But truth be told, I had a hard time with the unresponsiveness to overtures, the missing positive reaction to suggested plans or events, get-togethers, dinners. At first, I cut her a lot of slack: "she is a busy person," "overloaded with work," "probably wants to go slow, not rush things." With time, the evasiveness became more intolerable, as was the failure to acknowledge emails and texts. Her equanimity, not to mention any proactive suggestions of her own, any positive gesture from her side was discouraging--I wondered what I needed to do to get her closer to me?.

I finally decided to become pushy and wrote a lengthy email complaining about an apparent lack of interest and my predisposition to cut our losses consciously. Brenda disputed my accusations:" Maybe I am not as interested as you are, but I want to continue seeing you," she said. I accepted her statement at face value and continued to seek her out, but soon enough, we seemed to revert to the same pattern of before.

She made attempts to correct and improve on impressions, but they were almost laughable. When I went on a trip to the west coast, she asked how I was enjoying Chicago; when I wore my "dress to impress" glasses for the nth time, she remarked that they looked good on me and I should wear them more often. These efforts at appearing interested were backfiring terribly, mostly since I was blessed (cursed?) by an excellent memory.

One night, as I drove her back home from the movies, I had another experience that left me disheartened. As she had done before, she turned towards me for a brief, not precisely passionate, kiss good night. I attempted a second kiss, and her reaction was to raise her eyebrows as if I had overstayed my welcome. Yes, I confirmed to her, I was looking for an 'upgrade' in our relationship. She gave me a full of small teeth smile, opened the door, and wished me "good night." It was not cold that night, but I felt frozen--as if an ice shower had been heaped on me. There was humiliation, frustration, and sadness.

I decided to throw in the towel. I was done! Again. But I decided to reflect on what was transpiring before shutting the door for good.

~ ~ ~ ~

I talked to him using the Woody metaphor: "Say you would have a conversation with one of the movie's characters that show the guy very confused about what he is feeling. A Woody Allen type of figure. How would he describe the situation?

"My mom raised me to be a proud man. She wanted me to hold my head high, not let anyone push me down, belittle me. But here I am, feeling smaller and smaller by the day, despite all my efforts to pull her towards me, to cause Brenda to begin considering me a viable partner for this last phase in our lives. I feel rejected, but without her saying that much. I just wanted us to be lovers".

"Have you been able to talk to her about what afflicts you?"
The Woody character asked: "You know, how it is portrayed in
'Manhattan,' or in 'Hannah and her Sisters,' or other movies I
have made."

"Once," he responded. "But she was evasive, in denial, not
willing to engage and confront realities.

I said to Henry: "Woody would now turn pensive, clear his
throat, and in a familiar high-pitched voice said: "I don't know,
my heroines are not like that. They react, counter, refute and
engage. The movie would turn dull otherwise. The ladies in my
movies are emotional enough to do so."

Woody is not a psychiatrist. But his sensitivity for people is
profound; he might as well be one."

Henry's response surprised me: "You just said the key words-
I finally reached a useful conclusion-- I had been pursuing a
person whose emotional quotient was extremely low. It was
endemic to her, and it would not change. It was comfortable
for her to continue in this vein. What did she have to lose? She
would continue to play her Stradivarius. There was no
emergency and no urgency to turn introspective and cause a
radical makeover."

"My good friend Dave, a lawyer, opined at one point that
emotions were driven out of him by law-school and several
years of practice. Maybe that explains Brenda's behavior. But
I know another David, a lawyer as well, who is much more
emotional. It matters little: explanations of why people are the
way they are, are just that. They do not change the facts. They
do not make them more acceptable, more digestible in this
case.

The other side of the coin is equally apparent: I needed a
partner whose emotional quotient is significantly like mine. I
need a person whose heart and mind are open and interested in
understanding me and my needs—the only way we could take
ourselves to a journey that would lead to a lasting
relationship."

The following week, Henry came back and reported what the
epilogue was:

"The day after I saw you, I got a text from her. It was in

response to an earlier query where I had attempted to plan more get-togethers in the following days or weeks. She mentioned two events she would be attending (strutting through?) and that her sister wanted to join her for a dinner family gathering. There was no suggestion to join her for any of them. Surprisingly, she also claimed not to be feeling well, coming down with another cold, perhaps. No reference was about "us," except she inquired how I was doing. More like what she would ask a colleague at the law firm she once presided. I made up a story about traveling to Punta del Este, which would be warm and fun. I did not mention when I would return or if I would return. I then went into Expedia and planned my trip. I am leaving next week."

Then he added: "I wanted to respond to the rudeness of her equanimity with the loud thud of my silence, and this is the best I came up with."

~ ~ ~ ~

Without a shred of decency

Rob Z. cried intermittently as he relayed his story; he clearly was despondent about the manner of the breakup:

Rose opened the door to my apartment with her key. She did her usual: She stretched out arms to each side and exclaimed, "Voila," as her face was exhibiting a big smile. The theatrical entrance suggested to mean, "Am I not gorgeous?" but it left me annoyed; I hate "Catch-22's"! Either I had to tell her how beautiful she was—which I considered a blatant lie or respond, a cool "Hello," which would irritate her. The odd makers would probably bet that the latter would not set records in the happiness books. Because I hated lying in general, and because I was busy preparing dinner, I opted for the hello, nonetheless. Some people have such a knack for telling little white lies. I consider these the epitome of falsehoods. There is so much premeditation in the act, and there is such disregard for the recipients' intelligence.

Over dinner, she told me that she had a surprise for me. I

was wondering what this one could be. She had had a few surprises for me in the past. They never amounted to much of anything. In the past, such announcements filled me with anticipation and suspense, eventually decompressing into nothingness like an untied balloon whose air is quickly dissipating. Still, this was a bit intriguing. It ends up being that she also decided to become a writer. She had read a few of my stories before they got published, mostly liked them, and sometimes noted that maybe she ought to be concerned if they were autobiographical (I assured her they were not). Now it was her turn, she declared. She had written up a sort of outline, a rough sketch of the story, and asked me to read it. She did not want a critique, but my thoughts; how she thought these were different remains a puzzle unless it was similar to her expectations regarding her theatrical entrance just discussed--just standing ovations, please!.

The following morning, while she was at work, I dedicated time to what she had written. It was a somewhat well-written diatribe about some people who were rich and inconsiderate. They were judgmental to the utmost and treated a family member who was getting married as not particularly worth much consideration. After all, he was a member of the substantially less wealthy part of the family. "Without a shred of decency" was the title she gave it.

I wrote an email just to make sure my words do not get misconstrued or falsified. I remarked that it was nicely written and had rhythm. What was left unsaid was that she needed to be careful not to sound plagiaristic. After all, "Poor Man, Rich Man" was not a novelty. She would need to find an angle that would make it read less unoriginal.

Coming to think about it, it was not that surprising. Despite all the somewhat impressive biographical factoids, she was just average. One should recognize her achievements and the "Dr." in front of her name. One should see it as noteworthy that she survived a nasty episode of betrayal leading to divorce. Nonetheless, in so many ways, she was a fairly unremarkable, middle-of-the-road person who would not try to take risks or adopt strong positions on politics, social mores, or anything. In saying so, I even take into consideration how loud she was in bed.

I had decided that throughout most of my life, I was seeking the special, maybe slightly neurotic but titillating woman that would make me want to see her as soon as possible, please her as much as I can, "bring the stars down to her feet" (I actually used that phrase once!). The time had come to accept that such a search, such criteria for selecting a life-partner, was futile. Instead, I needed to look at the positives. As my father used to say, "look down, not just up." She had achieved plenty; she had a reasonably significant position at the university. She had rebuilt her life after the divorce. So, what if she was not the most beautiful woman I ever dated. So, what if she was a bit trite and a bit boring. So, what if she were not as warm to members of her own family as I would want my partner to be? So, what if she was not friendly, offering generous praise when my friends invited us for dinner at their place. I expected her to compromise to my stocky build, to my limited sex appeal, to my mood swings. I should put up with this mediocrity.

The relationship was only a few months old at this point. But, one could say it had been intense. We traveled to Europe twice, to a couple of places in the US as well. We attended concerts and ate a multitude of dinners at the best restaurants in the area. For her 60th birthday, I planned to take her for a one week sailing from Split to Dubrovnik. Those Adriatic voyages have become the rage in the last 20 years. I wanted to see the area as I had never been there. More than that, I thought it would be an affirmation of our relationship and an opportunity to decide whether we could spend the rest of our lives together.

Maybe this all was rushed a bit. Perhaps I was fooling myself. Rose had told me that usually, she was tight-lipped, did not say much, did not often discuss her feelings. But she had not demonstrated any misgivings about us as a pair. Yes, she had remarked that she needed more time for herself, for her work, for her personal affairs. I accepted that and offered her any compromise that might seem reasonable. But other than that, there were no reservations or pushbacks.

She was about to take a business trip to Los Angeles and suggested I spend the night at her place as she packed her things. In the morning, I could drive her to the airport. We spent the Sunday walking through a mall, holding hands, giving each other pecks. It was all normal. I drove her to the airport; we kissed briefly as married people might do. Later that Monday, she confirmed having arrived safely, as a married couple may do.

Early the following morning, my cellphone announced a message had come in. I always kept the phone open; having children may make you do that. It was her. She told me she had not slept all night and needed me to call her as soon as possible. I had a quick coffee cup to make sure I did not sound incoherent and dialed her number. "Hi, she said, I have not slept all night. I have concluded that I did not love you anymore." Just like that! It could not wait for a couple of days when I was supposed to get her at the airport. It could not wait for a face-to-face conversation. She did this without a shred of decency, without any understanding of the pain it inflicted. It showed her to be not just mediocre but selfish and uncaring.

After a while, when a calmer consideration of facts replaced anger, I concluded that to some degree, she showed the same coldness that I noticed her demonstrate towards her family members. This behavioral mediocrity walks hand in hand with an evident lack of emotional depth, something that cannot be learned or bought at Amazon. You either have it or not. I suddenly recalled her showing me some pictures from the distant past when her parents arrived as new immigrants to this country. I vividly remembered being frightened by the "American Gothic" look of her parents—there was no happiness or emotional depth in those faces either.

I told this patient: "How do you probe for that emotional quotient. It is not like you could have your partner put a thermometer under the tongue. Unfortunately, I do not have a recipe. The only thing I can recommend to you is to walk into the relationship with eyes wide open. Do not ignore signals that can inform you about your potential partner's character. It seems that Rose gave you some indications when you saw her be cold to her own family. Also, give yourself time, don't rush things. The trip to the Adriatic sounds lovely, but it may have been premature.

~ ~ ~ ~

Mad Ella

Madness! When Charles R. started telling me his story, he began with this loud statement.

"For the umpteenth time in the last few years, I thought that I could finally put the search for a female companion to, pardon the pun, bed. I found a woman who appreciated me, was kind, smiled at me, and gave me a sense of desire and friendship.

"It only took one week, a short span of seven days, for an incredible, unexpected, thunderbolt-like reversal of fortunes. Suddenly, Ella wanted nothing to do with me! She was done with me before we'd even slept together. We just kissed— passionately, I would say—as we perused the view of Hoboken from her balcony. Then we had dinner and mused about what might come next. It all sounded promising.

"We never argued. Ella told me that she was happy that we seemed to see things in the same vein, had similar political views, the same taste in clothing, furnishings, maybe even art— understated and slick was our preference.

"Then came the text—not even a phone call. Our short affair was finito. It was so sudden, contradicting all that preceded before.

"I refuted via text: 'Just two days ago, you told me that your heart was jumping out of your mouth with the titillating expectation of our next get-together. You then noted how pleased you were that we were so similar and how much joy reading the poetry book I gifted you.'

"Her response was short and lacking any explanation—she just said she was sorry.

"I was so unnerved. I did not close the book on this. I accused Ella of being a cheap, conniving liar. She rejected my condemnation. Her denial felt empty. When I told her that her behavior was plain immoral—that she had no compunction about reversing herself like that, all she managed to respond was: 'If you want to feel deceived, please go ahead.'

"Wow! Was this the woman with whom I thought I could share a future? What is wrong with me?

"Lately, my relationship's absurdity sent me into a state of such confusion and sadness that I lost my appetite and was unable to get a good night's sleep. I just could not understand what had happened here.

"It all started with an exchange of 'thumbs up' on a dating site. I liked EV's looks (yes, I am ashamed to admit my attention to looks). Because the biographical profile seemed quite good (I did wonder a little about her apparent passivity and search for calmness), I contacted her.

"The conversation went exceptionally well. We discovered we shared similar upbringings; we could talk about Elena Ferrante, we were bilingual, and our outlooks on life matched.

"We chose to meet at a Greek restaurant—I chose it because I had enjoyed it before and it was close to where she lived. Driving over there, I smiled, thinking the staff might regard me as a terrific womanizer, meeting a different woman every month.

"We had a wonderful time. We talked incessantly for nearly three hours and decided to get together again very soon. I walked Ella to her car and gave her a goodnight kiss that was well received and reciprocated. Lift-off was indeed as smooth as they come.

"Three days later, I was supposed to have dinner at her place, but she unexpectedly got hit by a virus and canceled. Was it an indication of trouble? Could it have been a convenient lie? The thought briefly crossed my mind, but I decided to bury any worry or concern. My proclivity to get nervous and doubtful had struck; yet, my neurosis was irritating. After all, people do get sick—in Hoboken, in New York, even in Florida. We agreed to meet for dinner the following Thursday, assuming her bug went away.

For that Thursday, she invited me over. Looking at the view from her high-floor apartment was less impressive than she thought or I expected—just a parking lot and some commercial buildings—but I said nothing and hoped my face did not reflect disappointment. On the other hand, the kisses were passionate; we acted like teenagers. I noticed that she closed her eyes during these moments of passion, the way she might have when in her twenties. I did not close my eyes; instead, I noted that her thin lips were not ideal for kissing, but I let it slide as kissing was not the all-important factor in a relationship. It seemed we could proceed even further, perhaps in the bedroom. I thought it would be best to advance gradually and stopped there.

"Indeed, our voyage into happy-land continued smoothly. We both expressed hopes and positive feelings for a get-together four days later. We would try to make that Saturday into a more protracted affair. A late afternoon movie to be followed by dinner, and who knows what—one can always hope—after that. It seemed like a good plan. The film, a likely Oscar candidate, was more to my liking than hers. She had difficulties with the symbolic violence at the end. And dinner was not a pleasing experience either—though the food was reasonably flavorful, the waiter was rude, rushing us along even though the restaurant was nearly empty. And I had hopes that we would, once again, go up to her apartment. However, she made it clear that I should head home after dropping her off.

"As I drove home and reviewed the day, I sensed turbulence. What had gone wrong? Was it because I'd placed my hand on her thigh in the darkness of the movie theater? Was it something I'd said? We never disagreed, unless...

"Unless my eagerness to move ahead with the relationship, push it along, was so disturbing that she could not handle it. As we discussed our separate pasts, I told her that one of the things I regretted most about my marriage was the lack of communication. I made it clear that I hoped Ella and I would be different and discuss whatever bothered us to find a compromise. I was very willing to talk things over and expressed a commitment to adapt and conform. That did not seem to make a difference, as she never raised an issue that might have been problematic—instead, she just threw the door in my face and sent me on my way.

For once, I had to admit to Charles that I had no satisfactory explanation of what happened. It is a sad truth that human beings will surprise you. Their thinking and motivations sometimes remain hidden and cause a shocking statement or, even worst, an act that is so surprising and so unexpected that it makes you wonder about yourself. There is no way one can prepare oneself for something like that. "What you must do, I said to Charles, is move on and hope not to run into someone like Ella again. Take solace in the fact that though such people exist, they are a distinct minority."

~ ~ ~ ~

La Chillona

Eduardo M. came to my office two months ago and told me his story:

"I have been jilted seven times over the last three years. Seven! Is that a record? So I found myself confused and in need of answers when I recently shut down a relationship and refused to change or reinstate it when she pleaded for us to start over. I am here talking to you—the first time I've seen a shrink—because I need to understand what happened here.

"Tell me more," I requested. "How did you meet, your background, and hers? Anything that comes to mind."

"The woman, Ramona, is from Chile. And it so happens, I am as well. But I have been in the US since the 70s. I was one of those maligned "Chicago boys." Young men who attended the University of Chicago to study economics. We went there because it was the bastion of conservative, monetarist economics. The negative press came with our presumed association with the military junta and the terrible viciousness of that regime. But those who went back to Chile managed to bring some significant prosperity to the country. Okay, I am digressing because the theme always gets me going.

"Anyway, Ramona and I met at a get-together of Chileans held in Manhattan. I had heard of her, but we never met. Her name was known to me because when we were in our thirties, she was a somewhat renowned singer—sort of jazz and French ballads that we would associate with Jacques Brel, Charles Aznavour, Piaf. During our first meal, she told me that she toured singing Piaf songs for a year. Later at home, I Googled it and was able to confirm her story."

"That all sounds positive. I love Aznavour."

"Yes. So do I. When I managed to find a YouTube recording of her performance, I noticed, and to be honest, was turned off by the fact that she screamed her songs rather than singing them. She probably thought that was an excellent way to replicate Piaf. Because I am sensitive to noise, her screaming was irritating. From that moment onward, I tagged her in my mind as 'La Chillona'—the best way to translate the word is the strident, the shrill screamer. I kept that to myself.

I thought her singing style would not be enough to create a wedge between us, mostly since she no longer sings in public. These days she is a personal growth trainer in Long Island. Interestingly, I saw one of her taped training sessions—a lecture prepared for a California clientele—a lot less traveling is a must as we go through this coronavirus epidemic. She was screaming there too. It seemed to be a bit crass.

"I invited her to my place. Restaurants are closed because of the pandemic, but I can cook. 'Why don't you come over to my Mineola apartment on Friday night, and I will make you my special chicken piccata?' We hit it off quite well. We talked about Chile and our past successes and failures. She told me she'd divorced a husband of more than two decades about four years back. She mentioned that it left her with little wealth and a shaky financial future—especially now, with the economic shutdown. There were some intimate moments—kissing, touching, that sort of thing. But we decided to cool it and get together two days later at her place.

"Her studio in Long Island was cute if small. To give it a romantic atmosphere, she lit lots of candles. She made dishes I love—humitas (made of corn and white cheese, it is delicious—you should try it!) and a mix of fish and mollusks, which was also delicious. I spent the night there. It felt good. Because she was very vocal during sex, I resurrected the 'chillona' tag.

"The next morning, while having breakfast, I found out some very unpleasant news. She told me that the only source of potential wealth was a life policy on her ex-husband. If he died, she said—and stressed that he was quite sick—she would stand to gain a fair amount of money. Knowing this, she religiously paid the monthly premium, even if it cost more than the monthly car payment for her Hyundai.

"I started feeling distaste, but also some animosity. I wondered how we would go on but decided to keep my feelings under control. The story made me sick to my stomach. You tell me, Doctor, am I crazy? Why does this so revolt me?"

"Go on," I said without answering his question. "We can discuss it later. I want to hear the rest."

"I saw a TV on the wall and asked her what service she used. I had an idea of how to lower the cost. She told me she only watched Netflix. She had no cable, nor did she follow the local news. Talking about politics, I also found out that she was rather ill-informed. These were turbulent times for the country, but she had little to no information about what was going on. I was incredulous.

"I went home. On the way, an assortment of tidbits bombarded my mind—the great sex, the screams, her plot to become wealthy. I had no clue about the numbers, the policy's value, nor did I want to know. I am very aware that wealth for one is different for another, but that was immaterial. Her political and social ignorance in the middle of a crisis for the country. Why did I feel like running?

"The next morning, I called her and simply said, 'Ramona, we are just too different. I don't think we are a match.' She was upset. She started crying. But I had turned cold. I tuned out.

"Had this been the end of it, I would not be sitting here asking you to help me get things straight in my head. Relationships between men and women, especially at this stage in our lives, should be based on a meeting of minds and souls. Did the issues I was upset about seem marginal? Why was I delving into minutia?

"However, once I came back from a day of unfocused work, I discovered a long message left on the answering machine. It was a loud, shrill diatribe in which she called me all sorts of names. She used pieces of information I had shared about my past against me—to paint me in the worst possible colors. Ostensibly she was getting even. What it did, though, was make me feel vindicated. The following morning, she left a text on my cell phone in which she apologized for the previous message. She was feeling hurt and betrayed. She'd had such high hopes for us. I concluded that she just was acting irrationally. Then I thought that maybe I was a passport to a more stable economic condition. In any case, this is the story. Please tell me what your trained mind thinks about this."

"Did you see the movie Blue Jasmine? Woody Allen directed it, and many liked it. Your story is not that unusual. Many see marriage as an elevator to a better, more luxurious life. You might have found it more distasteful because of all the other things that you did not like. I suggest you reflect on the extent to which you would have felt different if she were quieter, more socially and politically aware, and still sexually pleasing. In other words, can you distill the important from the tangential? But there is another issue: you seem to feel guilty you stopped seeing this woman. Maybe because you sense you inflicted pain on an ex-Chilean like yourself. Anyone must be respectful of their wishes and act according to self-interest.

~ ~ ~ ~

Jasmin's Self-Centeredness

Amram C. told me this in our first session:

"It is a recurrent theme, doctor, and I want to know if, perhaps, I am just too sensitive in my distaste for this type of behavior. I keep on bumping into women exhibiting the same personality traits, and when I got so frustrated and discouraged about Jasmin, I decided it was time to seek professional help."

"Yes, Jasmin is another dating site connection. It is what is in vogue these days. We emailed each other short messages and decided to have a phone conversation. I felt that we had much in common: the ethnic background (we both are descendants of immigrants from the Middle East (her parents are Iraqi and mine Lebanese), the higher education (we both have advanced degrees), and the fact that we are both writers (she writes plays and skits, I write stories)."

How about I send you some samples of my writing, and you send a couple of plays? I said as I thought it would bring us closer even before our first get-together.

She agreed, and soon enough, we attached our writings to short emails. Her email was curt, certainly compared to my effort, where I tried to be more endearing. I wrote: "I hope these two pieces please you, that you get to know me better through them, and that these writings provide a foundation for something special someday. I hope the sun shines on your day." When she responded: "I think it already has," I got excited; I thought we were getting somewhere.

I received her material the next day and dedicated a lot of time to read through them carefully. I found weaknesses in both (too repetitive, too cutesy, too shallow), but there were many positives. I wrote to her about those without mentioning any of the negatives. I said: "Your humanity comes across in the way you love your characters, even those that are a bit shady."

She responded with some measure of restrained and self-effacing pleasure: "So happy you liked it, and your comments are possibly too generous." She continued: "I have not yet read your pieces, but let's see if I can steal some time to get around to it." I told her I would prefer it if she would not hurry.

I was disappointed with the next email: "I have read your first story, but I was so tired I did not fully understand what you were after. It could be interesting to reread it when both eyes are wide open." I did not show any unhappiness and just expressed the hope she would find the time.

A day later, a second mail from her was more positive. She finally saw the point I was trying to make. She also said: "it is well written; I am so glad I had both eyes available this morning." But now, she explained, she was so tired.

Two days passed before she reviewed the second piece. It details a story taking place in Berlin. She wrote her email in three somewhat lengthy paragraphs. The first two had to do with her experiences while traveling in two European cities: Lisbon and Amsterdam-- how she felt, how she thought people behaved. Any relationship between what she wrote and my story was, at best tangential. The last, shorter paragraph noted that the love story seemed "a bit cold."

I was not happy. It seemed like a very self-centered response. I thought of writing something like: "What if I reviewed your Fire Island play by discussing my adventures as a young man in Miami Beach." Instead, to salvage what seemed like a sinking ship, I just wrote that I was disappointed that it looked like she did not understand that the love relationship that seemed "a bit cold" was strained because of the opposite political positions of the two characters involved.

Her response was swift and borderline nasty: How could I demand her to see what I wanted her to see; "we write whatever we write, and either the reader gets it or does not." Of course, she was right about that. But what about her going on a self-centered voyage in the first two paragraphs? Why couldn't she afford me the same courtesy I gave her? My reply was short; I just stated that I did not demand anything from anyone in the past and would never do that in the future; that is a principle that I hold dear. I wished her a wonderful week. Silence ensued.

"Was I too sensitive? Is it okay to accept this type of selfishness time and time again? How does one handle this?

I told Amram that we all need to set the boundaries of what is acceptable and not. But that is easier to pass across about specific behaviors. Can we establish the same limitations concerning personality traits that we do not like? Much more problematic as it may seem like outright manipulation, it may smell like trying to change a person's inner being. Can you say to a person: "You look very selfish and self-centered? Yes, of course, you can. Is the other person allowed to tell you to take a hike, because she is who she is, again a resounding yes! Can we criticize you for being hyper-sensitive? Some are more, and some are less. You are who you are. Can you be more tolerant? Can you accept a considerable variation in terms of that trait? I think you probably will say that you can. But if it gets to be too much, just move on. It is not worth it to get overly aggravated.

~ ~ ~ ~

As noted before, there are common themes in these stories. And it just occurred to me that I never had a female patient whose issues had to do with a falling apart of an amorous relationship. I have no idea why that is the case.

These stories seem to have several common strands; one such strand is that we want our partner, the person we enjoy a lasting, meaningful relationship with, to fit some ideal human being. The somewhat amorphous, undefined model of how that person should be, how she should behave, what personality traits she should exhibit becomes both: a measuring stick and a recipe for disaster. Why? Because the model is not even clear to the owner dreaming it up. It, indeed, is not conveyed to the other person. "You should not be self-centered; you should not be dishonest; you should not be deceptive." Even if these are general criteria most of us could agree upon, they hover over the relationship like a dagger, ready to fall on the fragile thread and destroy it. It may be challenging to get these men to accept being more humble and not expecting dreamlike life-partners. A healthy dose of temperance would have been best for these men. I just don't know how you acquire that wisdom.

It gets even more complicated. Because of sexual desires, the ticking of different biological clocks—the obvious female one, and that one afflicting both sexes, the one that brings you closer to the "over the hill" point when dating obtains a different meaning. Because of the fright of remaining alone, we often accept the unacceptable, dismiss the inappropriate, pardon the unforgivable. We might see what is wrong with the relationship and still get up the next morning to invite more trouble, just because of the fear of dying alone.

Two things struck me as I reflected on these individuals and their frustrations, complaints, bitterness. Like Woody, they were obsessed with the physical appearance of the women they wanted to love. Maybe these men could have been happier if they looked for a less physically attractive but much better human being. The other is that, like Woody, they could be accused of being egotistical. They did not seem to look at the possibility their behavior was as annoying as it was perceived. Misanthropes are partially blind.

WEENY SALCHICHA

The mind plays curious games with humans; they even confuse animals that may think that what they experience is real when it's not. It may just be the result of the twisted human mind and how it deals with a pet.

My name is Salchicha. My owner, Andrew, gave me that name even though I am not Spanish. In fact, there is nothing in my ancestry, even remotely Spanish. But Andrew, who used to be called Andres in Ecuador, is a Spanish-speaking person, and he knows—he told me so—that dachshunds are called *salchichas* in his home country. And that is why he gave me this name.

Salchicha also has a more common meaning. It is what we commonly call a sausage in the US. And in fact, the edible and the breed have a similar appearance—a somewhat elongated body with no significant changes in shape from beginning to end, excluding head and tail, of course.

But if you thought that I was just some typical dachshund, not so. Andres was annoyed when others referred to me as salchichita—a diminutive, an affix that aptly described my smallness. When he took me to the doctor for the first time, the assistants and even the doctor laughed disparagingly at my size. My owner was so embarrassed he swore never to go back to that establishment.

Now we all know that dachshunds are lovely, cute creatures. And so am I. Wagging my tail as I waddle from place to place at no high speed, despite the tremendous effort put into each step. During my first year and a half, I swiveled from one corner to the other for no practical purpose, as all dogs do, and waved my tiny tail with a great impetus to show my happiness. That was when I had been young and didn't know better. Eventually, I became more bashful and was content to hide.

The problem, as stated, was that I was tiny. Even within the universe of Dachshundia, I was small. When I was born, my mother—a normal-sized dog—had been perturbed by my smallness. She'd looked at my paws and had been instantly horrified by their insignificance. She shed a tear and howled to the heavens. Even if one would limit the comparison to miniature dachshunds, I was what one nasty man had called "a shrimp."

I am not a shrimp. Don't taste like one and don't want to be considered fish or human fodder.

My smallness was a terrible embarrassment to my owner. He even told me he had all sorts of nightmares about it. He developed an inferiority complex because of me. This issue was accentuated when we visited with friends, especially the ladies. They would say, "What a tiny salchicha you have, Andres! So cute!"

He did not think it was cute at all. He was frustrated by my inability to grow bigger. I was not only short, but also thin. Andres felt I was incapable of standing up for myself. He kept me at home, afraid to bring me out to the public, to the neighborhood street where other dogs might humiliate me.

At some point, Andres met Ivette, and they seemed to hit it off. For a while, he told me he was thinking of keeping me a secret. He was not going to introduce us. One night, they came in after dining out and drinking a bottle of wine. They were kissing and touching each other's half-undressed bodies. It was at this point that Andres introduced me to his girlfriend. She shrieked and laughed while pointing at me. He was so upset by her reaction. Once he recovered from his shock, he asked her to get dressed and leave the apartment.

Following that awful experience, Andres turned into a reclusive anti-social person—he went to work, came home, made dinner, watched TV for about three hours, and went to bed. Day in and day out. On weekends, he watched a lot of sports. Once in a while, he would get together with his sister and her husband. Most often, it was for a couple of hours at their house in the suburbs. I tagged along but tried to remain unnoticed, which wasn't hard for me as I rolled into a tiny brown ball and turned into a speck. On the way back, Andres commented that humans had nasty, vicious propensities.

Andres decided to investigate if I could get bigger in some manner, enhancing my girth and length. Perhaps some medications, some special diet, and some stimulants. He went from one doctor to the next and got no relief, no solution, no suggestions. The veterinarians echoed each other as they mechanically shook their heads and stated, "Nature is what it is. You can't force it."

He googled endlessly, searching for a possible solution. He even investigated Chinese medicine—some of his friends had sworn by it as the cure for all ailments. These attempts bore no fruits. He was frustrated.

Andres was the kind of guy who had a hard time taking "no" for an answer. His parents said that he was stubborn and taciturn. One teacher had described him as obstinate. When, as a child, his teacher had told him he could not paint to save his life, he'd sat in his room and spent hours working at it. One day, he'd come into class with a painting that everyone admired. When, as an adult, everyone argued that the machines the company had imported from Germany could not be integrated into the production line, he spent many hours with a German-speaking friend to understand the manual and find a workable solution. In my case, he wanted to cause change to take place but was hitting one wall after the other.

Three years later, while watching a sports show, Andres caught a testosterone advertisement geared toward older men.

"Hmm," he said out loud, "maybe I granulate the medicine and feed it to my Salchicha as part of his daily mix of dry food. What if it works? Can it possibly hurt the poor guy?"

He did not know enough about chemistry to make an intelligent decision, but he decided to try it because he was desperate. He ordered a bottle and waited for it eagerly—sometimes checking his mailbox twice a day.

The thirty capsules bottle arrived on a Tuesday, and I noticed

Andres working hard at turning the hard pill into powder. He mixed the powder with every meal for the next month. After a month, with the bottle spent, and as Andres examined me while giving a tummy rub, he confided that he sadly saw no changes. He also told me that he was happy that my stool was normal and I had not vomited.

He could not see that my muscles were getting a bit tense, and I felt a bit stronger. I had no way to communicate that to him except by employing a foolish grin.

Halfway through the bottle, in a moment of despair, Andres ordered a package of three additional bottles. He continued turning the capsules into powder, and I continued devouring my breakfasts and dinners as heretofore.

I was halfway through the second bottle's stimulants; my blood was rushing through the veins with force, and my muscles were getting stronger and springier. Even Andres noticed that I looked fuller and that my leg muscles had bulged a bit. He was excited and smiling more.

My problems came when no one was watching. When all the lights went out, I was lying on the pillow where I usually slept. My legs, my whole body, would be so tense, so erect that I could not relax and fall asleep. I would move from position to position, try to curl up, try to lie on my back, keep my legs up, and go from one side to the other, but nothing helped; I had a tough time relaxing and enjoying the deep sleep of yesteryear. During the day, I felt sluggish, but I could not manage a nice siesta.

Once I finished the third bottle, my legs were bulkier, my torso felt more robust, and, according to Andres, it seemed like I had a meaner look, a nasty grin. It was as if I was aware of my new countenance; remembering how I had been treated earlier, I now displayed a sarcastic smile. But, as stated, all this was not without cost as my new body refused to relax and curl up for one of those typical dog naps. Even at nighttime, when Andres turned off the lights and the TV and moved to his bedroom, I was so annoyed by my inability to relax and limp off into night dreams. In my discomfort, I would howl so much that Andres would get up, take me out of my crate, and try to pat me or massage my belly to calm me down.

Andres, on the other hand, was much more relaxed about his

relationships with others. He invited friends over. He was incredibly proud to show me off to his girlfriends. He seemed to have a new girlfriend every few weeks. He would come home with a girl, start kissing, and soon after that, "Please meet Salchichita." None of the new girlfriends made disparaging remarks about me, though not all were as enthusiastic as Gloria, who could not stop caressing me and kissing me. I felt terrific when she displayed such affection.

About two months later, I started having pain in my lower belly. Andres saw some bumps in my skin but did not think they were the result of the pills I had been swallowing earlier. When I began making sounds of discomfort, he took me to the doctor. The vet immediately suspected that I had developed MCT (mast cell tumors). He wanted to take me under a scanning machine to see if cancer had spread and whether it was stage I or II cancer. As I listened, the doctor explained that those mast cells were actually good for dogs—they prevent inflammation. But when the mast cells multiplied, they had a negative effect and caused multiple skin tumors. If they metastasized, they could attack the liver or spleen.

After further inspection, it became clear that I needed to go under the knife to remove those bumps. Furthermore, I required chemotherapy because the disease had developed into stage II cancer. Treatment had to begin immediately. I was no longer a skinny creature but a dog threatened by an illness that would affect my skin—instead of being scrawny, I became a creature with strange, unattractive bumps, and, worse than that, cancer threatened my sheer existence.

When Andres took me for the required surgery, he was in tears. He knew that it was likely to be painful, and even if partially sedated, I'd feel aches and discomfort during the convalescence period, as parts of my body were shaved and covered with bandages. My body would itch all over, and I would stubbornly try to peel off those strange paddings, but curtailed by a cone limiting my snouts access. Andres was also anxious about handling the chemo treatment and how long it would take to recover from the ordeal.

In the evening after the first chemo session, Gloria and Andres had dinner at home. I was on my day cushion, groaning with discomfort and very sluggish. My stronger muscles had turned limp as the surgery and treatment made me weak.

Andres turned to me and just said, "I am so sorry."

Gloria lashed out. "It is always the same! People get pets, dogs, cats, parrots, and instead of just caring for them as they are, they try to make them look cute, strong, beautiful, trick performing, and in the case of horses, performing dressage exercises. For what purpose? With what objective? Do they really think that the animal is happier when wearing a stupid pink bow, or, even worse, a green hat on St. Patrick's, or performing, repeatedly, the same trick that is most likely uncomfortable? No, Andres, just as in your case. The act is a selfish act with the sole purpose of making you look better. Of showing you off. As if the poor Salchichita reflected on your personality, of your prowess. Of your qualities as a man."

Andres lowered his head, turned toward me, and whispered, "I hope you get well soon."

But Gloria was not done yet. "People do the same with their children. They create a new human being, and instead of giving her or him all the tools, all the knowledge, emotional support, and love so that this young person can live a fruitful, enriching, joyful, and productive life, they create a little monster. They can be proud of that creature because it reflects well on them, emulating them with all their positive and negative personality traits. They dress six-year-old boys and girls in tuxedos and silk or chiffon dresses that normally would only be seen in the vitrines of Saks Fifth Avenue during the Christmas season. And they think this is cute and that the kids look so good in these clothes, and all this does is tell everyone that the parents are wealthy. How to twist the minds of a young child as to what matters in life!"

"I get your point, Gloria," said my owner. He knew that she had hit the nail on the head. The effort to turn me into a super-dog had backfired terribly. He buried his face in his hands and did not say much until they turned the lights off in the living room. I do not know what happened or what was said when they retired for the night.

As the veterinarian predicted, the chemotherapy was successful in redressing my condition. The surgery removed the bumps, and the scalping openings healed. It took some weeks, but eventually, I felt healthier and looked much better.

I noticed a change in Andres's attitude to all matters concerning me. He was a lot less interested in showing me off. He made sure I only ate top-notch healthy dry food without grains. He went on walks with me and was patient about my pace, my sudden change of direction for no particular reason, and the abrupt stops that were not precipitated by anything that he could understand.

Gloria was a constant presence at home. Despite her harsh words about what Andres had done to make me sick, she seemed to take it all in stride. I noticed a change in her behavior; she appeared purposeful and analytical, as if she had some plan. Gloria patted me twice in the morning before she left and again when she came back in. Gone were the hugs and small kisses. She did not even look at me while giving me those little pats—it all seemed very mechanical and shallow. As she walked through the main door and toward Andres with those very noisy stilettos, I tried to get her attention—whether by wagging my tail frantically or just walking next to her, making joyful noises, she always treated me to the same response. When Andres would suggest that we all go out for a walk, she would say, "You go ahead, I have some work to do," or "Why don't you send him to the balcony to do his thing and stay next to me?"

Notwithstanding, I was elated to see Andres very involved in the preparations for the wedding day. He and Gloria had ample discussions of how many would be invited to the wedding party, what food would be served, who would officiate the ceremony, and what music would be played at the party. When the day finally came, Gloria's niece, Blanca, looked after me. She stayed in the house for the wedding day and subsequent honeymoon. I liked her enough and was not upset to have her substitute Andres. After all, it was for a good cause—he seemed to be so happy about getting married. I heard him give precise instructions about the feeding, playing, walking that I liked. I was grateful for his concerns and efforts to make me feel good.

I had a different reaction when, three months later, Andres told me that he would pack my things and move me to Blanca's place for good. Gloria was pregnant, and she would rather not have to deal with me and my needs when the baby is born. What happened to all the prophesied love showered on me by Andres and Gloria while I was sick and convalescing? What happened to Gloria's long declamation of animals and children's rights to have a good life? How did they think I would feel being shipped off as an inconvenience?

As the days passed, waiting for my imminent departure, I looked more despondent. My eyelids drooped. I looked more like a basset hound. I no longer held my head high. I stopped showing happiness with a hectic wagging of my tail. Instead, one could often see me crunched in the corner with my head facing the floor.

As far as I was concerned, my life would never be the same. Gone were the days when I took the leash in my mouth to lead Andres to the elevator, to head to the streets. No longer would I chase the little orange ball that he tossed across the living room. He no longer would say, "Go ahead and shake your cobwebs," as I rattled my body and took a little hop before approaching my food bowl.

Laureate Saul Bellow said it best: "More Die of Heartbreak." Cruelty is not necessarily limited to physical mistreatment. Sometimes, it is purely emotional.

MY COUSIN GIG

He was a legend from the time he was a teenager—at least he was famous in our extended family. He did not know it, but his American relatives enjoyed gossiping about him. You could say, with a smile, that his name spanned countries and continents. Since our family did not have a *Cosa Nostra* member to whisper about or a famous scientist to read about in the papers, it was good to have him as a routine topic of conversation—at least, that's what I concluded when I turned into an adult. This story recounts snippets of his life I heard at home, or through the grapevine, or—eventually—from his mouth. Here and there, I comment based on what I saw during eventual personal encounters.

He was born Giancarlo DiSalvo, a rather common name in Sicily. Most called him Gianni, just as his parents endearingly called him. Living in metropolitan New York, thousands of miles away, I heard about him the first time when I was about sixteen. We were just one year apart—I was older—and the stories elicited curiosity rather than jealousy, fantasy-like images rather than a strong desire to emulate.

My mother and two aunts frequently oohed and aahed about his looks—how cute he was, how, despite his age, he looked so masculine on his Vespa. Soon enough, they told stories of girls fighting over becoming his girlfriend. They looked at pictures of him on his motorcycle in the main square, wearing sleeveless and mostly unbuttoned shirts. They commented on how they might have fallen in love with him as well.

Come on, ladies! He was barely fifteen years old!

One of these forty-year-olds would say to the other, "He looks like a young Marlon Brando," or "Ah, that Roman nose, strong chin," or "And that physique, those already defined muscles!" I thought they were exaggerating a bit, but I also was impressed with how much older he looked. I imagined him surrounded by girls while holding court in the middle of a popular *piazza*. One way or another, the aunts said, he got wind of all the commentary about him and smiled with unabashed satisfaction.

Years later, I learned that though the parents were highly indulgent, they made sure to inculcate in their son a calm and pleasant demeanor. "Don't look for fights. Do not look for disagreement. Look at the positives of each situation. Smile often, frown rarely. Be compassionate." These traits stayed with him for a lifetime.

At sixteen, Gianni asked his father if this approach would turn him into a pushover. His father reflected on how to best answer, took some time, and finally was quite thorough. "What do you have to gain from argument and strife? Think about what will make you live a happy life; if you smile, come to some good arrangement, and take advantage of the opportunities, you will end up living a pleasant life. If it all gets done in a gentle, smooth way, the resolution of any disagreement will be even more rewarding."

Gianni was not sure he understood everything his father, a clothing store manager, said to him but smiled and nodded.

Gianni's popularity extended and magnified during those late high school years. The best description of him was that he was a "heartthrob." I even heard about that in distant Queens, NY. My mother exclaimed at dinnertime, "This Gianni, Mamma Mia! The girls are all over him. He is so popular!"

A piece of *salsiccia*—the famous Italian sausage—got stuck in my throat when I heard her exclaim those words. Maybe I was thinking about my limitations in conquering members of the opposite sex. Since I was of nearly the same age as Gianni, the comparisons were only natural. I had a hard time finding a girlfriend, let alone being fought over. Later in life, I learned that

Gianni was not at all embarrassed by the heartthrob accolade. For decades, he frequently mentioned it, even to strangers, and continued to describe how the girls were eager to kiss him and flirt with him.

Gianni was no superstar in school. His grades hovered just above the minimum acceptable. He did not bother to read books or spend long hours preparing for exams. He was not interested in academic excellence, preferring to focus on his social life instead—switching girlfriends often. Making sure he didn't get any of them pregnant was a top priority. He told his close friend Carlo that he would be devastated if a girl got pregnant. Either he would have to marry her and cut short these fun times or pay for an abortion with money borrowed from his father (a prospect that frightened him).

One might say that success breeds success—especially if you make sure others know about it. He did not mind regaling others with stories of how girls chased after him; he smiled and described details that elucidated his popularity. Most listeners did not react negatively to his narcissism; they just saw this youngster describing reality and enjoying the particulars. Since he hardly ever experienced any pushback, he continued talking about his "stardom" well into his sixties.

Other than social life priorities, Gianni was keen on two hobbies: soccer and the movies. He loved playing and watching soccer, rooting for "Juve"—the short name for Juventus FC—even if their home stadium was in Turin. He was also adamant and eager to see as many movies as possible. He was primarily interested in American films portraying good-looking men, and he paid close attention to their demeanor, their poses, their attire.

By the time he turned eighteen, the idea of trying to make it in Hollywood, once just a fleeting thought, became a fully embraced goal. Knowing how much Gianni wanted this, his parents worked on enabling this venture. Thank goodness for *La Famiglia,* he would live with his mother's cousin in Culver City, at least until he gained some economic footing of his own. He would look for one of many acting schools and Berlitz to improve his very rudimentary English. His family might also help him find work as a bartender or waiter at some Italian restaurant. And so it is that in mid-July of 1977, at eighteen years of age, he kissed his parents goodbye, had a farewell party that, in a nutshell, broke the hearts of many girls while boosting the spirits of several young men.

~ ~ ~ ~

America! The first thing Gianni asked for when his uncle and aunt greeted him was to take him to a place where he could see those big letters spelling H-O-L-L-Y-W-O-O-D. In his exuberance and naiveté, he thought he'd already made it! He thought it would be as easy as driving his Vespa through the Piazza Verdi and being stormed by a dozen girls. Exuding his typical self-confidence, he saw no reason to change his demeanor once in Los Angeles. After all, it was America. He smiled with self-assurance and was happy seeing people smile back—at least in California. The early encounters with family and their friends who were Italians like him, spoke Italian, had the usual happy-go-lucky attitudes, loud voices, and those, so typical, hand expressions made him feel at home. The transition seemed easy and smooth. He went to bed during these early days thinking that soon enough, he would be on billboards. He was such a fan of the movies; now, he would relish being in them. He loved James Dean in *Giant* and John Wayne in *Rio Bravo*. He was convinced he could emulate their style and performances.

Three months later, Gianni showed signs of frustration and disenchantment. He had such difficulty mastering conversational English, pronouncing words correctly, and acquiring a richer vocabulary. His uncle Alberto, whom he later described as gruff, told him that even in the movies, he was supposed to enunciate what is in a written script. "You can't sound like an Italian that just got off the boat, Gianni." Alberto was a no-nonsense supervisor of a construction crew and was quite impatient with Gianni and his flippant attitude. As Gianni confided in me years later, Alberto possibly wanted him to succeed or go back to Sicily—but definitely be out of his house.

With the prospects of an acting career stalling, Gianni became concerned about how he would make a living. Staying at his relatives involved listening to his uncle's admonitions, and life was complicated enough without it. At acting school, he met a Costa Rican who worked all evenings at a bar in the Hollywood area.

The man told him he could probably help him get a job despite just having a tourist visa. "In this country, the bureaucracy is as convoluted and inefficient as it is back home. No one will know your status," he commented. "Between tips and wages, you could earn several hundred dollars per week, and you could even sneak in a free burger and beer when it is less busy."

Gianni started working at that bar, and a week into it, knew a few regulars by their first name. Linda was particularly keen to talk to him. Gianni noticed that she came in and left alone. On Tuesday of his second week, he asked her why she was always alone; she responded by propositioning him. It might have surprised many, but not him.

"What time are you done with work, Gianni? I will pick you up, and we will go to my place, okay?" She seemed to be thirty-five or so—older than him for sure, but he was keen to find out about American love.

Florence followed Linda—everyone called her Flo. Then came Marie and Penelope, who liked the shortened Pen. All had common traits—they offered to harbor him in their flats or houses, and all three were either wealthy or, at least, comfortable. Though he had one-night stands with Christie and Martha, also women attending the bar, Gianni dismissed them because, though relatively young and attractive, they lived in small studios in a lower-middle-class neighborhood.

The ages of the other three varied from the mid-thirties to the early forties—many years later, as he described his life in California, he told me that he liked these older women because they introduced him to so many new things: fine-dining, art, real estate, fancy clothing, and jewelry. A couple of ladies he recalled years later even took him shopping so that he would look good when they went out together. He was not embarrassed telling me that. I still see him grinning with pride.

The news spread like wildfire in the family. I found out about the new developments from the chatter as gossip was a significant pastime during the juicy Sunday night dinners. And by "juicy," I am not referring to the savory food but the spiced-up detail in the stories. At one of these gatherings, my mother told Dad, "There you go, Humberto, we now have a gigolo in the family." And, in a sarcastic tone that did not escape me, "Something we can all be proud of."

That night, when I closed my eyes, I smiled. I would now call Gianni "my cousin Gig," pronounced with a hard "G" like the word *gigolo*. I would keep it a secret, or at least I would try to hide what this name meant and its origins.

When Gianni went into the third month of his relationship with Liz, a novelty for those who kept track because it had lasted longer, many concluded that he thought this woman, in her early thirties, was special. In fact, decades later, Gianni told me that with Liz, and for the first time, he sensed that sex and passion were mixed-in with real affection, shared values, and common preferences and tastes. She also was the first one to show interest in helping him find a career. She pointed out to him that it had almost been a year since he'd arrived in Los Angeles. He already was too old to be a footballer and obviously could not make it in the movies. Might there be something else he was good at? Something he excelled at when he was a Palermo youngster?

He recounted later, "Quite accidentally, the conversation landed on the fact that, as a teenager, I was rather good, even lauded, for my dancing moves. Liz turned to me and said, 'There you go, love, you have the looks, the aptitude, the body, the full package to become a ballroom dancer. Women love to learn ballroom dancing, men less so, but they are dragged along by their wives and do not dare contradict them. You would need to learn the steps of dances like the cha-cha, bolero, foxtrot, and waltz, but this should not be hard for you. You may even compete in tournaments and make a name for yourself.'"

Gianni told me that he'd hugged her in a way he'd never embraced a woman before. And then he asked naively, "Wouldn't I have to become a citizen for all this to work out?"

Liz, having been married twice before, and very much the practical sort, did not hesitate. "If you are asking me if we should get married, my answer is that considering everything, it probably is a smart choice. But you need to promise me that you will do everything possible to earn a living."

Gianni hugged her once more and said, "Of course, love."

And so it was that Liz opened the doors to citizenship for Gianni, and a primary concern of his was lifted. From his perspective, Gianni knew this was a practical decision rather than a patriotic step. He did not have strong feelings about his new country—he was not particularly interested or fond of its history or politics.

He and Liz watched the news one evening, and the "Contra affair" was being discussed. At first, he thought someone in Washington had had an affair with a woman. Liz laughed at him and said, "One-track mind!"

He was, of course, amazed by the multilane highways and the immense shopping malls. It occurred to him that living in this country was pleasant, offered more opportunities, and was generally more financially rewarding than Italy.

"The essence of life," he remarked to me once, "is to make the most of it, always, at all times." (He tended to repeat words to make sure he was understood). America offered plenty of recreational facilities to satisfy his hedonistic tendencies.

It took a few months in a dance studio to learn the steps of various dances. Still, Gianni was very conscious that, as bothersome as these instructions were to his free-wheeling self, he would have to comprehend and accept the discipline and rigor of ballroom dancing. Obeying instructions was not easy for him, and because he'd been so well-liked, no one countered this trait. Now, his wife and sponsor demanded that he be a breadwinner, and Gianni felt that a dagger was dangling from a thin thread over his head—he could not afford to be frivolous. Citizenship was a process, he knew, and it might be snipped in a nanosecond if Liz turned her back on him.

When he finished the course, he began attending ballrooms and offering himself as a partner to a crowd of wealthy ladies. Liz was okay with that; she was not the jealous type, had a busy career as a mid-level manager in an international advertising agency, and wanted her husband to succeed. She had fleeting thoughts about his possible infidelity, especially when work forced her to travel to Europe, but decided no good would come out of fretting about it.

Brenda, whose skills as a dancer were above the average clientele, suggested that Gianni be her dance partner at a competition in Las Vegas. He consulted with his wife—she approved wholeheartedly and promised to be in the audience. Their second place-finish made everyone happy. Brenda was so excited that she compensated Gianni with the full $5,000 prize. That was the most money he'd ever made! But that fact he would not disclose to Liz, Brenda, or anyone else.

Gianni felt more relaxed about his new profession because his excellent result in Vegas got him more clients and higher-paying contracts as a dance partner. He asked Liz whether it was too early to launch a studio where he could teach dancing. Liz was effusive about the idea but thought he needed to wait till he got approved for citizenship.

Gianni was a bit miffed by this. "What has one to do with the other? You asked me to succeed in this career, and I think this would be a good step in that direction." Liz told him that there was a need for capital investments to launch something like this—the real estate, the décor, the equipment, the advertising, all these cost money. It would be much easier to get a bank loan as a citizen.

He turned to his parents, hoping he could get financial support, but they informed him that none was forthcoming.

"Dancing studio?" they asked. "We do not even understand what this is and why you would be doing something like that. Maybe you should think of coming home to work with your father in the clothing store."

What they did not tell him was that they were peeved by how he had treated them. That he only wrote to them every few months and not even long letters. They also did not like his behavior toward the family members who had hosted him during the first weeks. "He did not show enough appreciation," they complained. "And eventually, he left without even telling us where he would be staying."

The late 80s economic downturn created stress for many; it did not spare Gianni and Liz. He became anxious when he got a significant number of cancelations, even from some of his most adoring clients, and Liz got laid off. Suddenly she was a lot less kind, positive, and loving. As often is the case, even sex was affected. Gianni was particularly nervous as the immigration process was still ongoing. The final interview with the INS officer had been scheduled for the middle of April, three weeks after Liz was fired. When they arrived at the local INS offices, they were barely talking to each other. The large woman interviewing them seemed to be in a bad mood as well.

"So, you came here as a visitor, on a tourist visa, to see

beautiful California and stay with relatives. Suddenly you meet this American woman, elope in Las Vegas. And you, young woman, file to give this man American citizenship. We see many Latinos, Israelis, and Italians who get married to an American woman just to get citizenship. Could it be that you two are just another case? What evidence can you give me to the contrary?"

Gianni, usually calm in the face of conflict and insults—precisely like his father taught him—was ready to lift the desk and toss it on top of the INS woman. He was irate. His character was being questioned, and his intentions were described as nefarious. He felt Liz's hand on his leg. She sought to calm him down, make sure he did not explode, and scuttle his application for good. She still cared enough about him to protect him from himself.

Three months later, they got the confirmation that Gianni's citizenship petition was approved. His status in the country would never be a cause for sleepless nights. A scant eight months later, Gianni and Liz decided to split—first as a trial separation and six months after that for good. Years later, he told me it seemed that they were bored with each other and their routines, and they did not care much to listen to what the other was doing.

I asked him if he felt distraught at that time, and his response surprised me a bit.

"Stuff like this happens, cousin. You must take it in stride. You can't get too upset." The matter-of-fact, emotionless words, I can say today, meshed well with the rest of his personality. At that moment, I, a person who was most often surrounded by full-blooded Italians, thought he sounded like a robot.

Several months after his divorce, my family got word that Gianni was about to move to the New York area. We did not know precisely why. My father made some noise, suggesting he was worried Gig was coming to ask for financial help. Ended up being that—why are we even surprised?—he had met this woman, Denise, who lived in Brooklyn and worked in Manhattan. She had convinced him that the go-go '90s accommodated a sizable group of middle-aged women who wanted to learn ballroom dancing. They sought out venues where they could dance the night away, whether in Manhattan, the Boroughs, or Long Island.

I finally got to meet my cousin Gig. I learned we shared a passion for sports. While I was a lot less adventuresome in my relationships with women, I did not envy his success. However, I was sociologically intrigued by him. I was a social science major, and social as well as political epiphenomena always piqued my interest. None of that had much to do with my profession as a business consultant for one of the larger Boston-based firms, but it still intrigued me.

I immediately noticed his unusual walk. It was as if he knew that women would be following his still-handsome profile with their eyes. To me, it seemed that the ground he walked on was a personal runway. Another cousin once said that he had "the dancers walk; he is always gliding across the dance floor." I was bemused by the affectation involved in that strut. I was less euphoric about his willingness to talk about how often women propositioned him, even if it was for a one-night stand. I thought it was outrageously self-promoting. But he would just laugh it off as "one of those things" and casually switched topics. His attitude always seemed *legere* in those days, even concerning Juventus, the soccer club. Early on, I found out that he was a big fan. Surprisingly, a few months later, when Juve fell on hard times, he claimed to love Barcelona because of Cruyff. I thought to myself, "No sports fan does that!" I decided that he was not the one to look for when it came to consistency.

But you could talk to him about movies forever. Not so much about books, not even Italian authors like Umberto Eco or Calvino. When I once mentioned Eco, he raised his eyebrows like I had said something in Russian.

He was almost always willing to join you for a baseball game (I quickly convinced him to replace the Dodgers with the Mets; "Heck, I am a New Yorker now," he'd said). And he was happy to join you at the tennis US Open in September, or some Broadway show, as long as the tickets were not too expensive or someone else paid for them.

Through several sources and connections, many linked to Denise, Gianni finally set up a small studio where he taught ballroom dancing. There were aspiring Broadway actresses who wanted to hone their dancing, middle-aged women who found this an excellent way to break from the daily routine, and older women who were eager to convince themselves that they still had plenty of sex-appeal. He continued to attend competitions from time to time and won one of the top three prizes in four such events over two years.

Denise and my cousin lived together but never married. It was the end of the 20th century. Because they had no interest in having children, there was no particular reason to put their relationship in that straitjacket—those were presumably Denise's words. Gianni, tight-lipped, and even secretive about personal choices, shared with me what they had discussed. I concluded that he just needed to justify that choice. There was a conservative strand in my cousin—maybe something Sicilian—that suggested that a couple living together should also wear matrimonial rings.

9/11 had a massive impact on the world, and particularly on New Yorkers. From the conversations I had with my cousin, it had awakened a need to be more immersed and informed in all matters of politics and international affairs. He told me that Denise would sit long hours in front of the TV, incessantly sobbing over stories of firefighters and first responders who perished in that horrific event. He also said that he never felt more American and was angry at those who wished to harm this country. When I asked him if he understood the perpetrators' motivations, he was adamant.

"I do not care. You just don't kill babies, old people, women, and men; you don't randomly murder because you are upset."

When I asked him about his acquaintance with the conflict between Arabs and Israelis, he was equally curt.

"I probably know a lot less than you, but it does not matter—you just don't massacre people in this horrendous way." Then, he amended, and as if making a solemn pledge, he sternly said that he "would become better informed."

As if turning a new page in his life story, the new century brought Gianni an appetite to read more about what was going on in the world. On the other hand, and though he was now getting closer to his mid-forties, his casual, happy-go-lucky approach to life remained unchanged. Still, he wanted to come across as more aware, not appear ignorant during dinner conversations with friends. At one point, he slipped and disclosed that Denise once scolded him for being boorish and embarrassing her. He told me that at that moment, all he'd wanted was to bolt and leave everything behind. But he'd remembered his father's words about maintaining his cool during an argument and said nothing. He was miffed at the reprimand but chose to take Denise's words at full value. He would pay more attention to matters miles away from his usual frivolity and enjoyment of life.

They say that Sicilians do not forget; they just wait for the right moment to pay back. The vendetta came two years later as Gianni told her that he thought they should go their separate ways; he just had fallen out of love and wanted out. Denise only found out the truth a few months later. He had met a very wealthy woman who showed serious interest in him but would not seek his company while still sleeping with Denise. At first, he had been reluctant to succumb to her ultimatum-like conditions, but Sarah's wealth and the prospects of a life of excess were a great attraction.

At least, that was my interpretation. I must mention Gianni was too secretive and smart to admit to this self-indulgence and selfishness. He had told me, at one point, that as he was getting older, his concerns of economic survival were rising. I agreed with him that Social Security benefits would not be enough to keep him afloat. That even if he worked part-time as a senior, the income would not amount to much. He needed to build some sort of retirement nest egg to have a decent chance at a comfortable retirement. But I also acknowledged that his income from dancing instruction and competition prizes was probably not significant enough to save the kinds of money necessary to build a retirement fund. It was not difficult to surmise that Sarah would be a much easier path to resolve his quandary.

Sarah loved the opera and convinced my cousin to join her for the annual tour of extraordinary operatic renditions. They went to Verona to see their version of *Aida* with elephants, horses, and a vast cast—all of which impressed him. He went with her to La Scala in Milan to watch a Don Giovanni's performance, which left him cold. In contrast, he told me that the Berlin performance of the *Magic Flute* touched him. Sarah also loved ballet, so they went to St. Petersburg and Moscow to watch *Swan Lake* and *The Nutcracker* in the evenings while visiting the Hermitage and the Pushkin State Museum of Fine Arts during the day. No longer were expensive Broadway tickets an issue. I even got invited to join them a couple of times—each time we enjoyed an elaborate dinner at fancy Palio or the less fancy but excellent Osteria al Doge. I also joined them for the music I love most—jazz—at my favorite venue, Smoke, which I introduced to them. Because it was on Broadway and 106th St., Sarah was reticent. When she yielded, she insisted on taking a limo both ways. Once there, though, she relaxed and had positive things to say about the music and the food.

I only met Denise once, when my cousin moved to NYC; I got to know Sarah a lot better. A born and raised NYC woman who never was left for wanting, she had the kind of education that many would envy—private schools, Barnard, and Yale Law. She practiced law for a short time, and when her father died, took the reins of the retail chain he had founded. She lived in a gorgeous Park Avenue apartment. Exquisite Kandinsky, Chagall, and Miro paintings decorated the high walls, and bronze and glass sculptures of top-line modern artists further enhanced the furniture. It was clear she had high standards. Summers were spent in two large residences on Martha's Vineyard and Fire Island. Interspersed were trips to the festivals of Verona, Salzburg, and Montreux. She loved the *Salzburger Festspiele* best because of the mix of theater, opera, and classical music. She was cautious, conservative, unwilling to engage in anything deemed risky. At the same time, I noted and respected her social values, which were a lot more generous toward minorities—whether they were Black, Latino, or gay—than those of other wealthy and conservative people I had known over the years.

If I ever saw the two on different sides of an issue, it was at the time of the 2016 elections. Sarah saw the election of a Democrat as endangering her wealth while, and Trump was unequivocally supportive, likely even enhancing her financial condition. She made no qualms about how important this was to her. Gianni, on the other hand, had become an ardent supporter of Obama. He told me that he cried when Obama won the 2008 elections to become the first Black president. Gianni saw it as a confirmation that America was broad-minded, willing to give a chance to anyone. He abhorred the Republican candidate. He thought he was systematically ensuring that the gap between rich and poor remained extensive. That this was utterly inconsistent with his current lifestyle, interests, even his work was glossed over with a smile. If someone pointed out the contradiction, he swiftly and adeptly changed the subject. As usual, he was more than willing to walk away from a possible argument.

It is still remarkable that as far as I could tell, this political stance was the only subject-matter on which Gig remained steadfast. Considering that it clashed with Sarah's beliefs made it even more impressive. From what I could tell, he made sure not to discuss politics with her—it would be counterproductive. And it seemed that Sarah concurred, staying far away from inciting any dispute.

Appreciating his willingness to go to the art events she so liked, Sarah compensated him by getting first-tier tickets to the European soccer Champions League finals held in Kyiv one year and in Cardiff the next. He also enjoyed the JP Morgan Box for the semis and finals of the US Tennis Open and near-court seats at Wimbledon. Life was good.

One familiar friend told me once that Sarah was older than him by about eight years. But it did not bother my cousin. "She is kind and most interested in us having a pleasant life—maybe you could even replace 'us' with 'pleasing me.' My life is wonderful right now."

As unhappy as she was to engage in anything risky, she consented to his new interest in fast cars. He urged her to join him on a trip up I-95 to Acadia National Park. It would give him the chance to push the pedal of his new Porsche Carrera, a birthday gift he called his *new toy*. It would be perfect, he told her—he could go past 160 mph without much effort. He reported with a good deal of glee how she had been a bundle of nerves but had laughed hard in a feeble attempt to suppress it.

I reflected on that story and wondered why he needed to race his car. Was it that he needed new thrills because he was saturated by the glittering components of his carefree life to the point of boredom? Or maybe it was to balance out the demands for attention Sarah required of him. Perhaps it was just that he was trying to introduce her to an edgier lifestyle better fitting his own. Maybe a bit of all.

Gianni had closed the dance studio when he joined Sarah's life of luxury and pleasure. It was not an immediate decision, but he ultimately concluded that a late fifties dance teacher was not likely a success story. He agreed, however, to serve as a judge in top-level dance competitions. He even appeared on TV for a competitive dance show—his good looks had stayed with him, and with Sarah's connections, getting this TV gig was easy.

Sarah was elated to accompany him for a few competitions but then understood it would be smart to give him some space—occasionally allow him to roam around alone. It was not necessary to hear Gianni's commentary about this—I knew he enjoyed these breaks.

In mid-February 2020, he found himself judging a competition in beautiful Verona. He loved that city with its exquisite walkway between the *Arena* and Piazza delle *Erbe,* and being in Italy always felt right. The competition would last for about a week, and he would stay for two more days to enjoy the city.

On the eighth day, he suddenly felt very unwell. It was as if his throat was closing on him—he had this horrible dry cough, and that night he suffered terrible headaches. He called Sarah daily, and that morning's call was hard. He felt he could not talk and breathe at the same time. She arranged for him to fly home immediately; she got a private plane with a nurse on board. Once he arrived at JFK, a limo was ready to take him to Lenox Hill Hospital. Everyone knew that the coronavirus was raging in Italy, as it had before in China, yet few knew how to deal with it and help those afflicted. There was a concern that older people succumbed to its pulmonary invasion and were victims of a myriad of collateral damages. Still, Gianni was only in his early sixties, and Sarah was sure he would be okay. She consulted with the best doctors that dealt with pneumonia and pulmonary infections, and they gave her hope that he would overcome this.

Unfortunately, Gianni's autoimmune system was not robust enough to fight off the virus. The amassed liquid impacted the lungs, internal bleeding caused blood clots, and the doctors decided to induce an artificial coma to prevent major organs' collapse.

Three days later, doctors told Sarah that one of Gianni's legs had to be amputated to prevent septic shock and death. Sarah cried out, "How can this beautiful dancer lose a leg! How will he be able to deal with it when he wakes up?" The doctor was unwilling to tell her what he feared most—that he would never wake up.

It was clear that the ventilator was very difficult on Gianni's system. After the amputation, when bleeding was brought under control, the doctors did a tracheostomy. It made breathing a bit easier, even though it was still machine-assisted.

After a full month of ordeals, Gianni finally opened his eyes. A couple of days later, he slowly began responding to commands to follow a doctor's finger as it moved from right to left. Three days later, with Sarah at his side, he discovered that he had a mutilated stump where he once had his left leg. Sarah told me later that day that his face contorted into a wry smile. Totally in line with his character, he accepted his fate without drama. No tears were shed.

I wondered if Sarah would abandon him now that he was damaged. I did not think I knew her enough to venture a guess. But she had gotten divorced twice before and possibly had bolted out of other relationships that did not involve matrimony. Thus, I was concerned she might now seek distance from Gianni.

Old age makes most of us wiser. As we get to the end of our existence on this planet, we find ourselves excusing and tolerating more, accepting the facts and actions that we might have rejected, or run away from, in the past. Sarah showed devotion, caring, and the kind of empathy and altruism she might not have shown before. Yes, she had been generous to many—she was a patron of the arts, she was charitable—but some might have suggested that those were the actions of someone looking to bolster her social status. When she cared for Gianni's recovery, from convalescence to moving around with a prosthetic leg to slowly injecting him into their social life as they had lived before, she was indeed a terrific life-partner.

Eventually, I was allowed to visit him at the rehabilitation center, where he was learning to walk again; these visits were quiet. During his first week back in the Park Avenue apartment, we had a surprisingly profound conversation. As often was the case lately, Sarah allowed us some privacy and excused herself, alleging an important meeting.

He said, "This coronavirus pandemic is the planet telling us that there is no abuse without retribution. There is no excess without a penalty, without a cost. And the price has been tremendous. Not just my leg and my forever-damaged lungs, but the suffering of so many people. And it is not over yet, and who knows when it will be over? All those tens of thousands of people that died were probably not the main culprits of the excess. They were not necessarily the primary transgressors—they were not even the most egregious violators. The way nature acts out its revenge is nasty and indiscriminate.

"And you know what else, cousin? Humanity is showing itself in all of its current poverty. Nations blame each other to extract monetary compensation for each soul lost as if that would bring them back. Politicians, especially this president, blame everyone except themselves because of the narrow-minded objective of winning the coming election. None of this will bring back any of the thousands who have died, committed suicide in despair, or lost their livelihoods for good. States are stealing from each other access to ventilators. Countries block their own citizens' entry or exit stranded on a cruise ship infested to the hilt.

"The situation is so awful that one needs to be strong not to despair and jump from a high-floor apartment window. Husbands and wives are fighting, friends turn their backs on each other, insults are flying, and there is such a level of stress that comforting words, benevolence, and acts of kindness are not easily found. Yes, I know there are important exceptions—I also watch the news— but they pale next to all the ugly things I hear about."

Gianni was not the most eloquent speaker I ever heard, but his words rang honest, intelligent, and passionate. I thought many were thinking along the same lines but could not communicate their thoughts with such genuineness.

Five months later, at his behest, Sarah and Gianni moved to Palermo. He needed a new environment, far away from the last few months of New York City's pain and suffering. Sarah, all too keen to make his life better, acquiesced without a hitch. I feared that my cousin Gig and I would never speak again.

Nearly a year later, I reflected on cousin Gig. Distance gifts you the clarity of perspective; time presents you the luxury of analytical contemplation. Gianni, I concluded, had gone through an interesting evolution. He'd started as a youngster whose physical attributes were his full essence—a sexy heartthrob, whose profile created a picture that many may have deemed a caricature. This was the trampoline to a long period of near-thoughtless hedonism when he'd exploited that physicality to survive, enjoy day-to-day life without worrying about his future, the larger society he traveled in, or the broader historical component of sometimes earth-shattering events.

With age came the very gradual, careful tiptoeing into a broader understanding of his social environment, current politics, the consequences of deeds and misdeeds. As he went about it, without the direction of a teacher, a classroom, or the consistent guidance of reading material, he fumbled around and found himself confused. Still, instead of giving up, he continued trying.

By the time he hit his health crisis caused by the virus, he was able to survive its psychological effects—the demoralizing impact of losing a limb. Because he had evolved into a man with a deep-seated perspective on humanity and nature, a much more sophisticated understanding of politics and society, he was no longer the hedonistic person who would have been destroyed by just looking at his stump; he no longer was the happy-go-lucky hunk from *Piazza Verdi*.

Ultimately, it is only in our own hands whether any one of us can grow as a person.

ABOUT THE AUTHOR

Dr. **Michael Ranis has lived in** five countries, visited more than fifty, and is fluent in six languages. *After Opaque Blue*, his first publication, Ranis explores old and new crises, personal changes and other themes in this book.

Born in La Paz to German Jewish emigres who met in that city, Michael was exposed to all the beauty of Latin America and all that is so attractive about Jewish ethical traditions. He chose to migrate to Israel at the age of fourteen (1966). His interest in political matters being a direct consequence of that decision. He received his B.A. from Tel Aviv University (Philosophy and Science of Developing Countries being dual minors) and a Ph.D. in Political Science from the University of Chicago.

Michael taught several courses involving European politics, the Middle East, and Public Policy at Hamilton College and Swarthmore College. He taught for four years before turning his interests to finance, obtaining an MBA (New York University) and entering that industry. He was active in investment banking and portfolio management from 1986 to 2016. Most of his employment was in New York, but he also spent five years in Switzerland and almost as long in London.

Michael has two children. Ethan and Sophie (Julia) Ranis. He also has a beautiful baby granddaughter.

Though interest in arts and music play a significant role in his life, Michael is an avid and accomplished bridge player. He has achieved a number of good results in national and international tournaments. He has embarked on a literary career late in life to challenge himself to write like those he admired.

www.ingramcontent.com/pod-product-compliance
Lightning Source LLC
Chambersburg PA
CBHW071431260626
47170CB00008B/2676